THE MINDHUNTERS
WHAT THE
DEAD KNOW

KYLIE BRANT

Previously in The Mindhunters Series:

Waking Nightmare
Waking Evil
Waking the Dead
Deadly Intent
Deadly Dreams
Deadly Sins
Secrets of the Dead

For my readers, with thanks

ACKNOWLEDGEMENTS

Sometimes I can get lost in the research for a book, and this time around that's exactly what happened. Once again many generous souls stepped forward to help fill the voids in my knowledge. A huge round of thanks is owed to Christine Buckley, who arranged for the oncology answer; my favorite (retired) coroner, Chris Herndon, who is never too busy to answer dead body questions; Floyd County Supervisor Mark Kuhn for replying to my county government queries; Dusty Rolando, for descriptions of the Upper Peninsula, and Joe Collins, who knows more about weapons than I can fathom.

DNA questions were ably handled by Blaine Kern, Chief Forensic Consultant / Laboratory Director, Human Identification Technologies. When I listen to him I realize I should have paid more attention in science class!

Doug Boyle, trapper extraordinaire, answered all fur harvesting and trapping questions, of which there were many. Doug had but one request—that he not be made the villain :) You'll have to judge for yourselves whether I honored that request.

A big thank you to Sheriff Robert Hughes, Alger County, MI for taking the time to answer my endless questions about the job and procedures, with a few hypothetical murder questions thrown in along the way. Much appreciation for continuing to answer follow up emails entitled 'just one more thing...'

I can't thank you all enough. As usual, any errors are the author's alone and undoubtedly due to not asking the right questions.

CHAPTER 1

The frigid air slashed like razors in her throat, turned to flame in her lungs. Keira Saxon focused on the repetitive muscle activity. Kick. Stride. Glide. Kick. Stride. Glide. She'd hit the zone thirty minutes ago. When she'd stopped thinking about the twinge in her knee. The knot between her shoulder blades. Moved past thoughts of the havoc a jailer's long-term absence was having on scheduling. Her skis cut through the gauze of winter white, and for an all too brief period exertion wiped her mind as blank as the fresh snowfall. No worries. No memories. No grief.

The ribbon of smoke was a smudgy thread against the stone gray sky well before her dad's house came into view. She still thought of it as his, even nine months after his death. He'd built it for his new bride nearly forty years earlier. It had taken only three years for his wife to tire of it, and of him. It had been another four before she'd left, with their only child in tow. And yet when Keira thought of home, it was this cabin, with its circle of towering pines that she longed for.

Slowing, she took both poles into one hand so she could push the goggles to her forehead. Her tracks from where she'd left the porch nearly an hour ago had been obliterated by a set larger and wider. Snowmobile. The tread mark from the machine ran close to the front steps of the home. And the size twelve boot prints leading up and back from the front door were definitely not hers.

The nearest of her neighbors was four miles away, and none of them were the type to show up unannounced. She didn't even notice the item on the porch until she was directly in front of the steps.

A small red and white cooler. The same color and type that her dad had used to pack a lunch in on the rare occasions he had enough free time to go fishing or hunting. A twin to the one he'd taken with him on the day he died.

Nerves jittered in her belly. Carefully she stepped over the track from the vehicle and leaned her poles against the balustrade before unstrapping her snowshoes and toeing out of them. Climbing the steps, she skirted the new footprints to squat before the cooler. Recognition slammed into her when she saw the familiar black writing on the handle, done in bold strokes with a marker: *D. Saxon.* Danny Saxon. Sheriff of Alger County, Michigan for thirty-two years before his death. Deputy for ten years before that.

She took the handle in one gloved hand while she pressed the button to open it with the other. Vapor quickly formed as the cold air met the pink item inside. Keira reared back. She'd been present at enough autopsies to know it was an internal organ of some type, although badly damaged. What she didn't have the expertise to determine was whether the organ was human or animal. Her gaze rested again on the name printed on the cooler before she surged to her feet.

Running down the front steps, she made her way to the garage. Alger County had gotten six fresh inches of snowfall last night, which slowed her progress. It took her two tries to punch in the code to open the garage door. Distantly Keira realized her hands were shaking. She fired up the snowmobile inside that got as much use as the pickup in the Michigan winters and took off, following the vehicle tracks that looped around the front of her property and through the perimeter of pines, to the denser woods beyond.

There were three hundred miles of snowmobile trails in Alger County, thousands in the Upper Peninsula, but she wasn't on one now, and Keira's speed reflected that reality rather than the urgency that was pulsing through her veins. There could be any number of obstacles hidden beneath the drifts, so she followed in the other vehicle's path to avoid them. As the trees crowded in around her, she reduced speed even more. That didn't prevent her from brushing too near a drooping pine branch weighted with several inches of fresh snow. When it dumped down her back, Keira grimaced and gave a shake. Despite the layers she wore, a trickle of ice snaked down her spine.

The five acres of the property overlooked Lake Superior shoreline to the northwest and bordered the Hiawatha National Forest on the south. She'd never tried to ride the sled on the densely wooded land, but she'd hiked it often enough. There were paths crisscrossing the property that she knew as well as the back of her hand. With a flicker of unease, she recognized that whoever had left that cooler on her porch seemed to know her property equally well.

When the path she was following zigzagged to a groomed snowmobile trail, she realized she was in the forest. The trail was maintained seven times a week, and although it hadn't been plowed today, the base was significant, even for February. Given its proximity to the Great Lakes, northern Michigan received about two hundred inches of snowfall yearly. Winter tourism was big business here.

But it hadn't been a tourist who'd left that item outside her door.

After ten more minutes of following the curves and turns of the track, she slowed the vehicle before cutting the engine. The early morning scene was eerily still. A cardinal's trill split the silence. An older model black and gray Polaris sat motionless in the center of the path thirty feet in front of her. Woods hugged either side of the trail. Boot prints led from the sled into the dense firs to the right.

Keira's nape prickled. Had the vehicle run out of gas, causing its owner to take off on foot? Or was its driver hiding in the woods, waiting for her?

That sort of paranoia had served her well on the streets of Chicago. However, Michigan's Upper Peninsula was differentiated from the city in more than mere miles. The bulk of crime here was theft, drugs and assaults, in that order. Leaving a cooler with dubious contents on her porch didn't even rank on that list.

Except for the fact that it had belonged to a dead man.

Keira pulled off her gloves as she dismounted, leaving them on the seat. Pulling the key out of the ignition, she unzipped her pocket, slipping it inside as she approached the other sled. Circling the vehicle, she lifted the hood, reached her hand toward the engine. Still warm. It could have been here for ten minutes or so, but not more than that. She unzipped the pocket of her coat, pulled out her cell, and checked for reception. The signal flickered between one and two bars. Not exactly promising, but better than she'd get once she was further in the woods. She took a couple pictures, noting the lack of license plate on the sled. She sent the photos to Phil Milestone, her undersheriff, and then followed up the act with a phone call.

"Yeah, Phil, you at home?" She scanned the tree line to her right. Silvery birch trunks glittered intermittently among the denuded trees and pines. The prints disappeared between a cluster of fat firs.

"You'd better hope I'm at home since I'm standing here bare-assed naked." Milestone's voice was more than a little cranky. "Just got out of the shower. What do you want?"

She smiled. She'd known the older man since she was nine and he'd been something of an honorary uncle. None of the others on her staff would dare be nearly as familiar with her, even the ones she'd known for years. They were still feeling out their new sheriff. Trying to get a handle on how similar—or different—she was to Danny. Keira wasn't yet sure herself.

"I sent you a couple of pictures. Have Hank compare it to any reports we've gotten on stolen sleds, would you?" She stopped, squinting at a distant flash of color through the trees. Unable to make out the source, her attention reverted to her undersheriff as she gave him a brief run-down of the events of the morning.

There was a moment of silence. Then, "Could see someone stumbling across the cooler and returning it. Wasn't at the scene where the…where Danny was found. You sure it's his?"

"Hard to mistake that scrawl." Trying to make out anything in that knot of foliage was futile. She couldn't see more than five feet into the thickly wooded border.

The vegetation would lessen somewhat once she was a hundred yards inside it. And the snow would make her quarry easy enough to track.

"Wrote like a third grader."

A puff of vapor formed as the quick laugh of agreement escaped her. "That he did. And someone being neighborly might fill it with baked goods before returning it. Maybe turkey or venison. Pretty sure whatever's in it isn't edible."

"You trailing 'em?" The older man was wide-awake now, his earlier grousing tone alert. Businesslike.

"Got as far as mile marker 36 on the Hiawatha trail behind my place before he abandoned the sled."

"Might be a she."

"Don't know too many shes around here with size twelves, but it's possible, I guess. Tracks lead into the forest. I'm going to take a look."

"Watch yourself."

She disconnected, slipped the cell back into her pocket and unzipped her coat enough to reach inside it. Withdrawing her weapon from her shoulder harness, she scrambled off the trail and looped around the cluster of pines the tracks had disappeared into. If the sled's driver were waiting in the cover of those trees, she wasn't about to walk up on him.

The forest interior was more shadowy than the trail had been. Given the look of the sky, the sun wouldn't be making an appearance anytime soon. Even so, the footprints were easy to pick up leaving the pines near the trail. Weapon in hand, she followed them for another ten minutes until they disappeared into another row of firs.

She halted, squinting to discern any movement in the trees. This copse wasn't as dense as some of the others.

By angling just a few yards to the left, she was able to make out a trail of prints leading out of the trees before her. Without a second thought, she walked into the pines. And moments later realized her mistake. As she drew closer, she could see that the prints were deeper. Not as distinct. Someone had walked out of the group of trees. And then turned and retraced his steps.

Instinct had her whirling. There was a blur of movement to her right. The whiz of a long object cutting through the air. Throwing herself sideways, she squeezed off a shot before something made contact with her head and everything went black.

———

The cardinal's song was the first thing she heard when her eyelids began to flutter. The sound was difficult to pick out from the cacophony in her brain. With a supreme burst of effort, she managed to open her eyes. Sitting up proved much more difficult. Once she attained an upright position, Keira cursed, long and fluently.

Memory returned sluggishly. She turned her head sharply to look around, the movement amping up the din in her brain. But there was no one in sight. A stout stick rested in the snow several feet away. The top of it was bloodstained, presumably from its contact with her head. Her gun was inches away from her freezing fingers. Keira got to her knees, hissing in a breath when her vision grayed. After it had cleared, she reached for the weapon, brushed it off made sure the barrel was clear before replacing it in the holster. She paused a moment to take stock, then prodded gingerly at the area above her right temple. Her fingers came back bloody. No shock there. She didn't need a tactile investigation of the second large lump on the back of her head. Both injuries sang a duet of pain that reverberated in her skull. It took more effort than it should have to rise to her knees, then, unsteadily to her feet.

She swayed a moment as she scanned the area. There was a muddled mess of footprints only inches from where the battle had taken place. None pointed away from the area, so she figured her assailant had headed back toward the sleds. As she began following them, her gaze sharpened. Tiny cast off drops of scarlet could be seen here and there next to the footprints. Blood. A grim sense of satisfaction filled her. Not enough to collect for later testing, but at least her attacker hadn't gotten away unhurt.

The satisfaction dissipated somewhat when she arrived at the trail. Her gloves were lying on the path, but both machines were gone. The bastard had taken her sled.

————

"You look like shit." Dr. Tony King, Munising Clinic's newest general practitioner, drew on gloves and reached into the cooler Keira had brought. Since he was doing her a favor, she resisted the urge to punch him. Knowing his words were true didn't lessen their sting. She'd spent the walk back to her place calling and alternately wheedling and bullying him into making time for her ahead of his patients. Alger County didn't have its own coroner or morgue. But King had done a rotation in pathology for the medical examiner in Lansing, an experience he constantly talked about. She figured he might know just enough to answer her questions.

"And people wonder why you haven't married." Her tone was caustic. She and the man didn't have the best of relationships. Perhaps because he'd gotten word that she'd dubbed him King Prick shortly after he came to town. "A sweet line like that, women should be flocking."

"I know, right? The position remains open for qualified candidates." He laid the pink tissue on a counter he'd covered with sterile paper in one of his exam rooms. Fetching a magnifying glass, he added, "In case you're hinting that you'd like to audition for the job. You can start tonight."

It was probably her imagination that the man's presence notched the pounding in her head to jackhammer levels. The three Tylenol she'd swallowed earlier hadn't made an appreciable dent in her headache. Not for the first time she found herself missing Doc Ressler, the former owner of the practice and one of her father's oldest friends. The man had retired six months earlier, and King had replaced him. Keira met the man only once before requesting that her medical files be transferred to a women's clinic in Marquette.

"I need you to identify the organ—it is an organ, right? And tell me if it's human or not."

"Yeah, you said when you called, along with your usual pleasantries." Since he was closely inspecting the contents from the cooler she didn't respond. No use antagonizing him even further before he gave her some answers. "Where the hell did you get it? Looks like a twelve-year-old tried a resection with a pen knife."

Her cell vibrated, and she moved to the hallway to answer it. "Hey, Pammy." The younger woman constantly had Keira reconsidering whether to require uniforms for her dispatchers. The only thing that had prevented her so far was that they rarely met the public. Which was a good thing, since Pammy's style was somewhat schizophrenic. Currently, she was going through a Goth phase, which was preferable compared to the punk look she'd sported last month. Keira had known her since she was a little kid. The woman was sharp, which earned her some latitude.

"Your sled has been found, in what has to be the world's shortest investigation in history."

"Where was it?"

"It was left a mile inside the forest entrance on County Road 62. Tow kit still attached. Hank found it when he went to join Phil. Radioed it in. You didn't answer so I called. He said they'll dust it for prints, but…"

Yeah, but. The guy was likely wearing gloves, because of the weather. Prints were a long shot. DNA wasn't. "Tell them to check it for bloodstains." There hadn't been enough to collect for lab testing, but maybe her assailant had bled more freely on her sled while he was attaching the towlines. Hearing an exclamation from the examination room, her attention fractured. "Keep me posted." Abruptly she disconnected and returned to find King staring at the sample she'd brought with horrified fascination.

"What?" She rounded the table to join him, peering more closely at what she was now certain was an organ of some sort. "Do you know what it is?"

"I had a cat once during residency." When King sidled a bit closer, Keira shot out an elbow to keep him at a distance. "It used to bring me disgusting things. Dead mice. A snake once, even. This little gift of yours tops that big time."

Useless to spend a futile moment longing for the days Doc Ressler had worked here. "Get to the point, King. Is it human?"

Returning his attention to the specimen, he prodded it with a scalpel. "That I'm not sure of. What I am certain of is that it's a liver, at least part of one. And it's diseased. Likely cancer, although it would require testing to be positive."

The news hit her like a hard left jab, summoning an immediate visceral response. Pushing the reaction aside, she asked grimly, "Anything else?"

"Well, there's this." He pointed to the center of the mass.

Keira leaned closer. She'd already noted that it was badly damaged. But there was something white there, nearly covered by the surrounding tissue. She could see the small slices in the organ now, surrounding the area he was indicating. "That looks like...bone." A rush of bile surged to her throat, a response she hadn't experienced since she'd been a rookie. Keira looked at the doctor. "Since when does a liver have bones in it?"

With delicate precision, he used the scalpel to pry the item from the surrounding tissue. Once it was freed, he laid it on the counter. They both stared in silence for a moment. The bone at the end of it glistened white, but the flesh was badly mangled. Despite that fact, however, there was no mistaking it for anything other than the upper half of a human finger.

———

"Dr. Carstens is on his way from the lab now." Adam Raiker waved Keira to a seat and then rounded the gleaming desk to his chair. "I hope your trip down was uneventful. At least the weather is decent. The cold snap we had before Christmas set records."

She sank into the butter soft leather chair gratefully. It had already been a long day, and she still had the plane ride home tonight. "Compared to northern Michigan, the temps in the DC area are positively balmy." She'd landed in Dulles, rented a car and driven the remainder of the way to Raiker's compound in Manassas. The level of security she'd gone through—even as an expected guest—made the airport measures pale in comparison.

Keira studied the man surreptitiously. She'd never met Raiker before, but there were few in law enforcement that hadn't heard of him. The man had been a profiling legend at the FBI during his tenure there. The reason for his departure were evident in the scars on his hands and throat, and the black eye patch he wore over the eye that —according to rumor—had been carved out by the serial murderer he'd been trailing.

"I appreciate the fast turn-around time." It'd been only four days since she'd met with King, and she'd spent the first twenty-four hours examining all the angles before making a decision about how to proceed.

Raiker's shrug was negligible. "I know how it is working in the field. Waiting weeks or months for tests to be completed in the state labs. Time is an investigator's most valuable asset." His smile was slight. "And Raiker Forensics has the resources."

They certainly did. The man had cherry-picked the finest scientists and investigators across the nation to staff his company. It boasted experts in every possible forensic specialty, internationally accredited labs and investigators trained by Raiker himself. All these services were available to law enforcement agencies and select private customers. For a price.

His laser blue gaze shifted as the door behind her opened. "Keira Saxon, Finn Carstens."

Keira twisted around to look at the man approaching. Six foot, streaky brown wavy hair and hazel eyes with the face of a martyred saint. The mental observation was immediate and instinctive. But the kick in her pulse was solely due to the laptop he had tucked under one arm.

"Ms. Saxon." Carstens gave her a quick smile as he headed to the conference- sized table to the right of Raiker's desk. "I think I have the answers you asked for. And maybe a few more questions."

Something clutched in her gut as he fussed with the computer for a moment. There was a fleeting instant when Keira wondered if she wanted the answers at all. She had the feeling that whatever the man had to report was going to tilt her world on its axis.

She elbowed aside the emotion and settled back into her chair. Anything had to be better than the gnawing uncertainty that had dogged her for the past several months. "Anxious to hear what you found. I didn't want to send it to the state lab until I was sure of what we had." That wasn't the only reason she hadn't involved the Michigan State Police. Not by a long shot. From the look in Raiker's eye, she had an uneasy feeling that he suspected as much.

"Here we are." The content on Carsten's laptop screen was now displayed on a huge screen mounted on the wall next to the table. He threw a quick look at her. "Hope you aren't queasy."

Keira's voice was wry. "I was a Chicago beat cop for six years. A homicide detective for five years after that."

The man nodded. "What you see first are the items you shipped down to us in their original state." Both were shown close up from several different angles. It was the severed finger that drew her attention. Kept it. Given the size of the knuckle, it had probably belonged to a male. But like the size twelve footprints she'd followed a week ago, she couldn't rule out a large female.

"The organ is most definitely a liver, and human." Regardless of her earlier words, Keira's stomach gave a sudden lurch. "The portion you sent is from the right lobe." He switched to the next picture, with several frames showing only the liver, this time in thin slivers, each magnified. "There's evidence of advanced cancer here." He used a penlight laser pointer to indicate a spot on the large screen. "Here. And here. Hepatocellular carcinoma, specifically. The most common form of liver cancer, but rare in this instance as there's no accompanying cirrhosis."

The words hit her with the force of a runaway locomotive. She attempted to speak. Could summon no voice. Moistening her lips she tried again. "What about the blood sample I sent you?"

Carstens turned to fully face her. "I ran a series of familial DNA tests triangulating between the liver, the amputated finger and the blood sample. The liver presented the most difficulty, as formaldehyde had degraded the organ to some degree. However, I was able to find a small sample suitable for testing. Short story is the liver results showed a 99.99 per cent probability of paternity to the individual who provided the blood sample. As for the severed finger…"

There was a roaring in her ears. The rest of what he was saying was lost on her as her mind grappled with his revelation. The memory of her father's voice drowned out the scientist's.

It's advanced, Kee-Kee. And it's aggressive. The radiation is just to shrink it before surgery. And I haven't made up my mind about taking that step. We have to be realistic about my prognosis.

Screw reality. She'd clung to hope long after the time her father had accepted his fate. He'd wanted to avoid a long drawn out death, and she'd wanted that for him, too. But neither of them would have chosen the way his life had ended.

"Ms. Saxon?" The low timber in Raiker's voice was no doubt linked to the jagged scar that traced across his throat. His tone was concerned. "Are you all right?"

"The blood sample was mine." It took effort to smooth the slight hitch in her words before continuing, her gaze on Carstens. "What about the finger?"

The man shook his head. The sympathy in his expression was almost as brutal as his earlier words had been. "No match. Although DNA testing showed that it belonged to a male, it didn't match your father. It had been disarticulated at the second knuckle, likely using a large bladed knife with a smooth edge."

"I'd assumed a male victim, given the size of the specimen, but appearances can be deceiving."

"It could have been female," he agreed. "My great-aunt Edna had hands the size of small hams. Watching her shuck corn was a terrifying experience."

She recognized his attempt at humor for what it was. Couldn't summon a smile. There was no way to lighten this news. It took everything she had to squelch the tumult of emotion frothing inside her.

Carstens continued. "The hemorrhagic tissue present indicates the victim was alive at the time of amputation. The nail had been removed some time before. At least a week from the signs of partial healing evident."

Raiker rose from his desk to walk across the room, his limp more pronounced than when he'd led her into the room minutes ago. A cane rested against the side of his desk. He hadn't used it earlier, either. She wondered if the injury to his leg was yet another reminder of his time imprisoned by the killer he'd been hunting.

The thought was a welcome distraction, and she seized on it gratefully. Anything to avoid thinking about the forensic scientist's revelation. He'd validated her absolute worst fears. The ones too awful to share even with Phil Milestone.

"Drink this." Raiker pushed a short glass into her hands, and her fingers closed around it reflexively. "Fifteen-year-old Scotch made for sipping." He headed back to his chair. "Although a good gulp wouldn't be out of order. It's not every day a person learns that their mystery home delivery consisted of their father's liver and a stranger's severed finger."

Somehow his brusqueness was easier to accept than Carstens' sympathy. She took a long drink. The liquor scorched a path down her throat. She sipped again. Felt steadier.

"There was no formaldehyde present in the finger." Finn Carstens' voice was quiet. "How long ago did your father die?"

She swirled the amber liquid in the glass, her eyes trained on the resulting eddies. "It's been nine months. One of those rare weekday afternoons he'd gone fishing." Or rather, he'd had a doctor's appointment and had taken leave the rest of the day. He'd been tolerating the radiation fairly well. She'd been glad at the time to see him taking an interest in his old hobbies. Tipping the glass to her lips, she continued, "He took his pole, his rifle and the same cooler left on my porch a few days ago. When he wasn't home for dinner, I started calling." Useless to berate herself for not checking in earlier. He'd deserved a few hours of solitary time she'd thought. There'd been no way of knowing that she'd never see him alive again.

She raised her head, looked at Raiker. "I checked out all his favorite fishing spots. Found his truck, but no signs of him. I alerted his deputies, who organized a search party. It was later expanded to include a tracker and a scent dog. Took three days to find him, in the national wilderness area, nearly five miles from where he'd left his truck." She hauled in a breath, mentally avoiding the image that threatened to rise. "Animals had gotten to the body. There was a bear's den nearby. Coyotes in the area. The state medical examiner's office conducted the autopsy. Findings were inconclusive, due to the damage from the scavengers." The blood spill meant he'd been alive when he'd been attacked. She prayed every night to a deafened God that he'd had a heart attack and was unconscious well before… Her mind skittered away from the thought. Seized on another.

"We recovered his pole, but not his rifle or, until last week, his cooler." The missing cooler had always bothered her. It wouldn't have been unusual for her dad to carry extra ammo packaged inside it along with his lunch. What had he encountered that made him think he'd need it? "Two shots had been fired from his weapon. The bear in the vicinity was caught and sedated." , "There was a wound in its flank that could have been made by a bullet grazing it." Her voice was as grim as her memory of the scene. "The area is overgrown and untamed. Didn't make for a great crime scene." With no evidence of foul play, there had been a few realistic, if gruesome scenarios to explain what had happened to her father. All of them were stomach churning.

Finn seemed to be choosing his words carefully. "So the condition of his internal organs…" He let the words hang delicately.

"The body was found on its side and had been disemboweled by the scavengers. The clothing chewed away. Much of the skin was missing. Some of the ribs and smaller bones."

"The reason I ask, Ms. Saxon…" Finn waited for her attention to shift to him. "The hole in the liver. The one that the portion of finger was inserted into. Examination of the surrounding tissue showed minute traces of gunshot residue."

Her fingers tightened around the glass until her knuckles whitened, the wash of shock almost numbing. Was it better to have answers at all if they verified the darkest fears that had lingered since May? "There was no brass found in the area.." No evidence that his predator had been human. But even with a metal detector, the evidence technicians had been faced with an insurmountable task. The Rock River Canyon Wilderness was over forty-five hundred acres in the Hiawatha Forest, and a roadless unit. The terrain was rugged. She couldn't imagine what her father had been doing there. But whatever urge had caused him to hike five miles from his fishing spot had ended up killing him.

Comprehension seeped in. Solidified. Her father had been murdered. Shock and anguish gave way to a surge of scalding fury. Nine months. That's how long the killer had walked around free. She'd buried her father. Accepted condolences. Gone through his things. Bowed to the pressure brought to bear and accepted an appointment to fill out the rest of his term. And all that time, the killer had been doing what? Watching. Waiting. And given the severed finger, likely something even more sinister than that.

A fierce ball of rage lodged in her gut. "He might have stumbled on something in the forest. Poaching. A meth lab. Or he was shot by accident, then the killer left him there to die." She surged from her seat, the liquor splashing precariously close to the rim of the glass she held. "Unless…he was lured to that exact place. Deliberately." To an area where it was all but certain that the territory, coupled with the nearby wildlife would destroy the crime scene. And then the killer had covered up his involvement by removing all signs that would point to homicide. Including removing the organ that the killer's bullet had passed through.

"Did your father have anyone in particular who would want him dead?"

Keira gave a bitter laugh. "He was the sheriff for three decades. That list would number in the hundreds if I started looking at everyone he'd put away." She knew because she'd already begun making a record. Some nights it was easier to focus on the unanswered questions she had about his death than it was to face the nightmarish possibilities that sleep would bring.

"And now the killer is making it personal. He wants you to know what he's done."

She nodded at Finn's words, lifting an unconscious hand to her new shorter haircut that just brushed her shoulders. "More personal than you know. Four days ago my hair was six inches longer. When I got home after the attack and checked out my injuries, I discovered a chunk of hair missing." Her gaze went to Raiker. "Whoever the killer is, he likes to take souvenirs."

The other man leaned back in his chair, his gaze fierce. "Finn, were you able to lift a print from that finger?"

"No. It had been, for lack of a better word, skinned."

Keira returned to her chair, sank into it and drained the remaining Scotch. "Maybe the killer took something from me because he'd sent along something of his. Sort of a...exchange." Perhaps it was the alcohol, but the shock was wearing off, leaving only the anger behind. Could it be that bold, that blatant? She could think of no clearer way to throw down the gauntlet.

I'm here. I've been here all along. Come and get me.

"It might be a warning," Finn said quietly. His eyes were sharp. Shrewd. As if he could read her thoughts. "You could be his next target."

Keira smiled thinly. "If that's what he has in mind he should have killed me when he had the chance. I don't plan on giving him a second opportunity."

————

Boone expertly skinned and fleshed the last beaver. He had another name, but this one fit him better. His mother had wanted to name him after Daniel Boone, the famous trapper. That would have been a helluva lot more suitable than the one he'd been saddled with by his old man.

There wasn't much in season in February, but it had been a decent haul today. Fourteen coyotes, twelve beaver and eleven foxes. His catch would have been higher, but at one dam he'd released several of the beaver caught in his snares. A trapper with ethics didn't wipe out an entire habitat. It paid to leave seed for future re-population.

Finished with the task, he scooped the meat into a Ziploc and strode over to the chest freezer, carefully laying it flat on top of the other bags. He rarely ate anything other than game at home, although he did his share of dining out. Dizzy's Bar did a mean steak, and Claire's Diner had the best pie in the county, including his mother's, not that he'd ever tell her that.

It took discipline to become an expert trapper, and he had that, in spades. He was a hunter by nature, the best on the UP, and likely in the whole state. But he downplayed that fact. His hobbies demanded a certain amount of discretion.

The VersaTube shed was the newest structure on the property. He'd erected it a few years ago and had eventually torn down the old barn that had once stood nearby. Spread the concrete pad beneath it with the help of a couple of buddies, and that, with the addition of the foot-wide grated floor drain that ran the length had set him back a couple years' profit from selling furs. It was air tight, making the wood-burning stove he'd installed more than adequate heat.

He carefully hosed down the area where he'd been working and gathered up the carcasses to dump in the bin by the stove. It had hurt to release the marten he'd caught today, but not only was it not in season, he'd already gotten his one allotment for the year according to the Department of Natural Resources regulations. DNR was God when it came to hunting or trapping, and it paid to make sure it was regularly pacified.

When his work area was spotless he picked up his knife and cleaned it in the utility sink next to the freezer before turning his attention to his current guest. The man was slumped forward, naked, his arms shackled to the stout pipe running overhead. Over the past couple of weeks, he'd grown a patchy dark beard, and it contrasted sharply with the pallor of his skin, except for the dozens of areas of pink puckered flesh dotting his body. The bandage where his finger had been amputated was stained with blood and pus. The long strip of flesh removed from his flank was healing poorly. As Boone approached him, he could smell the infection oozing out of the man's pores, and his stomach twisted in disgust. His captive had deserved his fate, but in the end, he'd been a disappointment. Boone was ready to be done with him.

The back wall was lined with trophies, carefully arranged on shelves he'd built himself. There were a few animals that had been worthy of a taxidermist. The rare cougar that had been feeding off his catches while they were still in the traps. The feral pig that had taken two bullets and still managed to slice his leg with its tusks before dropping. The gray wolf that had eluded him for damn near a year before he'd finally tracked it down. The coyote that had attempted to chew its leg off to free itself from the trap. In most respects, animals were far more cunning than humans.

But there had been a few worthy specimens. Several jars lined the shelves with trophies he'd taken from those who had made a contest of the hunt. His gaze lingered for a moment on the empty jar in the center that should have contained the heart of Danny Saxon. The former sheriff had been a wily opponent. The healed gunshot wound in Boone's side was evidence of that. But his triumph had been spoiled when he'd slit the man open and discovered his adversary had been sick. Real sick, from the looks of his liver. The yellowness of his skin should have been a giveaway. What would have been his crowning achievement had turned anti-climatic. It had taken long months for Boone to fully regain his strength after his injury. He'd used the time to plot his next contest.

The hank of hair he'd taken from the woman was tied with fishing twine and draped over a nail protruding from the center shelf. She'd been much too easy to ambush; one reason he never targeted females. They never made a challenge of it. But she'd been faster than he'd expected, and damned if she hadn't grazed him in the shoulder. He could have gutted her for that act alone, as she lay bleeding and unconscious in the snow. But that would have been self-defeating. Because the woman was a tool, and she was going to be instrumental in setting up his next competition. One with the worthiest adversary yet. It'd be the best test of his skills so far, and his eagerness to begin burned like a fever in his blood.

Boone stroked a finger down the silky red-gold strands for good luck before striding toward his captive. Contempt filled him when the man cried out and cowered at his approach. Like a dog, beaten too many times by its master. Domestication did that, to animals and people. And while it was unlikely he'd ever meet anyone as unfettered by social mores as he was, very soon now he'd take on the best the state had to offer.

He drew a key out of the pocket of his Carhartts and reached up to unlock the man's handcuffs, turning away indifferently when his captive fell to the concrete floor. Going to one of the shelves, he retrieved the man's clothes and crossed back to drop them before him. "Put these on. You're leaving."

His head jerked up, disbelief warring with hope in his expression. "I need help. I need a doctor."

"So get your clothes on and go find one."

Leaving the man to dress, the trapper went to the garage door on the rear of the structure and pressed the button to raise it. Night fell early in February. The property sat on thirty acres and was heavily wooded, which made it seem even darker. He waited impatiently for his captive to get to his feet and stumble toward him before hesitating in the open doorway. "Keep going. A doctor lives on the next property. Just through those trees there." When the man made no movement, Boone felt a flare of impatience. "Or maybe I was wrong. Maybe you aren't as anxious to leave as I thought." His lone step forward was all the impetus his captive needed. He began running in a lurching clumsy gait for the cover of the trees beyond.

It wouldn't be sporting to watch the direction he took, so Boone withdrew into the building. He'd stripped his Carhartts to his waist earlier while he worked, and he drew them up now, zipped them and pulled gloves and a facemask out of his pockets. It was colder than a lumberjack's dick out there.

Next he went to his weapon bench, took a couple minutes to consider before taking down his crossbow. He selected only two arrows, because if he needed more to bring down that sorry specimen, he'd give up all his weapons for good.

He fixed a miner's hat over his stocking mask, turned on the light's tab, and—bow and arrows in hand—followed his former guest out of the building and into the woods.

Hunting time.

CHAPTER 2

The room was silent when Keira finished speaking. She sat back, giving her deputies time to digest the results she'd gotten in DC two days ago. God knew she was still struggling to accept it herself.

Brody Boyle was the least senior deputy and usually worked nights. He spoke first. "I don't know, Keira. That sounds a bit far-fetched, don't it?" He glanced at the deputies on either side of him. "I mean yeah, I can see how maybe Danny met a bad end. Came up on somebody doing something illegal. Seems like he might've got himself shot in that case, but the killer sure wouldn't stick around to cut out his liver. Less you think the bear did that, too." He gave a short laugh that dwindled to a cough when no one else joined in.

"Try not to be a dumbass." Mary Jacobs didn't spare a glance for the younger man, who wilted a bit at her words. "I know it's a stretch, but make the effort." Her unflinching gaze fixed on Keira "I've read about the Mindhunters. That's what they call Raiker's outfit, right?" She didn't wait for her nod before continuing. "Best lab facility in the country and their investigators are supposed to be top-notch, too. Hard to believe something like this is going on in the UP, but if that's what the results say, you can take it to the bank." The woman was ten years Keira's senior and had been with the department for two decades. She and Brody spent the majority of their time on road patrol. But Keira would need all available manpower for this case.

"So have you called in the MSP yet?" Hank Fallon, her investigator, asked. His handsome face was set in grim lines. "Surprised they're not here taking over already."

"Obviously an impartial party needs to handle Danny's case," Keira said carefully. "However, the severed finger tells us there may be one more victim. The way it was delivered means the cases are intricately linked. To avoid the appearance of a conflict of interest, our office will be coordinating the investigation with one of Raiker's agents, who will act as primary."

She could feel the disapproval emanating from Phil, no less apparent for being unspoken. They'd discussed the results and her decision at length last night. The ferocity of his disagreement had surprised her, but she'd been undeterred. She'd followed all the proper channels for nine months, and it had led them to the exact conclusion that the killer had wanted them to draw. That knowledge burned. It was time to take control of the situation. Past time.

And Keira wouldn't take the chance of being completely shut out of her dad's case. She couldn't be.

Her chair scraped as she pushed it away from the conference table a bit and studied the sober faces watching her from the other side of the table. "Turning the case over to the Michigan State Police is a crap shoot. Maybe our office would provide some peripheral support to them, but our degree of involvement would be dependent upon the agents assigned. And they've already had their chance with my dad's case." She was gratified by Hank's nod. "They ruled it an accidental death, leaving Danny's killer to walk around free for months. Free to target someone else. That's why I contracted for one of Raiker's agents. He—or she— should be here shortly and will work hand in hand with our office. I think we all deserve that much."

Fallon perked up at the news. "Don't give a damn who's in charge as long as we get in on solving it."

"That's what I thought."

"Maybe the first thing we should consider is getting you round the clock protection," Mary suggested. There was a murmur of agreement around the table. "This guy clearly knows where you live, and he's already attacked you once."

The memory stung. Keira suppressed an urge to reach up to the knot on the back of her head. And the shorter hair below. "Wouldn't have been difficult to figure out where I live. The cooler, its contents—maybe even the chase and attack—were all part of his plan." So far, they'd been dancing to his tune. "He's already accomplished what he set out to do. I think it was like… an invitation, of sorts."

"An invitation?" The words came from Phil on a burst of indignation. "To what?"

"To his game." Everyone swiveled at the newcomer's voice. Finn Carstens stood in the open doorway next to Cal Holm, who volunteered part-time as office secretary. Keira gaped along with the rest of them. She'd expected a stranger, a full-fledged agent. Not Raiker's forensic pathologist.

"He's set up the board and he hand delivered an invite for Sheriff Saxon to play." Finn Carstens strolled through the door, unzipping his coat as he walked. "It remains to be seen just what his rules are."

"You said you were expecting him." The inflection in Cal's words made them a question.

"Yes." She indicated for Finn to take the seat next to her and Cal retreated, closing the door quietly. Keira had questions of her own, but they would wait until she and the agent were alone. "Finn Carstens from Raiker Forensics everyone. We have him to thank for the lab results."

"So…you're a scientist?" Brody's brow furrowed.

"Part-time. Many of Raiker's forensic experts are cross-trained as investigators." Finn shrugged out of his coat. He was dressed in a dark sweater, jeans, and expensive-looking leather boots that would do him very little good in the snow. A corner of his mouth pulled up. "Consider me a twofer. Raiker has mobile labs scattered across the nation. If the case demands it, Sheriff Saxon could requisition one and I would do the lab work myself."

His answer addressed one of the issues she'd had when he'd walked in. But Keira still wanted to speak to him in private about the extent of his investigative experience.

Her mind flashed to her meeting with Adam Raiker. He didn't seem like a man who would make a mistake about a matter like this. The realization alleviated a portion of her unease.

"You think the killer regards this whole thing as a game?" It was the first time Phil had spoken. "That he killed our boss for what? Entertainment?"

"It's early yet." Finn's foot touched one of Keira's as he arranged his legs beneath the table next to hers. "Way too soon for conclusions. But based on Keira's description of the attack, I'd say he was trying to get her attention. That ambush may even have been pre-planned, although it's equally likely that she followed him faster than he'd anticipated, so he improvised." He turned his head to look at her. "Once you hit that trail, how far could the driver have stayed ahead of you without being seen?"

"There are a lot of curves, so maybe only a quarter mile or so. But I'd hear the sled, and on the trail my speed would have been far faster than it had been in the woods. The snowmobile he was driving matched the report of an older model stolen the same week. I probably would have been able to catch him. Obviously towing it was an easy way to keep me from following. My sled was left near a forest exit."

"We followed his snowmobile's trail." Hank picked up the story. "We lost it when it crossed the highway, but it resumed on the opposite side. Three miles later, the tracks went off the path through the woods to an old logging road.. He must have had a pick up waiting there. Easy enough to back up to a snow bank and then drive the sled in the back. Throw a tarp over it and off you go."

"I'm guessing no one saw him."

"We put out a media alert. None of the tips have panned out." Keira glanced at the clock on the wall. Almost two. "My deputies took casts of the truck's tire treads, as well as the footprints on my porch, so we'll have those for comparison purposes. No prints were found on my sled or my weapon." There had been an off chance her attacker had handled it. "Likely he wore gloves. At any rate, we have pictures of the scenes at my house and where I was assaulted, as well as the trail he took making his getaway. I got a shot off before he hit me. I'm pretty sure I wounded him. There was slight blood spatter near his footprints leading away from the scene. We found more where he had his truck parked. There just wasn't enough cast off blood for lab tests."

Finn's attention jerked toward her, surprise written in his expression. "You were close enough to wing him? So you have a description?"

She grimaced. "I wish. Things were a blur, and he was all in black. Probably wore a facemask. We've checked for patients presenting with gunshot wounds at all the hospitals and clinics in the east and west peninsula, as well as with veterinarians. There have been four reports of treating a GSW since last week. All have checked out, and we can be certain not one was our guy. It could have been a flesh wound, which he wouldn't necessarily have needed medical attention for. Or he had someone he trusted to help him who wouldn't report it. We found no traces of blood on my sled when it was recovered."

She slid a thick file folder on the table over to him. "Copies of the photos from a week ago and the scene from where Danny's body was found." Using her dad's given name helped her retain a modicum of objectivity. She was going to need every ounce she could muster for this case. "You'll also find a list of everyone this office sent away during his tenure."

Finn flipped the folder open and—setting aside the packets of photos for the moment—picked up the list and fanned the pages. "Wow. You weren't kidding about his enemies. Given his position, I guess that's to be expected."

"I have the cases cross-referenced for which ones he had a personal involvement in, including dates. Each is coded for when he made the arrest or provided testimony that helped put a suspect away. I've started another list for other county residents that may have harbored some animosity toward him." Keira lifted a shoulder. Not everyone with a grudge landed in jail. And while the most recent incidents would receive priority if she were at the helm of the investigation, she knew that thoughts of revenge could simmer for years. Decades, even.

Sound filtered into the conference room. A raised voice. Cal's low rumbling tones.

She scanned the faces of her deputies. "Hank and Phil, you'll accept duties from Finn and report to him on matters dealing with the investigation." As undersheriff, Phil was second in command and primarily responsible for running the jail. But they'd all have to pull double duty in this case. "Mary and Brody will work with me looking into the identity of the second victim. He was alive when the finger was amputated and still may be. The clock is ticking on this one. You'll have to juggle your other responsibilities as they come up. Assignments will be handed out by the end of the day."

The thunderous pounding on the door of the conference room signaled that the meeting was at an end. Pushing her chair back, Keira rose. Everyone else followed suit. When the door burst open, the deputies skirted the man in the doorway as they filed from the room. "Sheriff Saxon." Alger County Commissioner Arnie Hassert's whole body fairly quivered with temper. "You and I need to talk."

Keira had been half expecting him. She nodded understandingly to Cal, who stood red-faced behind the other man. There was no stopping Arnie in a fit of pique. It seemed to be his normal state, at least where she was concerned. "Certainly. Can I offer you coffee?"

In response, the man flicked a glance at Finn. "You'll need to leave."

Her eyes narrowed at the man's autocratic tone, but Keira's voice was cool when she turned to Finn. "Now would be a good time for you to see Cal about having a photo taken for a temporary ID."

But it took another moment for Finn to remove his gaze from Hassert. "I don't mind sticking around."

The look in his eye, in his tone, took her aback. *Protectiveness.* It had been a long time since she'd seen that expression on a man. Keira almost laughed. After working Chicago homicide, handling a loud-mouthed quasi-politician like Hassert didn't even raise her blood pressure. "It's okay." Her gaze slid back to the man in the doorway. The commissioner's face was red and with his frizzy hair standing on end, she could almost understand Carstens' hesitation. "We'll speak later."

Finn took his time replacing papers in the file she'd given him before rising, collecting his coat and ambling toward the commissioner. He'd barely brushed by the other man when Hassert slammed the door after him and stalked toward Keira, slapping his hands on the table opposite her.

"You deliberately went back on your word!"

"How's that?"

Her question seemed to stop him for a moment. "You know as well as I do! We had an agreement. You'd run all extra expenses by me first before allocating new resources."

"You mean to run them by the board of commissioners."

The subtle needling found its mark. Pushing away from the table the man ran a hand through his hair, which stood out from his head like a Brillo pad wired with live voltage. "I meant the entire board."

She nodded. "Of course. And if I do foresee additional expenses, I'll be sure to do so. Now if you'll excuse me…."

"And what do you call the agenda item you added this morning? *Discuss special transfer of funds?* I'm here to tell you if you're going to ask for an addition to this year's budget, the answer will be no."

She shook her head, torn between annoyance and awe. If leaping to conclusions were a sport, the man would be an Olympian. "I assume you've spoken to Dorie." The woman was the county auditor. Part of her duties included acting as clerk for the commissioners. She publicized the agendas and took minutes for the meetings. It was a mystery how she kept getting elected to the job. She certainly hadn't been hired for her discretion. The woman had set new records tipping off Arnie about their phone call a couple hours ago. "I'm not going to ask for more money."

"Then explain that agenda item!"

Keira stood, taking a moment to enjoy the fact that at five nine she was at least three inches taller than him. "I'll do exactly that when the full board is in session. Suffice it to say, my request has already been cleared with the prosecutor and the state attorney's office. Now I'm uncomfortable having this discussion with you in a private session, absent the rest of the commissioners." She took a moment to enjoy the flicker of discomfort the words brought to his expression. "It'd probably be best for both of us if we leave this conversation for tomorrow afternoon."

The man straightened, then yanked a stocking hat from his pocket and pulled it on. "We'll do just that.

Don't be surprised if the board turns down your request. You know the strain the county budget is under."

The man had a one-track mind and the comprehension skills of a three-year-old. "I look forward to discussing this with the commissioners." Keira walked to the door and opened it to urge the man to follow her. "See you tomorrow."

She watched him stride past her, his back rigid with his ire and wondered for a moment at the level of almost irrational animosity he seemed to reserve just for her. Because her dad had been slightly more than halfway through his current term as sheriff, a special election to fill his office hadn't been held. Instead, a committee comprised of the county clerk, county prosecutor, and probate judge solicited applications and chose a sheriff to fill out the term. Her selection had been unanimous. But it was an ill-kept secret in town that Hassert had actively tried to dissuade the committee from approaching her. Most of the time she could dismiss him as a harmless irritant, but other times—like today—he bordered on irrational.

Dismissing him with a shrug, she headed for Cal's desk and found it empty, save for Finn, who had perched a hip on the corner of it. He was studying the picture of her hanging on the wall just inside the door. At her approach, his focus switched to her.

"I had a desk moved into the conference room for you." She jerked a thumb over her shoulder to indicate the room she'd just departed. "It's stocked with the basics, but let Cal know if there's anything else you require."

He stood lazily and bent to pick up a briefcase next to the desk. She had the errant thought that a pair of blue jeans did far more for him than a lab coat.

Impatient at herself, Keira turned on her heel and led the way back to the room she'd just departed. "Shift change is in a couple hours. The names of the deputies at your disposal are in the folder." She stopped to face him, saw that Cal had returned to his desk and was on the phone. "I've arranged for your accommodations, and I'll be glad to show you to them. And to a decent place to get a meal after you settle in." She had to finalize her presentation to the commissioners for tomorrow's meeting, but she could always come back and work after dinner. She wanted an uninterrupted conversation with the man, and she was unlikely to get one here.

The intercom sounded. "Sheriff, Matthews on line two."

Keira stifled a sigh. She didn't know Tobias Matthews, a lieutenant with the Keweenaw Bay Tribal Police well, but she could already be certain that this discussion was unlikely to be pleasant.

"Go." Carstens was already walking by her to set his briefcase on the desk tucked into a corner of the room. "You don't have to babysit me."

After a brief moment, she took him at his word and headed to her office to take the call. With what she was paying for an outside investigator Carstens was right about one thing—she shouldn't have to babysit him.

———

It was an hour and a half past shift change before she looked at the clock on the wall and swore. Pushing away from her desk, she grabbed her coat and purse before striding out of her office to see if Carstens had given up and bailed yet. She paused in the doorway of the conference room, looking at the transformation that had taken place there in the last few hours.

Two wires had been strung across the wall next to his desk. The photos she'd given him hung from each, all punctuated with Post-its containing notes in a strong, bold hand. Drawing closer she realized one line of photos was from her attack; the other held the pictures from her father's scene. She scanned the ones from last May again, wondering if he'd see something in them that she hadn't on the countless long nights she'd stayed up studying them. The other wall acted as a makeshift bulletin board, where he'd used colored tape to attach a surprisingly large array of notecards.

"Looks like you're settling in."

When he looked over his shoulder at her, she saw that he was wearing a pair of narrow black-framed glasses. "I've got a start, yeah." He reached up to take the glasses off and set them on top of his desk before stifling a yawn. "Sorry. I got up at three to make my six oh five flight."

She walked closer to peer at the cards he had taped to the wall. They weren't arranged haphazardly at all, she saw now. The man's scientific brain probably wouldn't allow such randomness. One line kept track of the deputies' assignments. Another set of cards listed possible leads to follow. Two cards were alone. One was marked CODIS and the other ViCAP.

At the reminder, Keira gave herself a mental head slap. "I'll get you our access information to all the federal databases."

"I'll need them for state systems, but all of Raiker's agents have federal input credentials, which will get us a response far quicker."

She was surprised, but she probably shouldn't have been. It was another reminder of how well respected the Mindhunters were, since she'd only heard of law enforcement entities being given access. CODIS would only be useful if they got DNA from the offender, but ViCAP looked at crime patterns. Keira cocked a brow at Finn. "Think we'll get any hits on killers who cut body parts out of their victims and send them to family members with other people's parts inside?"

He rubbed his jaw, which was already shadowed. Of course, it would be since he'd been up for more than fifteen hours already. "I'm going to need more details to narrow the parameters of the search. And I hate to admit it, but I'm probably through here until I get some food. That burger I grabbed in Marquette is a distant memory."

"My offer's still good, if a little later than I promised. C'mon." Keira turned away from the display. She knew from experience that food refueled her thought processes. And hers had been fragmented all day. "You can follow me and drop your rental off. The two motels were full—it's the height of snowmobiling season here— but Turner's Landing is a decent bed and breakfast. You'll be comfortable there."

He powered down his laptop and got up to shrug into his coat, before sliding the computer into his briefcase. Snapping the locks, he straightened and turned toward her. "I'll follow you anywhere if you can promise that wherever we eat has steak."

She smirked as she led the way out of the room. "Steak? And here I'd pegged you as a vegan."

———

Although Finn had been willing to dine before checking in, at Keira's suggestion, he went to Turner's first to check in and meet the hosts. Their warm greeting made him feel a little churlish about his earlier plans. So much so that he spent twenty minutes trailing along as they gave him a tour of their cozy home, while turning down their repeated offers to make him dinner. He'd dropped his briefcase and bag off in his room, taking time only to change into the warmer snow boots he'd brought along. It was already clear that walking through snow and ice every day wasn't going to do his leather pair any good. Nearly a half hour had passed before he and Keira were finally seated at a rickety wooden table in a cramped establishment that looked more bar than restaurant, although at the moment he wasn't fussy.

A curvy startlingly blond waitress expertly wound her way through the crowded tables toward them. "Did you go on a fishing trip yesterday, Keira?" The woman gave Finn a slow wide smile that revealed a crooked incisor and more than a hint of mischievousness. "Because from the looks of this one, you brought home quite a catch."

There was an intriguing hint of color in the sheriff's face as she pulled off her gloves and shoved them in her pocket. "This is a colleague of mine, Tiff. And we're both starved. We'll take the special if you still have filets available."

"If we don't, I know where Diz stocks a few he sets aside for emergencies, and he's not here to catch me. I'll come through for you." She fluttered her lashes at Finn. "What'll you have to drink, flatlander?"

"Ah…" Distracted for a moment by the name, he glanced at Keira and saw she was watching the exchange with visible amusement. "Blue Moon, if you've got it."

"We do. Just water for you, Keira?"

"That's fine." The woman had bustled on to the next table almost before Keira got the response out of her mouth.

"Flatlander?"

She unzipped her coat and draped it over the chair. "Anyone who heralds from the flat land to our south. Not from the peninsula. And those of us who live under the bridge are trolls." His expression must have mirrored his lack of comprehension because she went on. "The Mackinac Bridge in St. Ignace connects the upper and lower peninsulas. Tiffany is a Yooper, born and bred."

"UP. Yooper. Got it." He divested himself of his coat. "Does that term apply to you, as well?"

She was given no chance to reply as the waitress had returned, balancing a full tray on one shoulder with ease. "Nope, Keira's not a full-fledged Yooper, because she only lived here in the summers before graduating college and thinking that shooting bad guys on the Chicago streets was more glamorous than life in Munising." Tiffany gave Finn a wink as she set their glasses on the table in front of them. "But we made some memories during those summers, and if you want to stay until after my shift ends and buy me a drink, I could be convinced to share some of them with you."

"Tiffany." Keira's smile was bright, but her eyes narrowed in warning. "Go. Away."

The woman flitted to the next table, leaving a throaty laugh in her wake.

"She's incorrigible. A horrible flirt. And my closest friend since childhood." There was a note of indulgence in her voice as Keira reached out and brought her glass to her lips, her gaze scanning the other occupants in the room as she drank. "My parents divorced when I was four, and I mostly lived with my mother. We bounced around some before ending up in Chicago. But I spent summers and Christmas vacations with my dad."

"Was it tough, going back and forth between two parents like that?" Finn tried the beer. Found it every bit as cold as he liked it.

Her shrug was a roll of the shoulders. "Having *no* parents is tough. Having two in different states was just a logistical obstacle. We made it work."

He took a moment to wonder if her father had approached the issue with the same matter-of-factness. It wouldn't have been enough for Finn with his child. Had the opportunity arisen.

Because the thought circled much too close to a wound that still throbbed, he shoved it away to consider the woman across the table as he sipped his beer. Her hair had been longer in the picture of her inside the sheriff's office and pulled severely from her face. The style had highlighted her tilted green eyes, narrow nose, and a stubborn chin. A face that surpassed mere attractiveness and bulls-eyed on compelling. She wasn't used to the shorter hairstyle made necessary by her attack last week. That was apparent from the impatient habit she had of shoving it back from her face. Ineffectually, because it barely grazed her shoulders and wasn't long enough to obey before it fell forward again, framing her jaw. Softening it in a way she probably despised.

"Corner table to the east end of the bar." At his conversational tone, her gaze flew to meet his. "The bigger one has prison tats and the spike studs the other is sporting on his leather bracelet come in real handy in a fight. I've seen a victim whose lip was torn away by one. Are they locals?"

"I only recognize one of them. The guy with the tats is Bruce Yembley. He's on the list I prepared for you." At that moment, the duo turned toward them and the man shot them a one-fingered salute. "He did twelve years of a fifteen year stretch at the Alger Correctional Facility for beating a man to death in a disagreement over a drug deal. My father testified against him." She raised her glass in a mock greeting before turning her attention back to Finn. "And Danny appeared at his parole hearings to make sure Yembley stayed inside to complete most of his sentence. Of course it helped that the man had been anything but a model prisoner. He was just released a few months ago."

Finn tucked the name away. "Who handles the issuance of gun permits and hunting licenses in the county?"

"The Department of Natural Resources is responsible for all hunting and trapping licenses. People can apply online or pick up applications at the local grocery store or Duane's Sports downtown." She must have caught the look of surprise on his face and added wryly, "Hunting is big in the UP. DNR tries to make the licensing as convenient as possible. My office handles the gun licenses and open carry permits. Michigan has pretty broad laws upholding its citizens right to open carry, but there are some restrictions."

He reached for his glass and sipped the beer, considering. "I read up on that—among other things— on my way here. In this job, I get sent to many different parts of the country. And outside it. It pays to research the laws of a region you're going to be working in."

She leaned forward, her gaze intense. "I was wondering about that. And your dual role for Raiker Forensics. How much time do you spend in the field on cases, opposed to in the labs?"

Her interest wasn't unexpected. Similar questions were directed at him in one way or another any time he worked in the field in an investigative capacity. "I've never figured it out, percentage-wise. I often provide both forensic and investigative assistance. I worked my way through medical school employed part time by a private lab, so I attained that experience early on. Completed a residency in pathology and then was employed by the Ohio State Medical Examiner's Office, where I often worked cases the Bureau of Criminal Investigation were involved in. I crossed paths with Raiker when he was consulting on one of them." He lifted a shoulder, his thumb tracing a circle in the condensation on his glass. "He contacted me months later about adding me as an expert consultant. I would only agree if it were a staff position that allowed cross training, so I wasn't in the lab or doing autopsies full-time." He drank to erase the memories that threatened and condensed the rest of his answer. "I serve in both capacities as needed. So far I've been happy with the balance."

Her expression said she recognized he'd left out far more than he'd chosen to share, but since she hadn't volunteered a helluva lot she couldn't complain. "So what part of the world have you seen since joining Raiker Forensics?"

He shifted in his chair to stretch out his legs, crossing them at the ankles. "Last month I was helping with the extraction of bodies from a swamp in South Carolina. Before Christmas, one of the cases I was assigned took us to Malaysia. Before that, I was in British Columbia."

"Really?" She sipped at her water even as her eyes scanned the occupants of the place. He wasn't offended. It was likely second nature due to her profession. After commencing his investigative training, he'd found himself doing the same thing. "I didn't realize Raiker took international cases."

"Occasionally." He didn't mention that the Malaysia case had involved the man's stepson being kidnapped and transported out of the country. Raiker had managed to keep a lot of the details out of the media, and Finn would respect his wish for privacy. Victims' families were seldom granted the same courtesy. Which made what he was about to ask Keira doubly difficult.

"Was your father buried or cremated?"

"He always said he wanted to be cremated, that it was ridiculous to waste land for a burial. Why do you…" Her expression froze. "You were going to ask to exhume him?"

He nodded, mildly disappointed. "There might have been something the state ME missed. Now that we know a knife was used to extract the liver, it may have been possible to find other similar wounds on the body. Perhaps some which were dismissed as marks left by the teeth of animals."

Keira sat back leadenly in her seat, her normally creamy complexion bleached of color. "That would have been a tough call to make. I have to admit I'm not unhappy that I won't be faced with the decision."

"Understandable." But she was still thinking about the possibility, he could tell. And he had a feeling that had it been an option, she would have eventually agreed. Because she was a cop, first and foremost. From their first meeting, he'd watched her tuck away her emotional connection to the case. And could guess exactly how much it had cost her.

A minute later she asked, "Do you think the killer might have removed something else from my dad's body besides the liver?"

"It's useless to speculate." But he'd bet she'd done more than her share of it since her father's death.

"Would it be possible to discover whether the same weapon was used on both the finger and the removal of the organ?"

"It's doubtful a tool mark comparison could be made, since the disarticulation is usually done with the point of a sharp instrument, as opposed to the blade. With a lab, I'd be able to do more tests to determine if the fingernail loss was due to a fungus or disease or whether a trauma caused it."

"Maybe its owner was tortured." Keira reached for her glass, drank pensively. "And he might still be alive." She gave a slight grimace, and she glanced at Yembley. "Wish I could say that I didn't know anyone around here capable of that."

"I assume you've been checking the missing person's reports for the state."

Her nod sent the curve of her hair swaying toward her face. "I've got two of my deputies compiling lists, but for now we're focused on the last nine months or less."

"Makes sense." Finn lifted his nearly empty glass to catch Tiff's eye as she bustled by. The waitress gave him a thumbs-up without slowing down.

Keira's index finger tapped against her glass. Her fingers were long and feminine, the nails short. "We have nine missing people in the fifteen county area that makes up the western side of the peninsula. Another seven on the eastern side. We're reaching out to the case detectives in those counties. But if we go back further, there have been a few reports in the last several years of tourists that have disappeared. Snowmobilers, hunters, fisherman." She fell silent when Tiffany came by to hand Finn his beer.

"Steaks are almost up," the waitress assured them before speeding off again.

Keira reached for her glass. Drank. "The UP is a beautiful area, but things can happen to the careless. A fisherman who goes through the ice on Superior may not be found for months, if at all. We have several wilderness areas on the western side of the peninsula. Not to mention the old copper mines in Keweenaw or the still worked iron mines in Gogebic. With well over a hundred thousand acres of forests and waterways…"

"Lots of places to meet a bad end." Finn moved his feet out of the way and straightened as Tiffany headed their way with two steaming plates in her hands. "Then there's always the people who disappear and aren't missed."

"Exactly." Keira unwrapped her silverware and placed the napkin on her lap. "This region is a great place for loners. More trees than people, with plenty of privacy. Last winter one of the deputies was delivering an eviction notice to a resident. The place looked deserted. No prints or tire tracks. The guy's pickup was snowed under in the shed next to the house. The deputy did a check and discovered the resident dead inside. From the stage of decomposition, he'd likely died months earlier."

It occurred to Finn that he couldn't recall a time when he'd sat across the table from an attractive woman and discussed decomposition. He decided he could get used to it.

"And I didn't even have to raid Diz's freezer," Tiffany declared as she deftly set the plates in front of first Keira, then Finn. Although for you I would have. Absolutely." She took a breath, beamed at them. "Enjoy. Kitchen closes at ten, and tonight I get off at eleven." She waggled her brows, looking from one of them to the other. "Any chance either of you will still be here?"

"Not likely, sorry." Keira wasted no time cutting into the steak and lifting a bite to her mouth. Her eyes closed in an expression of exaggerated ecstasy.

"What about you, fudgie?"

Mystified at the name, Finn shook his head and followed Keira's lead. He picked up his knife and fork. "She's my wheels."

Giving up, the woman blew out a breath. "Saturday. Keira, I'm not taking no for an answer. I've got the weekend off. Maybe we can even go to Powderhorn."

"I can't manage a weekend, but give me a call…" Keira began before their heads turned in unison at the raucous laughter coming from the corner booth.

"Tiffany! Get your butt over here." Yembley raised a bottle. "There are other paying customers in here besides that red-headed…" The rest of his comment was lost, but his companion's bray of laughter made it all too easy to predict.

"Asswipes," Tiff muttered and stalked toward the bar.

Finn gave the men in the booth a long look before returning his attention to his plate. "Does she need help with them?"

"She can handle those two." But all enjoyment had fled from her expression and her gaze fixed on Yembley. "If not…"

If not, Keira would. Her incomplete statement made that clear.

They both turned their attention to enjoying what was—in Finn's estimation—one of the best steaks he'd had in years. Their conversation was limited. He knew she was as attuned to the growing rowdiness in the nearby booth as he was. He wasn't sure how many beers the two had imbibed before he and Keira had come in, but they were doubling down now. They ordered again, shots this time, coupled with crude remarks to Tiffany. As Keira had indicated, the waitress handled them with barbed insults. Yet Finn noted the woman kept as far away from the booth as possible when delivering the next round.

"Hey, Pete." The voice was loud enough to be heard by every occupant in the place. "You know the difference between a ginger and a brick? At least a brick gets laid." Yembley and his buddy laughed uproariously. Finn caught more than a few surreptitious glances their way. Two tables abruptly vacated as the occupants got up with undisguised haste and went to the register at the far end of the bar to pay their bills. Clearly they sensed what had been brewing for the last half hour. One didn't have to see the clouds to feel a storm coming on.

"Think you're right, Bruce." Pete looked over his shoulder at them, revealing a grizzled jaw and a missing front tooth. "Desperation turns them redheads into lesbos."

"That true, sheriff?" Yembley called.

Finn tensed. The two were spoiling for a fight. And he would dearly love to be the one who landed the first punch. He glanced at Keira. With a calm expression, she continued to eat as though she'd gone deaf. But her back was rigid. Her fingers clenched around her fork. She wasn't as unaffected as she appeared.

"I'm talking to you, Saxon. You wearing your dead daddy's uniform, or did you get one special made for dykes?"

Tiffany propped her clenched fists on the men's table, her expression thunderous. "Get out. Both of you. And don't come back."

"Fuck off, Tiff. You don't own this place."

With great deliberation, Keira set her silverware down. Brought her napkin up to pat delicately at her lips. Then rose and stalked toward the booth. Finn stood and followed in her wake. With a subtle movement, she stepped in front of her friend, crowding her from her position beside the table. Finn took a step that placed him at Keira's side.

She wrinkled her nose. "You smell as gamey as the animals you trap, Yembley. You have running water at your place, right?"

The man's ugly obscenity had Finn's muscles tensing.

"Maybe it's just prison stench. Speaking of which, if memory serves, you're still on parole. Which means you're not supposed to be in a place that serves alcohol, or in the company of known felons. Now I don't know your friend here, but I'm guessing if we run his name we'll find a sheet as long as yours." Her voice turned hard. "So you have two choices. You can pay your bill and be on your way, or spend the night in jail before I turn you over to your parole officer."

The man laughed. "And who's gonna put me in jail, dyke? You?"

"Not sure she'd need any help. But if so, I'd be glad to provide it." For the first time, Yembley looked at him, his gaze assessing. Finn didn't need Keira's quick sidelong glance to know that his support was unwelcome. At the moment he didn't particularly care.

"C'mon, Bruce, it ain't worth it." Pete spit on the floor, narrowly missing the toe of Keira's boots.

"Wise choice, Pete." She moved back, and reluctantly Finn did as well to allow the man to stand. "What do you say, Yembley? Are you as smart as your friend here?"

"Smart enough to know you're as big a joke as your old man was." The ex-con slid out of the booth slowly.

Stood. "You just keep following in his footsteps. Maybe you'll wind up dead, too."

Keira and Finn stepped aside to allow the men to head to the register. Tiffany was already moving in that direction with their checks. As they returned to their table, Keira said, "Just for the record, I didn't require backup."

Finn waited for her to retake her seat before following suit and sending her a cool glance. "Just for the record, as long as I'm here…you'll have backup. Whether you want it or not." With her look searing him, he picked up his silverware and proceeded to finish the rest of his now cold meal. Keira had just started to do the same when her cell rang.

He reached out for his beer and listened unabashedly.

"When? Is there a car en route?" She stood and grabbed her coat. Finn set down the bottle and did the same. "I'll be there in fifteen minutes. Direct the deputy to establish a perimeter, but tell him not to go inside." She disconnected, donning her coat and heading to the door, calling out to Tiffany, "Hold my bill. I'll be back to pay it later."

"Where are we going?"

Keira shot him a startled glance as if she'd forgotten Finn's existence. "Not we, me. That was the night dispatcher. The alarm at my place just went off. Someone broke in."

CHAPTER 3

In the end, she brought Finn with her when she headed home, siren silent. Keira didn't want to waste the time it would take to drop him off. Not when adrenaline was churning in her veins, hot and urgent.

He was silent next to her as she kept in contact with her deputy via radio.

"Nothing out of place in front, Sheriff," Brody Boyle reported. "Phil's here, too. Your security lights and the alarm are on. I see a set of tire tracks out front. I'm going around back."

"There should be lights there, as well." The tire treads in front would have been hers from this morning. If the intruder were the same person who'd left the cooler for her to find, he'd likely approached from the rear of the cabin.

They waited a long couple of minutes before his voice sounded again. "One set of footprints leading to and then away from your back door. It's standing open. The window a couple feet from it is broken out."

"Check the rest of the yard, but don't enter the house." She disconnected, then contacted Hank Fallon to bring the evidence van. Putting the radio back in its holder, Keira sent a sideways glance to Finn. "At least we can cross Yembley off the list of suspects. Although I doubt he's above a little breaking and entering, he left the bar minutes before we did. There's no way he would have had time to get out to my place."

"Maybe that was the point," Finn suggested. "Make a public appearance so he has an alibi while an accomplice does the dirty work."

It was possible, she supposed, although Yembley seemed too impulsive for that sort of planning. Her foot pressed more firmly on the accelerator. *A game.* She and Finn had reached the same conclusion about the killer's motivation to involve her. It would take a stretch of the imagination to believe this latest action was attributable to anyone else.

The shrill of the alarm could be heard from the road before she turned down the long drive to the cabin. Joe Boster had a truck with a blade on it and had been keeping it plowed for as long as she could remember. It was clear now; it hadn't snowed since last night.

The strobe of two cruisers flashed through the barren trees as she made her way to the front of the cabin. Brody and Phil came around the corner of the house as she pulled up. Finn got out of the SUV. She retrieved her MagLite before going to join the deputies.

"There's a snowmobile track out back. Came out of the woods and looks like he left the same way."

Keira gave Phil a tight smile. "Of course he did." Whoever the trespasser was, his familiarity with her property was a detail to be examined later. Finn pulled out his cell and turned on a flashlight app to light his way as he went up to examine the porch and tried the front door. She followed the deputies around to the back of the cabin. The long wide porch hemmed all four sides of it. She could see the broken glass from the yard.

"No signs of movement inside," Brody told her. "Just one light on in the front room. Looks like he went in through the back window, and exited through the rear door."

She turned, half surprised to find Finn standing at her side already. The man moved fast and silently. Something to remember. Her gaze fell to the weapon in his hand.

"Let's enter through the front. Less chance of destroying any footwear impressions that might have been left."

Nodding, she told her deputies, "Cover the back. Brody, let Finn use your MagLite." Then she rounded the house again with Finn on her heels. Once she eased up the steps she set her flashlight on the porch to fish her keys out of her coat pocket to unlock and open the front door. Then, picking up the light she drew her weapon and pivoted inside the doorway.

In the cabin the alarm was ear splitting. The glow from the lamp she'd left on spilled as far as the hallway while leaving most of the room dark. Sweeping the area with the flashlight, she saw the front room was empty. With only a glance at the stairway that would go to the second story, she moved quickly toward the hallway ahead that acted as a hub for the other rooms. Kitchen, dining room, bathroom and utility area spoked out from the hall. The entrance to each space was dark.

Shadows huddled in the hallway, each shifting, and morphing as they passed. With her back pressed against the wall, Keira's light caught the glint of water puddles spotting the planked floor. Following them with the beam she saw the trail at the end of the hall coming out of the bathroom where the broken window had been. It stopped in front of the doorway to the kitchen.

Her heart was hammering. Stupid. The guy was gone. She'd bet the bank on that. She just wasn't willing to bet her life on it. She jerked her head toward the left and swung into the kitchen as Finn rushed by to check the dining room.

No one under the table. And there was nowhere else to hide in the space. Her chest easing a fraction she called, "Clear."

"Clear."

She heard him moving toward the back of the house, but rather than join him she played her light over the droplets of water on the floor showing better than words the path the intruder had taken. There was another small pool in front of the counter. She frowned. Her breakfast dishes were stacked neatly in the sink. Some correspondence she needed to tend to hung from a magnetized clip on the fridge.

And more water was on the floor in front of it.

"Bathroom clear." Finn's voice drifted in.

Moving back into the hall, she brushed by him to go to the utility area that connected the cabin to the double garage. Keira swung open the door to her left and peered into the remaining room. The washer and dryer were tucked side by side against one wall. Furnace and water heater were nestled nearby. She stepped further into the dark room, playing her light over the appliances and around the furnace.. "Clear."

Finn was closing and locking the door to the garage. "It's clear. Bedrooms upstairs?"

Nodding, Keira led the way to the stairway. But it didn't take long for them to ascertain that the three bedrooms, baths and office on the second story were empty. Her pulse slowed to a steady rhythm. The place was deserted. She could almost feel that much in the stillness in the air. But if she'd been home thirty minutes earlier the intruder would have walked in on her. Had he planned on it being empty, or had he hoped to surprise her?

"Whatever he wanted, his focus was the kitchen. The water on the floor in the hallway?" Keira flipped on the light switch in the kitchen as she re-holstered her weapon. "You see it again here."

"Melted from the snow on his boots. It's in the bathroom, too."

"He walked to the counter,"—she indicated his path with the flashlight's beam— "and then continued to the refrigerator. If it was food he was looking for, he's out of luck. I've been putting off grocery shopping."

Finn put away his weapon and pulled on one of the gloves he'd stuffed in his coat pocket. Stepping toward the refrigerator, he opened the door wide for her observation. The contents were paltry. A nearly empty half-gallon of milk. A carton of eggs. A six pack of beer. A couple of containers of leftovers. All had been there that morning.

The plate on the second shelf had not.

Dread pooled nastily in her belly. "The dish is one of mine. But I didn't put it there." Her gaze went to the cupboards above the counter where the man had headed. The plate had been taken from there, a match to the set of stoneware her father had kept for as long as she could remember.

"Let's see what he brought you this time." Finn pulled on his thick winter gloves before retrieving the plate and setting it on the counter. Keira awkwardly unwrapped the newspaper around the object, while avoiding touching the dish. She stilled when the item was uncovered. Then squelched the quick, violent lurch in her belly when she recognized it. A human ear.

"Jesus," she muttered, hauling in a deep breath through clenched teeth. "I think I'll request that lab."

"I was about to recommend it." He slid the plate around, crouched until he was eye level with it. "One thing I can tell you definitively without running any tests." His gaze lifted to meet hers. "The victim was dead when it was severed. And it didn't come from Danny."

She gave a short nod. A mental loop of the images from her father's crime scene replayed in her mind. "There were portions of each ear intact on his body." This one was complete save for the lobe, which looked as though it had been partially cut away. "You'll be able to run DNA tests on this and the finger."

"Yes. Do you have a large Ziploc?"

Keira bent to take one out of a bottom drawer and opened it. He rewrapped the specimen, slid the plate with its contents inside and secured the bag. Then he looked at her. "It needs to be kept cool. I hate to ask..."

"*Mi casa es su casa*," she said with dark humor. He opened her refrigerator and shoved aside the items on the top shelf to place the baggie and contents there. They'd be dusting the other shelf for prints, along with the counter, cupboards and refrigerator door. Keira had a sinking feeling they wouldn't find any.

She needed to shove aside the rising certainty that their efforts would be in vain. Master criminals were largely a work of fiction. While she'd investigated several puzzling homicides for the CPD, more often crimes were committed impulsively and sloppily. Whoever had been here could have made a mistake.

Besides the one he'd made murdering her father.

Together they headed out of the kitchen. "Do you have an EDL? There's a good chance we could lift footwear impressions from the areas beneath the broken window and the back door."

Her smile was fleeting. "As a matter of fact." She'd bought the Electrostatic Dust Lifter for her dad a couple Christmases ago. They often exchanged forensic tools as gifts because law enforcement resources were chronically limited. "Danny had exterior cameras mounted on all sides of the cabin. Unless they've been deactivated, I should have feed on the computer."

She went to the coffee table in front of the couch and turned on her laptop. While she waited for it to power up, she strode to the security panel next to the front door and punched in the code. The alarm was abruptly silenced. But its echo pounded in her ears. Keira used the radio on her belt to contact the deputies. "All clear in here. See you in the front."

When she and Finn went out the front door, meeting the two men as they rounded the house. "What'd you find in there?"

"Aside from the human ear in my refrigerator, not much." Phil's profanity was ugly and imaginative. "I didn't expect to see you."

Fascination bloomed as the older man hunched his shoulders, looked away. "Happened to be nearby, that's all."

After a moment, comprehension bloomed. "Betty Lawler lives near here." The woman had been Dr. Ressler's nurse before they'd both retired.

Phil glowered at her. "So what if she does?"

"Nothing." Keira couldn't prevent a tiny smile and Brody was grinning hugely. She didn't put much stock in gossip, but apparently the rumors she'd heard about her undersheriff and the nurse were true. "Just an observation. I think the excitement here is over for the night. Hank will arrive shortly. No reason for you or Brody to stick around."

The older man nodded. "We checked the cameras on the exterior of the house. All look intact."

"Ballsy," she muttered. "All right. I'll update you tomorrow." The two turned to go. Finn looked at her. "Let's take a look at that feed while we're waiting."

Keira nodded. "My thought, exactly." They re-entered the cabin and went to the computer, sinking down on the couch in front of the laptop. Overconfidence could lead to mistakes. It was time to see if her uninvited visitor had made one. Opening the security application, she quickly selected camera four, and the screen showed a dark picture of her back yard. She reversed the stream until she saw action on it. Then further to where the movement first started.

"Twenty-nine minutes ago," the man beside her murmured. They watched intently as a person clad in black came out of the woods bordering the back yard holding something in one dark gloved hand. The figure approached the steps. Climbed them. Then he stepped directly to the window, cocked the object in his arm and swung. "What'd he use? A bat? A bar?" she wondered aloud.

"Too narrow to be a bat." Finn leaned closer to the screen. "Maybe a stick or a metal bar." The intruder broke out the glass around the perimeter of the window before setting the tool on the porch and climbing inside the house. The feed went dark again. They continued to watch the monitor screen silently until the back door opened and the figure stepped out of the cabin, picking up the weapon he'd left and headed back toward the woods from the direction he'd come.

"He was inside just over two minutes."

He nodded. "Closer to three from the time it took to break in and enter. Knew exactly what he was doing and how he was going to do it."

Keira checked the time stamp on the screen. "Seven forty-six PM. How does he know I'm not at home? Or doesn't he care?" Switching screens, she brought up the camera from the front of the cabin and reversed the feed to examine the hour before the alarm sounded.

"Since you're pretty sure you winged him the last time the two of you met face to face, I'm guessing he made sure you were away. It's early enough that he wasn't counting on catching you asleep." Their gazes met. "Which means somehow he's tracking your whereabouts." His eyes were hard. Flinty. Or maybe it was a trick of the lighting because at that moment Finn Carstens seemed very far removed from the amiable scientist she'd met at Raiker's compound a couple days earlier. He looked every inch a cop. "Your vehicle is the only SUV in the sheriff's fleet, at least that I've seen. Easy enough to drive by and see whether it's in the parking lot. It was equally visible in front of the restaurant."

She nodded, frowning at the scene displayed on the screen until her phone pinged from an incoming text. After checking the message, she rose. "Hank's here."

"I'll help carry the equipment around back." They got as far as the front door before Finn turned to her. "You never mentioned…did you get an image from the cameras when the cooler was left on your porch?"

She grimaced. "I went out to ski. Was gone less than an hour. I'd locked the door but hadn't reset the security system. The cameras and alarm are on the same circuit." Keira had been kicking herself for the lapse ever since. The hyper-vigilance she'd practiced in Chicago had grown a bit more lax since she'd returned to her dad's remote home, and that was a mistake she wouldn't make again. "We should get a general idea of height and weight from these images, though." He nodded and headed outside to the van, not giving voice to the obvious: had the cameras been activated last week, she'd have images to compare.

Not—she thought grimly, as she followed him—that there was much doubt that the trespassers were one and the same. The macabre 'gifts' left each time made that obvious.

They set what they would need on the back porch. Keira helped Hank wrestle the spotlight into place to angle its beam toward the window. Straightening, she leaned in for a closer look.

"What'd he use to break the glass," Hank asked, surveying the broken panes. "Were you able to tell from the feed?"

"A club of some sort, no more than an inch wide. Approximately eighteen inches long."

Finn squatted on his haunches and reached into the kit for goggles. Handing each of them a set, he settled another pair over his head before taking the alternate light source and sweeping it over the split log siding beneath the window. Keira realized that he was looking for a mark or remnant of some sort that would supply a clue about the object used. After a couple minutes he stood, playing the ALS over the window. The handheld device was equipped with various light bands to search for prints, fluids or trace evidence.

"What's that?" She and Hank spoke simultaneously. Even before they got the words out Finn was bending nearer the object in question. A single dark hair was caught on a short jagged fragment of glass at the bottom of the casement.

"Bet he doesn't know that he left something else behind." He bent down and rummaged in the kit and rose with a pair of tweezers and a small coin envelope in his hand. Leaning in, he gently released the hair. Keira took the envelope to hold it open so he could place the short strand inside. Returning it to the kit, he switched the filter on the ALS device. Reading his intent, she squatted beside him and took out the fingerprint powder and brushes. Keira and Hank dusted around the bottom half of the window frame before leaning inside to repeat the action. Then, replacing the powder and brushes they got the tape and went flanked Finn as he played the ALS over the areas she'd dusted.

As expected, a mottled mess of prints showed. They painstakingly lifted the ones Finn pointed out. Danny had had all the windows replaced on the cabin a decade earlier. "I didn't see a flash of flesh in the video feed from the cameras. The figure was all dark. The chances of him leaving a print out here are pretty slim."

"Maybe we'll have better luck inside." Hank was affixing the latent tapes to individual cards. "He might have taken off his gloves there."

Finn bent to take out the EDL. "Probably ninety percent of physical evidence collected is useless. The kicker is, you never know which piece isn't."

———

It was after midnight when Hank Fallon pulled away from the cabin and nosed the evidence van down the drive. His taillights winked as the vehicle pulled around a curve and was lost from sight. They didn't finish until after midnight. It was only then that it occurred to Keira that she could have asked him to deliver Finn Carstens back to town.

She stopped on the second tread of her porch and pulled out her cell to call the investigator back, then hesitated. Turners wasn't on the way to the courthouse. Once Hank returned the van to the courthouse, he'd have to log in all the evidence collected tonight including, thankfully, the item left in her refrigerator—to keep the line of custody clear. She'd give Finn a ride herself.

Continuing toward the front door, she shook off the waves of exhaustion waiting to settle. It would be a late night. Likely the first of many for a while.

Stopping short inside the doorway, Keira cocked a brow at the man who was currently looking very much at home in her family room. Finn had his stocking feet on the coffee table in front of him, a beer in one hand and her computer balanced in his lap. He'd turned on the fireplace, she realized, and the warmth had chased away the chill that had permeated the cabin since they'd returned.

She leaned a shoulder against the wall. "You really took that *mi casa* thing literally."

Reaching for another bottle sitting on the table before him, he held it out. "Wanted to get a look at all the feed before we called it a night."

After a moment's hesitation, Keira crossed the room to take the bottle from his hand. She took a long drink before sinking onto the couch next to him so she could see the computer screen. "I didn't have a chance to review it all," she admitted, resisting the urge to nestle deeper into the overstuffed cushions. She tipped the bottle to her lips again.

"I retraced his steps while you were outside. Given the amount of time he was in here, there was no time for him to deviate from the path we found." He took a drink, his eyes never leaving the computer screen. "So you don't have to worry that he was anywhere near the upstairs."

Annoyance flickered. "I'm not worried."

"You should be." Now his gaze did leave the screen to fix on hers. "This is his game, and he's decided you're a key player. We don't know the rules or what to expect from him next. But he's targeted you twice. I'd say there are plenty of reasons to be cautious."

"Switch to camera one," she ordered, before seamlessly moving back to their conversation. "Caution isn't the same as worry. I've already alerted the security company and they'll be out to fix the window first thing tomorrow." Hank and Finn had managed to tape cardboard over the opening. It was neither weather tight nor burglar proof. "And I realize I have to figure a way to have these cameras monitored twenty-four seven. We've missed him twice." The words were released on a stream of frustration. The first time he had to have been watching the house. She'd left to cross country ski at first light. But tonight either he'd been following her, or he had someone else reporting on her whereabouts.

"I'm glad you've already considered the need to put a person on the security feed." They both watched the video from camera one in silence for a minute. "There's usually a way to log on to the feed from another computer as long as you have the password, so it would be easy enough to have someone at your office checking them round the clock."

"Yeah right." Broodingly she watched the screen, which currently showed the front of the cabin. "I'm already down an employee since I've got a jailer on medical leave with a broken leg." An idea formed even as she said the words and took root. Monitoring live feed wasn't a physical task. It might even be something that Chase Patten would welcome as a diversion from his forced inactivity. They could also use him to do phone interviews and follow-ups for the case if need be. She'd have to run it by the county's human resource director, but it was a possibility.

"This guy is familiar with your property. He might be equally well acquainted with your routine. And he doesn't care if he's caught on camera because he knows he can't be identified." Finn pressed a command to speed up the video.

"Maybe not his face." Whether it was the beer or the warmth from the fire, Keira felt some of the tension of the day melting away. She slouched a little lower on the couch. "But I'd peg him at five ten or eleven, one hundred eighty pounds from what we caught on camera. Unless he tried to disguise that, too." There would be only so much he could do toward that end, she thought, and he might not have bothered. It's not like an approximate height and weight were going to lead them to his door.

But maybe, just maybe some of the evidence they'd collected tonight would.

"If he dumps the body of his latest victim and it's discovered, it'll jumpstart the investigation." Although the man beside her didn't reply she sensed his dissent.

"What?" She turned to face Finn more fully. "You don't agree?"

"I don't think he'll dump the body. Wait." Their attention fixed on the computer screen, as something in the image seemed to move in the trees in front of the cabin. "What?" Finn peered more closely. "That's not a deer."

"A moose. A cow, to be exact." Delighted, Keira leaned forward as well. "I haven't seen one around here since I've been back."

The animal stilled as if alerting to some unseen danger, before bounding back deeper in the woods. "There are advantages to living out here, surrounded by nature," he decided. "The quiet, for one. In DC, it's never really silent. To truly leave behind the buzz of traffic you have to get quite a ways out of the metro area. And it's sprawling outward more every year."

Her gaze went to the wall of windows to their right. The shades were drawn now, but they opened to a breathtaking view of Lake Superior. The home had been designed to enjoy the surroundings, from the wrap around porch to the large windows that punctuated the split log walls. "My dad loved this place. I can't imagine him anywhere else." And try as she might, Keira couldn't picture her mother here at all. It was far away from the crowds and stores and the constant bustle that Lisa Brockton loved most. She'd hated everything about this area from what she'd told Keira, and had despised Danny's job. Which meant she'd never been happy with the career that her only child had chosen. Lisa was not shy about sharing her opinion on that, and on every other aspect of Keira's life.

Thoughts of her mother had her lifting the bottle to her lips again. "You said he wouldn't dump the body. Why is that?"

"He didn't exactly dump Danny's. He didn't hide it. Maybe because he thought the animals would do the job for him. Or because the place was remote and he didn't think it would be found. Or possibly because your father wounded him and he was unable to move a body."

Her head snapped around to look at him. "I've wondered...two shots fired from Dad's rifle, no brass found. There was always the possibility..."

He sped up the feed. "And we may never be certain. The killer has to know that he's leaving clues every time he brings something to you. I think that's intentional, part of this contest he's begun. He'll allow you to see so much and no more. That way he remains in control of what you learn. At least he'll think that."

"He's made me part of this." It was easier than it should have been to sit here and talk to Finn, a man she'd met less than three days ago. More times than she could count she'd sat just this way with Danny, discussing details of cases long into the night, shadows from a fire flickering on the walls. It was too easy to lower her defenses and give voice to fears that had up to now been kept private. "Why am I part of this? Was it about me from the beginning? Or about Danny?"

"When we have more details we can put a file together for one of the profilers on Raiker's staff and maybe he—or she—can answer those questions. We know the killer has chosen you now. Either because you're next on his list, or because he wants to engage you in a battle of wits."

She nodded. Some of what he was saying dovetailed with half-formed theories she'd wrestled with in the long months since Danny's death. And it was curiously liberating to be able to discuss her fears and conflicting ideas about her father's murder with someone who wasn't personally involved. Phil and Doc Ressler—heck, all of Danny's friends—had been battling their own grief. And much too concerned with comforting her to want to spend much time discussing theoreticals.

"He thinks I'm a tool." Her gaze went past the computer to the fireplace beyond, and she watched the gas flames hypnotically. "I'm not necessarily a target, at least not yet. But what's the point of leaving me clues if I'm not going to be around to put them together? He needs me to play, or there's no game. And maybe that's how he started with Dad, too." She examined the idea; decided it had merit. "Maybe he was the first participant."

"I assumed you've looked at cases that were being worked by the office at the time of your father's death." The low tones of Finn's voice coupled with the dim lighting and fire, wove a false sense of intimacy to the scene. False, because she didn't know the man. Not in any way that mattered. Frowning slightly, Keira set the half-full bottle on the table in front of her. Exhaustion could cloud thinking. She didn't need to compound the effects with alcohol.

"There wasn't anything that stands out." Because they were sitting close enough for their shoulders to touch, she moved surreptitiously away to widen the distance between them. "I've gone through everything in Danny's home office, and I can't see that he was working on anything in his spare time, either. He'd do that sometimes. Puzzle over a cold case, or work on finding patterns between current ones. Still, I'd been here for nearly three months before he died. He never mentioned a thing."

Finn looked up in surprise. "You were living here?"

She nodded. The memories that threatened were bittersweet, and not to be dwelt on now. "After he called and told me he had cancer I did some checking. Talked to the doctor in town, who was also a family friend. Found out that dad was downplaying the prognosis, which wasn't surprising, knowing him. I took leave a few days later and headed back here." It had taken only a couple weeks for her to come to the realization that she wouldn't be returning to Chicago. There had been nothing left for her there, even if it had taken her over a year to recognize that. "Danny wasn't happy about having a nursemaid, but he wasn't about to kick me out. Especially after I sub-leased my apartment." Keira smiled slightly. If she'd listened to her father, she wouldn't have had those precious last few months with him. The time seemed like a gift.

The clock on the computer caught her eye then, and she gave a mental groan. "We can finish this tomorrow. I have to get you back to town. You'd better hope the Turners still have the door unlocked for you."

With deliberation, he pressed the key that would halt the feed. "I'm not going back to town. At least not tonight."

Her eyes narrowed suspiciously. "What?"

"I'm not leaving you here alone tonight." His voice was amiable enough, but his expression was resolute. *Still waters.* She had the errant thought even as she was gathering her indignation. There was more—far more— to this man than met the eye. "It's unnecessary and careless. You've a window that isn't secure and a killer fixated on you. Tomorrow you'll get surveillance lined up, and the window fixed. But for tonight I'm staying right here. I'll just stretch out on the couch."

"Like you told me this afternoon, I don't need a babysitter."

"Good." He worked his shoulders tiredly. "I don't have a lot of experience in that area."

"Carstens." He cocked a brow at her sharp tone. "I am armed. I assure you I wouldn't hesitate to shoot if the intruder comes back, but we both know he won't. You can't stay here."

"Well, realistically, I can." The reasonableness of his tone set her teeth on edge. "You look like you're in pretty good shape, but it's not like you can pick me up and carry me to the car. Nor can you have your deputies do so because there's not one of them who would disagree that it's just common sense for me to stay tonight."

"I'm not a fan of pushy men."

A slight smile played around his mouth. "My mother calls it leadership skills, but I can see how you might regard my abilities in a different light. We've got about five hours until I'm guessing you're going to be up in the morning, so we can spend it arguing or we can catch some sleep. I'll text the Turners that I won't be there until tomorrow." He waited, as if for her agreement and when it didn't come he added, "Some women find stubborn men charming."

She bared her teeth. "And here I've always had an overwhelming urge to stab them in the eye. There's no accounting for tastes."

His smile widened. "Go to bed, Keira. It's been a helluva night."

She stared at him impotently, considering her options. It took all of a minute to realize she had none. So she rose silently and did exactly what he told her to do. It was with a small measure of satisfaction that she neglected to tell him that the couch he'd chosen was a lot more comfortable for sitting than it was for sleeping.

———————

"The commissioners want you there at two-thirty rather than three." Pammy waited as Keira switched her snow boots for the shoes she'd left there, then followed her through the offices. "Arnie called in about six-thirty and left a message. Apparently he's successfully convinced the rest of the board that your presentation is going to take longer than they'd allotted."

Keira squelched the urge to rub her forehead where a headache brewed. It had been brought on by Finn Carstens and was likely going to be topped off by the upcoming meeting before the board. Arnie would lead the charge, attempting to interrogate her about her decision to bring in an agent from Raiker Forensics. She had to believe that more rational minds on the board would prevail.

But it wouldn't hurt to keep some Tylenol on hand just in case.

"Do you have last night's…" Her words trailed off as the most recent incident logs were shoved into her hand. "Thanks, Pammy."

The younger woman tromped along beside her in black platform boots that bore a vague resemblance to the pair that Herman Munster had worn in a long-ago sitcom. "There's also been a missing persons' call this morning."

That stopped Keira in her tracks. "From whom?"

"Connie Abernathy. Seventy-nine-year-old female living on disability outside of city limits in Fair Grove Trailer Park. She's concerned about her son, Charlie. He's twenty-seven, lives on his own, but normally calls or stops in daily. He's done neither for eight days nor does he answer his cell."

Eight days. She did the mental math. The delivery to her porch had been six days ago. But the missing nail on the severed finger had shown signs of healing. How long would that have taken? She'd have to ask Finn.

Involuntarily she glanced at the conference room, which was dark. She'd dropped the man off thirty minutes ago and then gone to Patten's house to give the man the security access for her home cameras. Finn would have to shower and change clothes, and she doubted he'd escape the Turners before sitting down to eat the breakfast they provided their guests every morning. Which was more than she'd had to offer, even if she'd been so inclined. They'd established the paltry stocking of her kitchen the night before.

"Okay." Keira began moving away. She'd hope her early arrival would give her time to put the final touches on her presentation to the board. If she let it, the hours would be sucked away dealing with the everyday details of the job. "When Cal comes in tell him no calls or visitors until my door is open, except for emergencies. Oh, and I need to see Carstens when he arrives." She was almost, almost over his obstinacy from the night before. Especially when she'd come downstairs this morning and caught him rubbing his neck as if it were stiff. She'd been unable to spare any sympathy.

"You got it." Pammy clomped away.

Unsurprisingly the light was on in Mary Jacobs's office already. She stuck her head in the door to find the woman hunched over her computer. "Morning, Mary."

The woman's head jerked up. "Sheriff. How'd it go at your place last night?"

As Keira gave her a brief rundown Mary's expression grew grim. "Have you given any more thought to adding surveillance to your place?"

"Yes. I have an idea in mind, but I have to check some details. We got a missing person's report this morning." She held up a hand to quell the spark of excitement in the woman's expression. "I'm not sure the individual has been gone long enough to be the victim we're looking for, but it is a male. His mother called it in, and she's disabled, so take her a report to fill out. Pammy's got her personal information. Let me know what you come up with."

The woman nodded, and Keira continued quickly to her office. Something told her she wasn't going to get as much time as she wanted before the first 'emergency' arose today.

————

"As Mary and Brody work down the list of their assigned missing persons reports, the findings will be logged on the chart on the wall." After last night, Keira had decided to put Brody on days. They'd all take turns responding to calls that came in after hours.

She checked the clock above the door. She had an hour and a half before the meeting, and she'd skipped lunch. Experience had taught her it paid to have a full stomach for fortification. "I'll prioritize them and follow up with the case detectives if specific information is needed." She switched her attention to Finn. "Is it possible to tell the age of the victim the severed finger belonged to?"

He shook his head. "Forensically speaking those tests are in their infancy. At any rate, they rely on blood or tooth samples. Even then they can only come within about five years of accuracy, which for our purposes may or may not be narrow enough."

"But you already did DNA samples back in DC, right?" This from Phil Milestone. "What else were you able to tell about the owner of that finger besides the fact that he's male?"

"Even without the tests, it was easily eliminated as belonging to Danny Saxon," Finn explained. "The liver had degraded a great deal because it had been kept in formaldehyde. The finger had not been similarly treated. It had been taken from a live victim much more recently, probably no more than a week earlier."

"I only ordered the tests that would tell me if there was a match between the liver, the finger and my own blood sample. Finn has ordered a mobile lab, which will be here…" Keira looked at the man questioningly.

"It should arrive this evening." Finn looked around the table. "Additional testing will reveal whether the partial finger and the ear that was delivered to Keira last night came from the same victim. I should be able to determine race, gender and possibly any disease the individual is suffering from." He hesitated, and Keira knew intuitively that he was thinking about Danny. A DNA analysis hadn't been necessary to establish his cancer condition. The condition of the liver sample had made it obvious.

Useless to wonder now if her dad would have beaten the illness had he been given the opportunity. Because Danny's time had run out the moment the killer had targeted him.

"Once we have those results we may be able to zero in on a victim from our files. Or else discover that we have to go further abroad," Keira said, "and look at missing persons reports from the lower portion of

Michigan and Wisconsin. Until then we'll keep working the cases we have."

Hank nudged a paper across the table to Finn. "These names were on the list of people Danny helped put away. Those that I eliminated have been crossed out with the reason marked. Dead, alibied or back in prison. Five have left the state, and I'm tracking them down. The other two names belong to people who would be in their seventies now. How hard should I be looking at them?"

"We aren't ready to eliminate anyone at this point." Finn took the paper and scanned it quickly. "What we know about his activities so far indicate someone in fair shape, but they wouldn't require a great deal of strength or exertion. Check them out as thoroughly as the others on the list."

Keira pushed back her chair to signal the meeting was at an end. Hank left quickly, and she knew he was feeling the urgency that came from the double duty they were pulling, with this case on top of their other responsibilities. Theirs wasn't a particularly large department. Being down a jailer and tracking a murderer on top of it would be taxing on everyone. The fact that one of the victims had been their former boss meant there would be an emotional cost, as well.

Phil lingered in the room until Hank had left, then closed the door. Lack of sleep showed clearly on his face, carving the lines in it even deeper. "Before this goes any further, you need to see to the security at your cabin. Is that window fixed yet?"

She fought to keep a smile from her face. Despite his brusque exterior the man could be endearingly mother-hennish. "In the process. The security company got there a couple hours ago. They have to reset and check the alarm once the new window is in, and make sure the trespasser didn't establish a loop in the system that would allow him to circumvent it next time." She caught Finn's approving nod from the corner of her eye. "I've also tapped Chase about monitoring the feed from home, at least during my shift. I'll stop over there after my meeting and download the security app on his computer and input the access information."

The older man scratched his head. "Good idea. Will that screw up his medical leave?"

"Not sure yet." Keira picked up the files she'd brought in. "I'm going to let HR nitpick through that one. We might have to return him to part-time work on a conditional basis. I'll let them worry about it. He's eager to help out, and they've given the green light for computer work to proceed. And possibly some phone work, as well."

"It'll be good for him. Keep his brain from going to mush while he's recovering." Apparently satisfied, Phil went out the door.

Once he'd gone Finn inquired, "What are the culinary lunch options in town?"

"I was just going to grab something myself. We've got a couple fast food places." She noted the flicker of distaste on Finn's face so continued without missing a beat. "Claire's Diner is good if you have the time to wait out the lunch crowd. Otherwise, there's another sit-down restaurant and a great deli that will make sandwiches to your specifications."

He crossed to his desk, dropped some papers on it, then picked up the coat draped on the back of his chair to slip into it. "The deli it is."

"Afterward I'll take you by the county garage, and we can check out whether it's suitable for storing the mobile lab." They fell in step as she walked back to her office to set the files on her desk and then turned to gather her coat and purse. "The structure mostly houses county maintenance vehicles and includes a repair bay. If it's appropriate, I'll have to get permission to use it. The sheriff's department doesn't have access to the building on a normal basis."

"Hopefully you don't have to run the decision by the commissioners. From my brief meeting with one of them, I can imagine how that request will go," he said wryly. "Is the garage climate controlled?"

She had a quick sinking feeling in her gut. "I'm not sure. Is that necessary?"

His expression was somber. "It is. There will be a generator on board the mobile lab, of course, but a continuous proper temperature is necessary for the reagents and consumables."

If it meant an extra expense for twenty-four-hour heating, she'd have to agree to shoulder the cost. If they found out the county garage wasn't going to work there would be limited time to find another location that would be acceptable.

"We'll figure something out."

"Maybe Arnie will have some ideas." Finn jammed his hands in his pockets as they strolled toward the front door. "He seemed so helpful."

Stifling a snort, she stopped at Cal's desk to give him a schedule for her next few hours before switching into her snow boots and heading out the door. The radio on her belt crackled then, and she answered it while digging in her pocket for keys to the SUV.

"It's Jacobs, Sheriff. I've finished with Abernathy's report and talked to a few of the neighbors. Connie Abernathy was in a weakened state when I got there, and I called County Home Health to come out for a wellness check. But she's adamant she hasn't seen or heard from Charlie since last week when he brought her some groceries." Keira heard traffic sounds in the background and assumed Mary was in her car. "The next door neighbor can't recall whether it was eight or ten days since Charlie came around, but he remembers noticing his visit because he always watches for him since 'the kid' as the neighbor referred to Charlie is 'no damn good.'"

Keira crossed the lot, her boots crunching on the icy layer covering the pavement. "Did Ms. Abernathy give you any ideas of where to start looking for him?"

"I went to the place he'd been renting, but the landlord said he'd been evicted last week. Guess Charlie doesn't believe in paying rent. Had a phone conversation with the one contact his mom was able to give me, a girlfriend by the name of Zilly Peck."

"Name rings a bell." Keira searched her memory as she used the fob to unlock the vehicle and pulled the driver's door open. In the next moment the name clicked. The woman had done a short stint in jail for kiting checks in the past but had been working at the Kwik-E-Station since she'd returned to town. As far as Keira knew she'd stayed out of trouble since.

"What do we know about Charlie Abernathy?"

"No record, but also no known employment history. Peck claims she hasn't seen him in months, but she gave me the names of three guys to check out. A couple of them has had some drunk and disorderlies and other misdemeanors. They're both from town. The other is Pete Bielefeld. Just paroled out of Milan a couple years ago on federal drug charges for manufacturing and distributing. I spoke with his parole officer and got an address on him. He's living in Shingleton."

"Pete Bielefeld," she repeated, slanting a glance at Finn, who was fastening his seatbelt. From his expression, she could tell he'd made the connection. "Have Pammy text me a picture, and I'll need the complete address on him. I have Carstens with me. We'll check it out." Shingleton was an unincorporated township about ten miles away. She started the SUV and nosed it out of the lot. "I need a description of Abernathy and his vehicle if he has one."

"He drives his mother's, which I suspect is one of the reasons she's so concerned about his absence." Mary reeled off the descriptions, adding, "I'll follow up on the other two acquaintances."

Keira disconnected and pulled onto the road in front of the courthouse, squinting from the glare of sunlight on snow. "What are the chances that Pete Bielefeld is Yembley's buddy from last night?"

"The way the last several hours have gone?" Finn took sunglasses out of the inside pocket of his coat and put them on. "I'd say the odds are pretty good."

CHAPTER 4

Finn wolfed down the remainder of the sandwich as they pulled into a narrow heavily rutted lane hemmed by frost-painted brush and trees. The house wasn't visible from the road or from their position on the drive. If Bielefeld had selected the property for its privacy, he'd chosen well.

Neither Finn nor Keira had been surprised when the information from Pammy had come while they were at the deli. There was no doubt that the man in the photo was the one who had been with Yembley at the bar last night.

The drive led to a white clapboard farmhouse. The exterior hadn't been touched in a couple decades and old paint curled up from the siding, giving peeks at the slate gray beneath. Thick plastic covered all the windows. Torn pieces flapped lazily in the breeze as they pulled to a stop in front of the place.

"According to Pammy's info Bielefeld is self-employed as a carpenter."

Finn scanned the three outbuildings on the property. A navy pick-up with rusted out wheel wells was parked next to an older white minivan outside the largest shed, which was in only slightly better shape than the house. "Wonder if that one is his workshop. Neither of those vehicles matches the Abernathy car."

As they exited the SUV, the front door of the house opened and one of the men from the bar last night stood framed in the doorway.

"Sheriff." The man's gaze flicked to Finn and then back again. "What do you need?"

"I'd like to ask about a friend of yours," Keira said as they approached the porch. "May we come in?"

In answer, Bielefeld stepped outside, closing the door behind him. "Here is fine." His parka was unzipped. Either he had just gotten in the house or was just getting ready to leave it.

Finn scanned the area to their right. The nearest building—the one with the vehicles parked outside it— was a hundred yards away. Its rolling front door was shut. A thin thread of smoke plumed from a metal chimney on the roof. The window on the left side looked as though it was open.

"I got a lot of friends." Bielefeld's tone wasn't particularly congenial. "Who you looking for?"

"Charlie Abernathy."

It was hard to miss the flicker of surprise in the man's expression. It was followed swiftly by wariness. "What about him?"

"His mother filed a missing person's report this morning." Keira rested her foot on the first of the sagging steps. "When did you last speak to him?"

"Hell, I don't know." Bielefeld shrugged. "A month or more, probably."

"A month, huh. What did the two of you talk about?"

He looked bored. "How the hell am I supposed to remember that long ago? Maybe had a beer together. Sometimes he drops by after I finish for the day and we have a drink or two."

"Because as a parolee you wouldn't want to be seen in a bar."

Finn stifled a grin at Keira's pointed remark. The man seemed unfazed. "That's right. Wasn't my idea to go to Dizzy's last night. I wasn't driving."

"As part of your parole you're also supposed to avoid keeping company with felons."

Belatedly Bielefeld adopted a contrite attitude. "You're right. Absolutely. It won't happen again, Sheriff. I've been keeping my nose clean since getting out. The last thing I want to do is mess up."

"So what can you tell me about Abernathy?"

"Charlie?" The man seemed confused by the change of subject. "He's just a guy I see sometimes. I don't know that much about him."

"You have to talk about something over those beers you share."

The wind was chilly despite the bright sunshine. When it flipped a red-gold strand of hair across Keira's face, she pushed it away with an impatient gesture. The temperature hadn't topped twenty yet today. Finn detested stocking hats, but he was probably going to have to break down and buy one while he was here.

"We just bullshitted about sports mostly. Women."

"Yeah?" Keira seemed impervious to the cold. Her voice was conversational. "Was Charlie seeing someone?"

"Not since that last broad dumped him. That Peck bitch—gal," he amended. "You might check with her. I know Charlie still talked about her."

Several more minutes of questioning elicited no new information, so finally Keira and Finn turned back toward the SUV. Halfway to the vehicle Finn saw a flash and stopped, tipping his sunglasses down to stare hard in the direction of the glare.

"What?"

"In back of his workshop," he said in a low voice as she came to his side. "To the left. Looks like the sun bouncing off something metal. A bumper, maybe."

They exchanged a glance. "Let's check it out." They swerved and began walking in the direction of the building.

"Hey. Hey!" Bielefeld shouted. "Where you going?"

"Just taking a look around."

"What the hell?" Finn shot the man a look over his shoulder. He was hurrying down the porch steps after them. "You can't just roam around my property without my permission."

"Whose cars are parked in front of that building?"

"The pick-up's mine." Bielefeld had lost his earlier semi-cooperative attitude. His tone now was downright surly. "The van belongs to a guy who helps in my shop."

"What's his name?"

While Keira began questioning the man again, Finn walked past the building to get a better look at whatever was hidden behind it. He heard, "Where the hell is he going?" as he walked around the rear corner of the structure and took a long look at the vehicle parked there.

"Sheriff." Keira was already heading toward him, with Bielefeld on her heels. "Looks like Connie Abernathy's car." His gaze shifted to the other man. "Maybe you'd like to revise your story about not seeing Charlie in the last month. Because there's no snow on this vehicle. When's the last time it snowed, Sheriff?"

"Four days ago." Keira leveled Pete with a long look. "Did you have a memory lapse?"

"Honest to God, I got no idea what it's doing there." He tried for a baffled expression. Failed miserably to Finn's way of thinking. "I mean, maybe he's hiding out somewhere. He owes a lot of people around the county, I hear. Might have stashed it there last night or the night before."

"And then walked back to town?" Keira took the handcuffs off her belt. "Turn around. Hands behind your back."

"What the fuck. No. Hell no." Pete took a long step back. Then another. "I don't have a fucking idea why that idiot hid his car back there, but it don't got nothing to do with me."

"And you'll have time to explain all of that. In detail. Hands behind your back."

The man turned and ran. A dumbass move, but not an altogether unexpected one. Keira sprang after him, but Finn was faster. He chased the man down halfway to Keira's SUV and tackled him. They rolled, and when Finn was on top he barely had time to duck Bielefeld's meaty fist. He grabbed the man's arm and used his grip to leverage him over. "You just get smarter and smarter." With a knee pressed to Bielefeld's back, he kept him prone while Keira reached their side and handcuffed him. Finn took a few moments to search the man, coming up with a wallet, a wicked looking knife from a belt at his at his waist, and a video monitor in the man's coat pocket, much like the type used in baby's rooms. He handed the knife to Keira and jammed the other two items in his pockets before rising and hauling the ex-con to his feet.

"I want a fucking lawyer." Bielefeld was yelling now. "I know my goddamn rights and you can't come on my property to harass me."

With her hand on his bound wrists, Keira propelled him forward. Finn opened the rear passenger door on the SUV, and she ushered the man inside, then closed and locked the door. "And this is the reason my father refused to drive a vehicle without a cage in the back," she muttered. She opened the rear hatch and took out some evidence bags, dropping the knife in one. Finn handed her the wallet and monitor, which she stopped to study for a moment. "From the view on here it looks like he's got the camera mounted just inside the drive. I didn't notice it." She shook her head in disgust and placed it into another bag before checking the contents of the man's wallet.

"Neither did I, but that's not surprising with all the trees and brush out there." Finn stared down the drive. The road wasn't visible. A windbreak stretched across the property in the front and the drive was equally sheltered. "Man's either paranoid or he has something to hide." He paused a beat. "There's an open window on the side of the building."

Keira looked at him. "Ventilation?"

"That's what I'm thinking. Could be for fumes from paint or varnish. Or maybe something else."

She rocked back on her heels a little. "We have Abernathy's vehicle hidden on the property of an ex-con, who has obviously lied about seeing the man. Looks like exigent circumstances to me."

"Abernathy might be in imminent danger," Finn agreed. Ignoring the obscenities hurled from inside the SUV, he and Keira drew their weapons simultaneously. As one, they approached the nearest building. With her free hand, she gestured a count of three and pulled the handle. The door glided open with surprising ease. Finn had a moment to register the stench coming from the structure before they flanked the opening and aimed inside.

"Sheriff! Hands in the air! In the air!"

"Fuck!"

Squinting in the shadows, Finn peered into the building. Two long metal tables were set up side by side with a line strung overhead from which portable lights hung. The first table served as a makeshift counter and was topped with three hotplates. A man and woman in surgical masks stood side-by-side tending to pressure cookers.

"Use one finger to turn off the burners." Keira went no further than the doorway. Finn understood why. What had at first seemed like the overwhelming smell of cat urine was likely from meth being cooked. The material was highly explosive if mishandled. And the two standing before them didn't look exactly reliable. "Do it now!"

The flames from the burners were abruptly extinguished. "Now on your bellies, hands behind your head."

"This ain't our shit," the woman said. "Us being here don't mean…"

"Shut the fuck up, Chrissy," the man barked. She subsided into a sullen silence and got down on her knees.

Finn could see now that two more windows dotted the rear wall, with another on the right side. Black shades hung over the openings, but they moved in the wind. The reason for airing out the building was clear.

"I've got FlexiCuffs in the back of the vehicle." Keira reached into her pocket with her free hand and gave Finn the keys. Swiftly he went back and retrieved several pair of the cuffs and returned, keeping a sharp eye out for a third person. Neither of the two currently hugging the broken cement floor in the outbuilding was Charlie Abernathy. While Keira held the weapon on the two prisoners and used the radio on her belt to call for backup, Finn holstered his gun and secured their hands. Then he patted the two down. Neither had a weapon on them. Nor did they have any ID.

"I've got to get them out of here."

Finn helped Keira get the two to their feet and walk them to the vehicle.

"Look, if we tell you what you want to know, does that count in our favor?" the woman asked.

"Goddamn it, Chrissy, shut the fuck up!"

Keira pulled the man further away when he would have lunged at the woman. "I'll make sure the prosecutor knows that you cooperated."

"I don't wanna go to jail!" Chrissy screeched. "I got kids."

"I will fucking kill you, bitch."

"Shut up," Keira advised him in a steely voice. "You really want me to add making a criminal threat to your charges?"

Finn asked Chrissy, "Where's Charlie Abernathy?"

"Sleeping." She tossed her head at the man's murderous glare. "Inside there."

Without a word Finn walked back to the shed. There was only one possible place where Abernathy could be, and it was in the partitioned area they hadn't searched yet.

Finn stood in the doorway of the structure and took another careful look around. Against the far wall was a large stainless steel sink standing under an old-fashioned farmhouse pump. Two propane tanks and several empty water jugs sat beneath one of the tables. His gaze lingered on the tanks. The brass valves were corroded. They were likely used to transport anhydrous ammonia.

The extra table was littered with chemicals, rubber gloves, strainers, funnels, lithium batteries, and blenders. This wasn't a small-scale operation. While not super lab capacity, Bielefeld's setup would at least make him the largest meth manufacturer in the area.

Six-foot tall wooden shelves partitioned the interior from the left third of the structure. The racks were filled with enough tools to suggest that Bielefeld actually might do some carpentry work. They stretched from the back of the building to the front, with only an opening the size of a doorway. From where he stood, it looked like there might be a workshop of sorts behind them.

There was no light spilling from the space. The dim interior was softened only by the cast off glow of the bulbs strung over the cooking table. Finn moved further inside and realized that the shelves were double sided. Most were filled to overflowing with lumber, hardware and more tools. The one closest to him was stocked with baggies of various sizes. He picked one up and peered at the powder in it. Bielefeld had a large stockpile of product.

There were several large saws in the space set up on tables. He set the baggie back down on the shelf and surveyed the area. A few large pieces of furniture, in various stages of completion, were scattered about.

His gaze went to the window, the one he'd first noticed when checking out Abernathy's vehicle. From the way the dark blind moved he knew he'd been correct earlier. It was open to ventilate the structure. With good reason. The entire building smelled like a mixture of chemicals, rotten eggs, and urine. Which explained the masks the couple had worn.

There was a slight sound. Finn stilled, his ears straining. He didn't hear the noise again. He moved deeper into the space, dodging the scattered furnishings and caught sight of something in the corner. A jumble of blankets.

Tension radiated along his shoulders. He drew his gun again as he approached the area in question. As he moved closer, he could see the edge of a mattress on the floor beneath the covers. His sight was obscured by a large half-finished entertainment center.

Walking around the item, he caught movement from the corner of his eye. He heard the scream of a power saw. He leaped away. The saw went silent but sailed through the air to slam against his ribs. Finn stumbled. His assailant used the opportunity to dodge past him, darting around a tall cupboard.

Gulping in a breath, Finn raced after the suspect, holstering his weapon as he made a grab for a stocking clad foot as it was disappearing through the window. The man kicked wildly, managing to slip out of his sock. Finn lost no time tearing out of the building and around its corner, shouting to Keira, "There's a third one."

He got a closer view as he sped toward the car parked behind the building. Abernathy—and the man he saw through the window fit Charlie's description—was inside the vehicle doing a frantic search. Keys. He must not have them. Finn nearly tripped over something buried in the snow and realized the ground was littered with junk beneath the drifts. When the man looked up and caught sight of him, he threw himself across the seat to climb out the opposite side. Finn was there before he rounded the opened door.

Unlike Bielefeld, Charlie didn't run when cornered. He launched himself at Finn, and they both went down hard, slamming against the front bumper as they grappled before rolling in the snow in front of the vehicle. The man bucked wildly beneath him, dislodging him and crawling a few feet away. After a moment, Abernathy turned and reared back with something in his fist.

Breathing hard, Finn pulled his gun. "I advise against it." Charlie hesitated, then lowered his hand, dropping what looked to be a large metal gear of some type. He wiped the blood from his face. Feeling the telltale trickle crawling down the side of his head, Finn knew he was bleeding, too.

"Charlie Abernathy?"

"Yeah," the guy muttered.

"I'm happy to inform you that you're under arrest." Finn blinked rapidly. One eye was already swelling, impairing his vision. "On your feet, hands on your head." As they walked toward where Keira waited with the other two, Finn could hear the distant sounds of sirens growing closer by the instant, which was handy, because they were going to need more handcuffs.

Keira's eyes widened when they walked into view.

"Our missing person is found."

The look she gave Finn was touched with concern. "You need to see a doctor."

Now that the rush of adrenaline was ebbing, a litany of aches was beginning to make themselves known, with a drilling headache vying for first place. "As it happens, I am a doctor. Something tells me you're not going to make the commissioner's board meeting."

"Forgot all about that. I'll be tied up here for hours. I've radioed for an UPSET team. That's the drug task force that serves our county. Once the place is photographed and inventoried a Hazmat team will have to take over."

"How 'bout me? I need a doctor, too." Abernathy's voice was truculent. A few days' growth of patchy whiskers covered his face. "This guy tried to kill me. I'm gonna file charges."

"You do that," she said unsympathetically. "In the meantime, assume the position against the side of the vehicle."

"I need my other sock. My shoes and coat. Christ, it's colder 'n a witch's tit out here." As he griped, he turned toward the SUV and spread his arms and feet to lean against the left side of it.

"Your mother reported you missing this morning, Abernathy." Finn gingerly touched his left eye, which felt swollen. "How long have you been here?"

"Pete wouldn't let me leave."

"And why is that?"

The man's answer was lost as two cruisers sped into the yard, sirens wailing. Pitching her voice over the racket, Keira said, "I'll have one of the deputies take you and Abernathy to the clinic." She pulled a Kleenex out of her pocket and handed it to him.

Finn didn't reach for it. "Abernathy can go. I'm fine."

With an ungentle touch, she pressed the tissue against his forehead. "You look fine with that gash on your head. And you need ice on your eye to keep it from swelling shut."

He reached down and scooped up a handful of snow, pressed it to his eye and managed to avoid wincing at the contact. "I'll be all right."

"Yeah, you will," she said, turning as her deputies approached. "Because you're going to get medical treatment."

————

Finn wondered how many men had successfully out-stubborned Keira Saxon. He'd had a lot of time to consider the question while he waited in an exam room at the clinic he'd most definitively said he didn't want to go to. Brody Boyle had waited in another room with Abernathy whose bitching had been loud enough to drift into Finn's room.

The doctor was a type he'd never been impressed by. With a sarcastic demeanor glazed with ego, Dr. King had been competent, if not especially compassionate. Once he'd learned that Finn had no intentions of spilling details about Abernathy's arrest, he'd said little else, ignoring Finn's suggestions for butterfly bandages and stitching up his head with more speed than dexterity. After checking his eye and ribs, King had offered the brusque suggestion that he apply ice to both. The entire visit had been as worthless as Finn had imagined it would be, and by the time he'd left the waiting area with the deputy and prisoner his mood had soured dramatically.

Keira called five minutes into their ride to the courthouse. "You back at the office yet?"

"On our way. Things took a while at the clinic."

"The clinic? I figured you'd be seen at the hospital."

"Apparently the ER was busy with several people who had fallen today. Brody made an executive decision."

Humor laced her tone. "Please tell me you didn't see Dr. King."

Something told Finn Keira held the man in as low esteem as he did. "I did. Pleasant guy. He sent his regards." Finn had caught hints of a personal interest in some of the questions the doctor had leveled at him during the visit. "He said I was fine, by the way."

She made a sound of derision. "I know better than that. I'm not sorry I strong-armed you into going, but I feel the need to apologize to anyone forced to undergo King's not so tender ministrations."

The cloud over his mood partially lifted. "I'll find a way for you to make it up to me. In the meantime, my next order of business is to take a look at the county garage."

"That's why I'm calling." He could hear the sound of voices, a lot of them, from her end. "Brody can take you over after he books Abernathy. The county engineer, Roger Wilson, will meet you there in an hour. He can answer all your questions, and he'll be the one to give permission about storing it there."

"And the commissioners are on board with it?"

"They shouldn't be a problem." The vagueness of her tone had his senses alerting. She'd found a way around the issue, but obviously wasn't going to share it over the phone.

"I don't need the deputy to take me. Just give me the address and I'll drive the rental over. Is it in Munising?"

"Yes, just a few miles from the office. But Finn..." He heard someone shouting her name and knew she was running out of time. "Wilson can be a bit of a character. I'm always careful around him."

His brows skimmed upward when she signed off. As the courthouse came into sight, Finn recognized that he was almost as intrigued by what Keira had left unsaid as he was by checking out a suitable location for the mobile lab.

————

Roger Wilson was a few inches shorter than Finn, stout, with a full head of gray hair and mustache. Whatever had been behind Keira's uneasiness with him, the man seemed amiable enough when he met Finn outside the county garage. After exchanging introductions, the older man took him on a tour of the steel sided building. "Keira...Sheriff Saxon said you required a twenty-four hour heated area. Part of this structure is heated. The offices, break room, bathrooms and parts area have forced heat." The man moved as fast as he talked and Finn matched him stride for stride. "In the shop the mechanics bay has in-floor heat. I can't free that up, though. As you can imagine in this sort of weather, we have vehicles in constant need of repair. Two truck and motor grader bays are heated, as well, but they share a space." Wilson sent him a questioning glance. "I'm guessing you not only need heat, but security."

"The mobile lab can be locked, and it has an alarm system. But it would be best to be in an area that can be locked separately." They walked into the building portion that the man had indicated and Finn scanned it. Certainly it had the ceiling height and breadth to hold the lab, which was basically a modified RV. But the space was currently occupied with a grader and large dump truck.

"I can free up the bay if it isn't for an extended period," the man said. "When Keira…the sheriff called, I was glad to help." There was a flicker of emotion in the man's expression, one that disappeared too quickly to be identified. "Things can be shuffled around if I have an idea of how long it will be necessary."

"I appreciate your assistance with this." The warmth inside the building was a welcome change from the temperatures outdoors. Finn pulled his gloves off, shoved them in his pocket. "But I'm afraid I can't answer that question. No more than a couple weeks." If the case dragged on longer than that, Finn would talk to Keira about less expensive options. Raiker had told him that she was footing all fees for their agency herself. The arrangement was unusual. Occasionally they did work for heavily vetted private customers, but the bulk of their clients were law enforcement entities. Few in that field had the funds to pay for the services from their own pocket. Not for the first time he wondered how a former Chicago police detective could afford the expense.

"Two weeks." The other man looked relieved. "I can handle that. If you come with me, I'll get you a key to this bay. It will take a couple hours to get the vehicles in here moved."

They walked through the structure to the back of the building and entered one of the offices. An attractive mid-forties brunette looked up from her computer. "Roger. I didn't know you were here."

"Just for a few minutes." He went to a labeled pegboard that held keys and slid off all three that were hanging on one of the hooks.

The woman looked surprised. "The guys are going to be needing those when they come for the vehicles."

"I'll take care of it, Sandy." They left the room, with the woman frowning after them. Once outside it Wilson handed the keys to Finn. "The overhead doors are unlocked right now. You can secure them after we move the vehicles and get your lab in there." As Finn took the keys the man offered and slipped them into his pocket, Wilson went on. "What case are you helping the sheriff with?"

Remembering how Keira had referred to the man Finn offered him a half smile. "I'm not free to discuss it. What did she say when you spoke to her?"

The man released a bark of laughter. "Damn little. As close-mouthed as her old man, although a helluva lot more pleasant about it." He folded his arms across his chest, regarding Finn from beneath steel gray brows. "This is a small county. A smaller town. Came here nearly forty years ago and never expected to stay. But here I am. People talk, some who shouldn't. Word is out that something big is brewing in the county. Guess it'd have to be big, for the sheriff's office to bring in a mobile lab."

"Like you say, people talk," Finn said easily. Under the circumstances, he didn't want to offend the man, but neither did he have any intention of exchanging gossip with him. "In my experience most of what they say isn't worth listening to." He started moving in the direction of the door but stopped when the other man failed to follow.

"Fate has a helluva way of working out, doesn't it?"

Finn was beginning to understand why Keira had seemed so cautious about Wilson. There was something in the intensity of his gaze that was more than a little discomfiting.

The engineer's throat worked. "I never wished Danny Saxon ill. He probably wouldn't believe that, but it's true. I was wrong with what I did, but she had one foot out the door when I came along and Lord, there's not a man alive who could resist Lisa when she fixed on him. She was…dazzling."

At a loss, Finn picked through the man's words. "Lisa? Is that Keira's mother?"

"Keira's got the look of her, although her coloring and height favor Danny." He shook his head as if to dislodge the memories that crowded it. "At any rate Lisa wasn't interested in me so much as she was in a way off the UP. She found that eventually, with someone who could offer her a helluva lot more than I could." He shrugged. "Water under the bridge. Danny never had much use for me after that and I guess I can't blame him. There's no making up for past mistakes, but any favor I can do for Keira…maybe that evens things out. Just a little."

"I know she appreciates it." The words sounded inane, but he had nothing else to offer the man.

Wilson only nodded and moved past him toward the entrance. Leaving Finn to trail behind him and wonder how much Keira knew about the snippet from the past that the man had revealed.

———

It was nearly six o'clock before Keira stopped in the doorway of the conference room, looking surprised to find Finn still at his desk.

"We don't expect you to work around the clock, you know."

He twirled his chair around to survey her critically. "Same goes for you." There were mauve shadows beneath her green eyes that hadn't been there this morning. He could only imagine that the stress of the afternoon had put them there. "Everything cleared up at the scene?"

She walked in far enough to lean against the doorjamb and moved her shoulders tiredly. Although her coat was unfastened, she hadn't taken it off. He hoped that meant she wasn't planning to stay much longer.

"Hazmat won't finish until tomorrow." She tried, and failed to stifle a yawn. "You know that idiot Bielefeld worked in the same area where he made meth? Ran power tools in the vicinity of explosive chemicals? The stupid runs deep with that one."

"He had quite a stockpile of product in his workshop," Finn noted. "Unless he's got a helluva client base, he had enough to supply his customers in the county for six months."

"The task force thinks he's bigger than that. They kept hearing about a dealer serving a three-county area, but names were elusive. Now they have one. He'll be going back to prison, and I'm guessing his stretch will be even longer this time."

Finn rose and dragged a chair from the conference table over to her. "Sit." He accompanied the suggestion with a hand to her shoulder, exerting enough pressure to urge her to obey. "Before you fall down." The fact that she did so without protest was testament to her level of exhaustion. He propped a hand against the wall, leaned against it.

"He had a safe." She stifled a yawn with the side of her fist. "A big sucker, like the ones you used to see in banks. We found guns, money, and more product there.

His parole officer says he's been out to Bielefeld's place a few times to check on him, often unannounced."

"Which didn't do much good when he had the camera mounted alerting him to any visitors."

A satisfied smile curled her lips and the sight of it hit Finn like a quick left jab to the gut. Sleep deprivation. He moved his shoulders restlessly. Had to be.

"We found proof that our arrival had…ah… interrupted Bielefeld answering nature's call. Apparently he's not a multi-tasker in the bathroom. That's how we managed to take him by surprise."

He grinned. "Helluva way to get busted."

Her smile widened in agreement. "Hank has interviewed all four of them. Abernathy is claiming that he stopped out for a beer with a friend and he and Bielefeld had an argument about Charlie owing him money. He's saying Bielefeld wouldn't allow him to leave. That he took his phone and keys and forced him to cook to work off his debt."

"Could be true." Finn shifted when his position had his ribs howling in protest. "Which brings up the critical question of how he grew indebted to the man to begin with."

"I'm guessing a tox screen would show exactly why he owed him." Keira lifted a shoulder. "The female suspect—Chrissy Larson—says they were working around the clock all week. Bielefeld must have been planning to move a lot of meth."

"Maybe he was expanding his territory."

"Could be. UPSET has more information about that end of things. Thought those guys were going to wet themselves when they saw the haul in there."

"I'm not surprised." It had been a good-sized bust. He just hoped she made it home before she crashed. "You didn't mention finding records."

"Not in the shed or the house. Which is suspicious, because I don't see Bielefeld as having the smarts to keep the financials in his head."

Finn thought about that for a moment. "Didn't you say his buddy from the other night, Yembley, had a history of drugs?"

"Buying, not selling. At least back then." She slid lower in the chair in a boneless slouch. "So you said when you called that the county garage is all set. I was a little leery about contacting Wilson directly but as county engineer, the garage is really his territory. The commissioners would have just had to ask him for permission, anyway. The guy's got a weird affect, but I figured he'd be more amenable if the request came straight from me."

Abruptly sobering, Finn said, "I think it's safe to say that he's very accommodating where you're involved. After talking to him, I'm wondering why his name isn't on the list of people who had a grudge against your father."

Her expression stilled. "Why? What'd he say? I know Dad didn't like him. He never made any bones about that. Wilson used to come to my softball games when I was kid, although he didn't have any children of his own. I don't think he ever married. He'd come up afterward and talk to me about the game, gave me tips. Which was sort of weird, because I really didn't know him well."

Finn hesitated. There was really no reason to dredge up ancient history. If her father hadn't seen fit to fill her in on the source of animosity between the two men, maybe he shouldn't be the one to do it. He'd thoroughly check out the man on his own.

"You think Wilson had something against my father?" All semblance of relaxation had vanished. Keira sat up straighter, her gaze fixed on Finn's. "Whatever it is, you need to tell me. Even the tiniest bit of information can help make sense of an investigation. You know that, Finn."

"I haven't verified it.". As a scientist he was used to checking and re-checking data before presenting it. But he reluctantly repeated what Wilson had revealed about his relationship with Keira's mother. He watched her expression carefully for signs of shock. Of grief or disillusionment. He only saw the shock, which quickly turned to cynicism.

"Neither of my parents ever said a word, not that they would. But it sounds like Lisa. She still hates this place, and she hasn't lived here for decades. And…well," Keira stood.

"There are always men. Plural. So the news isn't unbelievable. As a matter of fact, it sort of explains the tension between him and my dad. They had words one day after one of my games. Danny wouldn't tell me about it but Wilson never came to another one."

"Which could have led to some pent up hostility," he suggested quietly. "Sure, your mother eventually left, but your dad still had you. Every summer, you said. Christmas break. He thinks you look like her."

Keira gave a throaty chuckle. "Not even in my wildest dreams." Her expression was genuinely amused. "Mom looks like a model for one of those miniatures. You know, those beautiful little statuettes that you're too afraid to pick up because it might break in your hands? I'm hardly the delicate type. I resemble my father."

Although he'd never seen pictures of either of her parents—other than crime photos—Finn was willing to bet that Wilson's assessment was closer than Keira's. She was tall and willowy. While she exuded a competency and confidence that bespoke strength, her features had a refined appearance that suggested she might have inherited more physical traits from her mother than she admitted.

"I think it's worth checking into Wilson." The cell in his pocket vibrated and he pulled it out of his pocket. "If only to eliminate him."

She shrugged. "Under the circumstances, I'm sure you're right. But I hope you alibi him quickly because I don't have any other ideas for where to park the lab."

Reading the message, he pushed away from the wall. "The lab is twenty minutes out." He texted a reply as he spoke. "They have the address of the garage, but I have to meet them there."

"Them?"

"Two of Raiker's employees. One is driving behind in a car for the trip back. They're going to drive as far as Gogebic County tonight."

"Staying in Bessemer?" At his nod she stood. "Under the circumstances this is more than a little pushy…but how long until we can expect test results?"

He crossed to his desk chair to get the coat he'd hung over the back. "Pushy? You sound like every law enforcement agent I've ever worked with. Normally the fastest we could promise is three days." He turned to shrug into the coat and noted her crestfallen expression. "But things move a bit quicker when a scientist has no other tests he's juggling at the same time. *Preliminary* results can be ready as soon as tomorrow, and that's barring any unforeseen complications."

"Preliminary?"

They fell in step together as they walked to the front of the offices. "All tests require validation. Most labs demand that another scientist confirm the results before releasing them. Raiker's lab protocols call for two individuals substantiating the data. Once I'm finished, I'll be sending the outcomes to his lab in Manassas. But I can give you tentative answers as soon as they're available."

She nodded. "I appreciate that." They paused inside the front door while they switched footwear. "So you'll run them tomorrow?"

Finn lifted a brow. "I'd planned on running them tonight if you'll fetch the evidence you collected at your place yesterday evening. Figured you might be in a hurry."

Excitement warred with concern in her expression. "No offense, but you look like you could use some rest. And it wouldn't hurt to ice that eye again."

He squelched the urge to reach up to touch the swelling. Cal had supplied an ice pack and he'd been using it on and off since his return. "I'll grab a few minutes here and there while I wait on the tests." Recognizing the skepticism in her expression he put a hand at the base of her back and gave her a gentle push. "Bring me the evidence. Then you'd do well to follow your own advice. Get something to eat before heading home." He recalled the contents of her refrigerator all too well. "Hopefully by tomorrow we'll have something that will provide a solid direction for the case."

Without uttering another objection, she turned and made her way toward the evidence room. Finn rubbed his hands over his face, skirting his swollen eye. He hadn't told her that sleep would have been impossible now that the lab was here. He was just as anxious for those results as she was. Not only might they lead them to the man who had ended Danny Saxon's life, the tests just might allow them to stop the killer before he decided to make Keira his next target.

CHAPTER 5

Oddly enough, Keira felt at loose ends as she drove home. When she'd offered to come and keep Finn company in the lab the look in his expression had approached alarm. He'd been quite clear about the need to avoid outside contaminants, which, now that she thought about it, was a borderline offensive way to refer to her presence there. But she got it. He was a professional and probably more than a little OCD about his work. Because she'd had the same accusation leveled at her in the past, she could appreciate the quality.

Keira couldn't bring herself to stop and grab something to eat. If her appetite made a return, she had cans of soup in the cupboard. Besides, Chase was probably waiting to be relieved of his surveillance of her property. It had likely been a bone-crushingly boring day spent watching the cameras.

Light snow was falling. She turned on her wipers. The forecast called for snow for the next several days. Had it come sooner, they might have missed the glare on the bumper of Abernathy's truck behind Bielefeld's shed. Once in a while, they caught a break.

The closer she got to her home the less anxious she was to reach it. She should have stopped by Tiffany's. It was the other woman's regular night off, Keira was almost certain of it. And Tiff was between boyfriends right now, a rarity in itself, and might have been free.

The moment she had the thought she discarded it. The case consumed her every thought. She wouldn't be good company, and she definitely wouldn't have responded well to her friend's good-natured prying for details. Better that she be alone to deal with her crappy mood herself.

As she turned down the long drive toward her dad's property—hers now—her headlights caught the faint tire treads ahead, and she slowed unease stirring. Joe Boster hadn't made them. There wasn't enough snow yet for him to plow. He'd likely wait until early tomorrow morning.

She hated the nerves that jittered in her belly. Nerves that were fresh and raw after the break in last night. The killer wouldn't have come back. Not because he didn't dare, but because it was too soon. Surely he'd wait for Keira's counter-move before reacting again.

Keira stopped the vehicle just as her phone rang. She answered it with Bluetooth.

"Sheriff Saxon."

"Keira, it's Chase. There's a vehicle in front of your property. I called in and had the plates run. Belongs to Tiffany Andrews."

Relief escaped her in a long stream of breath. "Okay, I'm just in the drive now. You can knock off until I contact you tomorrow."

"No problem." Chase's voice sounded more cheerful than it had when she'd stopped by earlier today. "Beats watching daytime TV, I can tell you that."

"If that's a bid for sympathy, you've got it." She could only imagine the dearth of programming. "I appreciate the call. Thanks."

She drove down the drive and passed the running vehicle parked outside her house as she made her way to the attached garage. Using the automatic opener, she continued into the space, parked and got out to discover her friend walking toward her, holding a grocery bag.

"I'm bored," Tiffany declared baldly as she hugged Keira with her free hand. "And I come bearing gifts. I figured you wouldn't kick me out if I brought food and wine."

"Depends." There was something about her blond friend that had a way of lifting her spirits, even when they'd been drifting dangerously close to moody moments ago. "What kind of wine?"

Tiffany followed her into the garage. Keira lowered the overhead door and unlocked the entry to the cabin. "I classed it up just for you, meaning it's not in a box. Does wine go with Chinese? Doesn't matter," she declared in the next moment. Keira paused to lock the door behind them, and her friend sailed by her toward the kitchen. "Wine goes with everything."

Interest stirring, Keira followed in Tiffany's wake. "Tell me there are crab Rangoons."

The woman threw her a look over her shoulder. "When have I ever failed you?"

Keira rounded up wine glasses while Tiff—with the familiarity bred of long friendship—went unerringly to the cupboard that held the plates. A mental image of last night's intruder doing the same flashed across Keira's mind. The woman turned with two dishes in her hand, stilling when she glanced her way.

"What?"

Forcing a smile, Keira shook her head. "Nothing. I'm glad you're here." She was a bit surprised to find the words true. The exhaustion that had been crowding in for the last couple of hours lifted a bit. She welcomed the distraction.

"Good." Tiffany opened a drawer and took out some forks. "You can talk me out of making a mistake with this dark, brooding stud that keeps showing up at the bar to talk to me. Steve, his name is. Steve Feller. He's hot in a sort of Marlboro man kind of way. Think he lives in Doty."

"He's a loser." The wine bottle didn't take much finesse since it was a screw top. Keira poured them both generous portions and carried the glasses to the table where Tiffany was dishing up orange chicken. "He's got some domestic assault charges against him. His wife had the good sense to get out a couple months ago, and when I sent a deputy with her to go back and get some of her stuff, he tried to interfere and landed in jail again. Not exactly a prince."

"Well, shit." Tiff's tone was philosophical as she reached for her wine glass. Lifted it in a salute. "Let's drink to the fact that this time I actually found that out *before* I slept with him. That's maturity, right?"

Amused, Keira clinked her glass against Tiffany's. "Definitely." She sipped, before setting down her glass to attack her food with an appetite that had been absent only minutes ago.

"Maybe I'm just feeling desperate because I heard the juiciest gossip that Dorie Hassert is getting laid." She nodded at Keira's shocked expression. "Yeah, that's what I thought. Haven't seen her with her mystery man yet, but word on the street is she's hinting to one and all that she's playing mattress tag with someone. Which makes me just a wee bit desperate. My mom says I'm destined to die alone." Tiffany hadn't lifted her fork yet. Instead, she took a long gulp of wine. "Of course, she also says I'm a bum magnet, so reason would suggest if that's the case, it'd be best to be alone, right?"

"Your mom needs to look in the mirror before leveling remarks like that to you." Keira rose immediately to her friend's defense. Rhonda Andrews had always had a revolving door on her social life, and some of the men she'd brought home had seemed more interested in the woman's teenage daughter than in Rhonda. "She's not exactly an expert on healthy relationships." Nor had she ever shown expertise in mothering.

"She didn't like your dad." Tiff set down the glass and picked up her fork. "I never knew why until a few weeks after his funeral. I stopped by with some groceries and she was in a melancholy mood. Blamed him for running off the one guy she now claims was the love of her life."

Keira paused with her fork mid-air. "He did? Who was that?"

"Not sure." Tiffany bit into a crab rangoon and let her eyes slide shut in ecstasy. "Heaven. I think it was the one that creeped us out. Remember the guy who hung around my room when you were over?"

"Mullet Head?" Tiffany had always hung nicknames on her mother's boyfriends.

"I don't think so. The one between Mullet Head and Beer Belly. Greaseball, I think."

Keira did remember the man and the way he'd made them feel. She hadn't had the words for it as a thirteen-year-old, but during that summer Tiffany had spent far more time at the cabin than she had at her house. She scooped up more rice and reflected on the news for a moment. "What did Danny do?"

"She didn't go into detail, but I got the impression he gave her some facts about the guy's past and maybe hinted DHS might think he wasn't the type who should be around kids. Because now she claims it was all bullshit, of course. He was a great guy." Tiffany rolled her eyes. "As were they all."

"Did you ever hear anything about Lori and Roger Wilson?"

Her friend leaned forward, eyes huge. "Your mom? With Wilson? Back in the day?"

"According to something I heard yesterday, yeah."

"No, but that would explain a lot. Remember how he used to come to our practices and games? I could ask around if you want me to."

Keira shook her head. "That's all right." She had a feeling Finn would quietly check out the man on his own. He seemed to have considered the details Wilson had provided as credible. As difficult as it was to believe that someone she'd known her whole life could be behind Danny's death, she had to face the fact that she may well know the killer. Alger County had ninety-five hundred residents. She knew many of them by sight.

Tiffany turned her attention to her wine, holding up her glass to admire the glint of the liquid in the light. "Maybe we're both destined to be alone. You had happiness within your grasp once before Fate, that noxious bitch snatched him away."

She could think of Todd now without that heaviness in her chest. The catch in her throat. The feeling of loss would linger longer. Like something unfinished had escaped her before she'd known for certain what she had. It was times like these that she knew she'd made the right choice to leave Chicago and its dead behind her. Keira had been up front with the committee when they'd approached her to fill her father's position. She had no idea what her long-term plans were. The job had helped ease the unusual sense of indecisiveness enveloping her. But there was still a part of her that felt like she was in a state of suspended animation. Maybe now a sense of new purpose would change that.

Finding her father's killer.

Deliberately changing the subject, she said, "I think you need to give Beau Chandler a shot." And then watched her friend choke on her orange chicken.

"You've got to be kidding me." She chased the bite with a gulp of wine. "He's okay looking but too damn quiet. And he's got a huge Adam's apple. Seriously, that's all I notice when he does talk, is that thing bobbing up and down like Cassie Winkelman's boobs when she jogs."

Now it was Keira's turn to choke at the mental image that accompanied the description. "It's not that noticeable." But damn if she'd ever be able to look at the man again without the thought in her head.

"I'm going to have to leave here to meet anyone that I haven't known my entire life." Tiffany gave a little sigh and pushed her plate away. "You've been telling me that for years. And you're right. I might go work on Mackinac Island this summer. Hell, fifteen thousand tourists a day, I'm bound to meet someone, right?"

"By the inside of a month, the tourists would be coming to see you." Memory struck belatedly. Keira got up and went to fetch her purse, which she'd left in the living room, coming back with a fifty.

"No. No way." Tiff shook her head violently. "This was my treat. You paid last time."

Taking her chair again, Keira pushed the bill across the table to her friend. "For dinner last night. I didn't have time to stop by and pay today like I meant to."

Her brows rising, the woman took the money and tucked it in her purse. "That's like a forty percent tip."

Keira tipped her glass to her lips. "The waitress deserved it. She had to deal with assholes all night."

"Not all night, but yeah, the jerk factor of those two increases parallel to their alcohol level." She surveyed Keira steadily over the rim of her glass as she drank. "So. Were you really not going to mention it?" At her silence, Tiffany shook her head. "Seriously. The way you tore out of there I knew something big was going down. And today I heard it was trouble here? What happened?"

The woman, Keira had often thought, was like human radar. "Where'd you hear that?"

"Over breakfast at the diner. Same place I heard that Dorie was boinking some mystery man. It's a hotbed of gossip." She made a c'mon gesture with her fingers. "So give. Someone broke in here?"

"He came in through a window, but he was long gone before my deputies arrived. Nothing was taken," she forestalled Tiffany's next question. "The alarm likely scared him off." She didn't share details of ongoing investigations with anyone outside the department, even though she knew she could trust her friend to keep a confidence. Tiffany may be a fountain of information about others, but she was as private as a vault when it mattered.

"Uh-huh." It was clear from the woman's tone that she knew Keira was sugarcoating the incident. "Did you talk to Yembley about it?"

"He left minutes before we did. He wouldn't have had time to get here."

She looked unconvinced. "Maybe not, but he might have a friend who could. I'm serious, Keira, that guy hates your family. It's not the first time he's gone off about your dad in there, and you. I've gotten in his face about it before but well, he's not an especially fast learner."

Keira reached out to touch her friend's hand. "I appreciate you sticking up for me, but if you see him again just give him a clear berth. He's unpredictable. Remember that." If today was any indication, the company he kept was, as well. "We took his buddy down this afternoon. Believe me, if there's the slightest shred of evidence that Yembley was involved, he'll be next."

Tiffany squeezed her hand. "I hope you kicked his ass. I'll try to steer clear, but if Yembley disses you again, I can't be accountable for my actions."

When Keira blew out a breath of frustration, her friend smiled wickedly and held up her wine. "To fierce women everywhere."

After a moment Keira gave up and reached for her glass. Tapping it against her friend's she echoed, "To fierce women."

———

"I appreciate you re-scheduling my presentation." Although she was less grateful for the seven AM meeting, beggars couldn't be choosers. The new time was just over the eighteen hours required for public notice under Michigan law. That might explain the absence of a representative from the local paper. The media only had to request the minutes of this gathering to compile a story. Keira was going to do all she could to make sure the minutes Dorie was taking reflected nothing worth reporting.

She sipped from the coffee she'd bought on the way and offered a polite smile to the five commissioners across the table. "The story will be in the paper today. The drug bust that prevented me from attending yesterday is likely the largest in county history and one of the biggest on the UP this year."

Her revelation set the room abuzz. She answered the most general questions lobbed at her while avoiding the specifics her office had withheld from the local reporter yesterday.

"Great work, Keira." Commissioners Stewart and Bailey spoke simultaneously. Two others nodded with enthusiasm while Arnie Hassert was noticeably quiet. Joni Stewart said with a smile, "Leading with news like that is an excellent way to tempt the board to grant this special transfer of funds request."

Chairman Tom Dailey gave a hearty laugh. "As long as it doesn't require the county to transfer more funds to your department for this fiscal year."

"It doesn't." Theirs was a small county and finances were perpetually tight. Arnie Hassert aside, she hoped she was never in a position to have to ask for additional monies after the budget had been set. "This is more of a housekeeping matter. I've hired a private forensics firm to assist with a homicide. Given the circumstances, it's imperative that my office avoids the appearance of a conflict of interest. The attorney general suggested to increase transparency I should give the money to the county and have you pay the fees from the deposited amount." She took the check from her purse and handed it to Dailey. "The county attorney can write up the necessary paperwork. The only responsibility the county has in the matter is to pay presented bills against this deposit and to refund any unused monies back to me after the case is closed."

The chairman looked uncomprehending. "This is a personal check." His brow furrowed. "And the amount…surely this firm won't charge that much?" Joni craned her neck to see and her brows shot up when she saw the figures on the check.

"Hopefully not, but I've also requested a private lab, so…" Keira lifted a shoulder, wishing that the meeting was already over.

"That's ridiculous." Unsurprisingly the outburst came from Arnie. "MSP can be called in to help with homicides. It's a waste to hire a private firm to do something our own state law enforcement can handle."

It was the moment she'd been dreading. Keira didn't discuss ongoing investigations with the board, and her deputies were trained to be tight-lipped, as well. She was cognizant that anything she said was likely to end up in the daily paper, and managing the information disclosed was second nature. "There are reasons the MSP won't be called."

"Conflict of interest." This was from Dailey. "You haven't been here long enough for there to be a case…" She gave an inward sigh when his mental light bulb seemed to go off. "Not…Keira, this isn't about Danny?"

"I can't confirm or deny the victim's name. " She waited for the uproar from the five to calm before going on. "I'm not at liberty to disclose much more, but the case is unfolding rapidly. The agent I've hired is primary on this case with my office providing support."

"It sounds to me like you're over-reacting, which is not a quality we need in our sheriff." Arnie's voice was sour. "You're not emotionally fit to be making these types of decisions, I said as much at the time. We had another interested party ready to apply for your position, one equally qualified…"

"That's enough, Arnie," Joni put in sharply.

Keira filed the exchange away to be examined later. "As sheriff of this county all law enforcement decisions in these matters are mine to make. I can pay the bills for this investigation through my personal account. That would have been my preference. Funneling them through the county isn't a necessity; it just makes things neater when it comes time to prosecute."

Rick Enabnit spoke for the first time. He'd been a friend of Phil's, Danny's and of Doc's, the fourth in the poker group who played together most Tuesday nights. Seeing the fresh grief in his eyes made Keira's burn. "We don't have the authority to second-guess the sheriff and Keira isn't asking for much. Given the situation, I think it's the least we can do to provide what support we can. I move that we deposit a personal check from Keira Saxon and use it to pay any and all bills for the private forensics firm she's hired."

After a moment's pause, Dailey said, "We have a motion on the table. All in favor…

———

Keira finished going over the interviews from the four they'd arrested at Bielefeld's yesterday, and squelched an urge to check the clock again. It sure as hell didn't make the time go faster. And it didn't make it any easier to resist the temptation to text Finn for an update. The test results took as long as they took. She was grateful they'd be available after a matter of hours, instead of days.

She turned her attention then to the missing persons reports. The deputies were whittling down the names, but there were still a lot of possibilities. If lab tests didn't come up with something definitive that would help them focus the list further, she'd start calling the case detectives herself. With the board meeting behind her, she'd have more…

There was a knock at the door and Phil stepped in. "I see you survived the board meeting. Still have an ass, or did Hassert chew it off?"

In answer she lifted a hip off the chair to show him that her butt was intact. "His teeth aren't that sharp. But I am glad it's over."

The older man pulled up a chair and sat. "Saw the press release. It won't satisfy Stella for long. She'll be in sniffing for more, mark my words."

The first thing Keira had done when she got to the office was to write up a carefully worded statement for the media. She knew Phil was right. Stella Cummings, the local paper's owner and main reporter, would certainly be hounding her for more details. They'd be forthcoming only when Keira deemed necessary. "I can handle her."

The man's expression was dour. "Woman's like a bloodhound on the scent for news, with a face to match."

She stifled a smile. There was no love lost between the undersheriff and Stella Cummings since the woman had a habit of misquoting him on the rare occasions he was forced to speak to her in an official capacity. For all the reporter's faults, she was good—too good—at her job, so Keira suspected the errors were purposeful. She'd often wondered if the two had a history, although she knew better than to ask the man.

There was another question she could put to him. "Do you know the source of Hassert's antagonism toward Danny?" Because it had started with her father, she realized that much. After she'd accepted the position, it had been transferred to her.

"Oh shit." Phil settled more comfortably in his seat, his angular face set in contemplative lines. "That goes way back. To before the little weasel became a commissioner. Let's see." He took a moment to remember. "Seems to me he was making some sort of complaint about his neighbor running trap lines on his property without permission."

Keira frowned. "That's a Department of Natural Resources matter, not ours."

The man held up a hand. "I said it started there. DNR got involved and whatever the outcome Arnie wasn't happy so he started making calls on the neighbor constantly. Accusing him of illegal burns, littering, stealing the newspaper out of his mailbox, petty crap. Danny finally sat the two of them down in an attempt to work things out, but Hassert accused him of not doing his job, favoring the neighbor, whatever. That had to have been a good ten years ago. The man knows how to hang onto a grudge."

An imperceptible chill worked over her skin. Not every grudge resulted in an arrest. She'd said as much to Finn earlier. How many people were out there harboring an imagined slight? People who wouldn't show up on that list she'd compiled for Finn.

She said as much to Phil and he lifted a shoulder. "Hell, no one could know that. And it's not enough to have wished Danny ill, how many had the means and opportunity to go through with it?"

Recalling something that Hassert had said that morning, she asked, "Were you interested in becoming sheriff?"

Phil shook his head. "I'm too damn old. Older than your dad, and he was planning to retire at the end of his term." Her expression must have alerted him. "You didn't know?"

Slowly, Keira shook her head. "He hadn't mentioned it." Maybe because dealing with his cancer diagnosis had pushed all other thoughts out of his head. Or because of the half-formed fear that planning for the future was a waste of time. "Arnie said they had someone qualified who was willing to apply."

"None more qualified than you." Under her steady gaze he admitted, "Likely he was talking about Hank. Hassert is full of shit, as usual, though, because Hank wasn't pushing for the job. You made it clear from the get-go that you were only going to fill the remainder of Danny's time."

She was learning all sorts of things today. Hank Fallon, as sheriff. Considering the idea, Keira couldn't fault the man for his ambition. He was a damn fine investigator and a seasoned deputy. Alger County would be lucky to have him. "He'll get his chance." She had a little over a year left in the position. And though she hadn't yet decided where she'd go from here, she knew she'd be leaving.

Phil gave a slow nod, the bald spot on top of his head glinting under the overhead light. "You're not long for this area. Knew that when you took the job, even before you told the committee the same thing. Your talents are wasted here. You just need to figure out your next step. Give yourself time to heal."

"Finding Dad's killer will go a long way in the healing process."

He surprised her by shaking his head. "You think so, but it won't. I want to catch the bastard as much as you, and yeah, there will be satisfaction in having him behind bars. But Danny will still be gone. And the only thing that will cure that loss is time."

Sound filtered freely through the door. She could hear the normal noises of the office, with phones ringing, people talking and the sound of heels clicking on the tile floor. They'd belong to Pammy. She ignored it all. Phil Milestone was a reticent man. These past few minutes he'd been positively verbose. The opportunity shouldn't be wasted. "Is that why you were against me hiring Raiker Forensics in this case?"

He shifted in his chair, looked away. For a moment she thought he wasn't going to answer. When he did his voice was reflective. "It wasn't just MSP on that crime scene. Multiple agencies were represented, and most of us from the department took part in the search. Whatever the state police missed, well, we did, too. We all bear responsibility for that, and it weighs heavy sometimes. But the inferences drawn were understandable. I've been all around it, every which way and I wouldn't have come to a different conclusion on my own. So, no, I wouldn't have excluded MSP based on the past. And I don't think your father would have wanted you to spend the life insurance money he left you on this investigation."

She smiled wryly. "Probably not. But I can't afford mistakes this time around. The killer has claimed at least two victims. And I'm going to do everything in my power to make sure there isn't a third."

As if he'd run out of his allotted reservoir of words for the day, the man only inclined his head before rising to leave. She didn't fool herself into believing that the gesture indicated agreement. Just that the conversation was over.

As the door shut quietly behind Phil, she checked the time again, and after waging a short inner war gave in and pulled out her cell. It rang in her hand.

Finn Carstens. Trying and failing to squelch the leap of her pulse she answered on the first ring. "Although I was just about to reach out and nag you, the fact that you called first means I didn't get pushy."

"Duly noted." She could hear the exhaustion in his voice. "There's a small space at the back of the lab that serves as an office. How soon can you get here? I have preliminary results."

———

Keira didn't break sound barriers getting to the county garage, but she did use the light bar on the vehicle and ignore all posted speed limits. She hurried across the lot and into the structure, almost as anxious to get out of the wind as she was to hear what Finn had to say.

Her steps slowed as she walked into the bay where he had the lab stored. He was leaning against the outside of it looking every bit as tired as he'd sounded on the phone. His streaky brown hair was mussed as if he'd run his hands through it, although she doubted he had. He'd be much too worried about contamination. A day's beard covered his jaw and a woman would have to be dead not to recognize how good it looked on him.

Keira still had a pulse. But at the moment she was more cop than female. "Tell me you found something we can use."

He pushed away from the side of the RV with a lazy grace that had heat pooling in her belly. "And here I thought your eagerness just meant you missed me."

Her lips curved. "I'd miss a guy with answers a lot more."

"You *did* miss me then. Because I've got answers."
He turned away to open a door near the rear of the lab.
"Probably more questions, but we have a direction."

She followed him into the vehicle and looked around.
The original use of the area had likely been a bedroom,
but it was outfitted with a table, a few chairs, and a
screen. There was a door that would lead to the lab itself,
but it was closed.

A laptop sat on the table with a sheaf of papers next
to it. "I've got all the results on the computer, but I ran
hard copies for you." He slid the pile of papers over to
her. "Here's the short version." Pressing a command on
the keyboard had images appearing on the wall screen.
"Congratulations to whoever took the snow cast of the
footprints from when you were attacked. That can be a
tricky test, but it gave us a great basis for comparison."

She leaned forward, anxious for the next image.
"To…"

"To this." The next picture showed a perfect imprint
taken with the EDL. He'd lifted impressions on the floor
beneath the broken window at her house and again at the
back door. "After a careful examination of the tread
captured with the snow cast and the footwear impression
caught with the EDL, I'm satisfied that the same footwear
was worn in both." He brought up the next picture,
which had an area on the inner sole enlarged. "I didn't
find any individual characteristics, but the signs of wear
on the tread will be unique to the individual."

Excitement flickered in her veins. They'd have to
make an arrest before they could search for the footwear
in question, but if they found it the evidence would be
damning indeed. "We can input this information into
the FBI's Footwear and Tire Tread database." The system
had vast amounts of manufacturer information. They

might even get the brand of footwear, which could prove more valuable to them in a town this size than in a city the size of Chicago, where stores were limitless. Unless, of course, the buyer had purchased them online.

He gave her a tired smile. "Already done. And I also submitted it to the forensic database at the National Institute of Justice. But I've got something better. The EDL also picked up trace amounts of animal feces. Scat, not manure. The molecular content shows it came from a meat eating animal rather than a domestic or farm animal."

Keira stared hard at him, mind racing. "So…wildlife. With all the forest in the county, we've got plenty of that." There was a sick stirring in her belly. There had been no lack of wild animals in the vicinity where her dad had been found. She took a breath, forced aside the memory. "Plenty of residents hunt, fish or trap in the area. And we don't always have to go to the wildlife. Sometimes they come to us. Remember the moose?"

His smile flickered. "I do. It doesn't tell us much, but it's something. So is this."

The screen filled with an eye-popping color-coded chart that she could make no sense of at all. "The DNA analysis. When I conducted the tests the first time, I only ran comparisons on the liver and the finger long enough to determine they weren't a match. Last night I did a full analysis on the finger and then another on the ear your intruder gifted you with. Not only did they match on all markers," Finn picked up a laser pointed and highlighted several columns on the chart, "but I discovered the ethnicity of the victim is primarily Native American." He cocked a brow at Keira. "Not sure how many on your missing persons list would fit that description."

"I don't recall that information being included for any of them, but I'd have to double-check." There were a dozen Native American tribes represented on the Upper Peninsula and a handful of reservations. A buzz of adrenaline started in her veins. The victim deserved justice. So did her father. And this just might be the first real step toward getting it. "As we noted before, we could be dealing with someone no one has missed yet, and he isn't in the database." She looked at Finn, noting his drawn expression. Despite what he'd told her last night, it was clear he'd gotten no sleep at all, and she felt a flicker of sympathy. So far his room at Turner's Landing had gone unused. Hopefully, tonight would be different.

"There's more." He flipped through images on the screen until he came to one showing a close up of the ear that had been put in Keira's refrigerator. "I told you that it had been severed post-mortem. But the lobe—," he switched to the next image which showed that area magnified—"had been cut off shortly before death." He saw her open her mouth and beat her to the punch. "And yes, it's statistically probable that the same weapon was used on the ear and the lobe, but not the liver or the finger. A much thinner blade was used for those."

"So cutting off the lobe could have been torture," Keira said slowly. "Or the killer might have been trying to hide something. An identifying mark, maybe?"

"Give the lady a gold star." Finn brought the next image up and Keira leaned closer to peer at it. "There was some sort of old trauma to the earlobe, and the killer didn't quite get all of it cut away. Some of the scar tissue remained. There was evidence of long-term healing, so it wasn't inflicted by the killer." He sat back, a satisfied expression on his face. "Identifying marks are routinely included in missing persons reports."

"And none of the ones on our list includes a descriptor like this." That didn't necessarily eliminate the ones they'd been looking at. The reports were only as complete as the information given to the case detective. They couldn't afford to overlook anyone on their narrowing list.

But she was already planning to expand on it.

"Thank you." Genuine gratitude laced her voice. "I know what it cost you to get all this done so quickly."

He worked his shoulders tiredly. "As much as I enjoy having you indebted to me, it's sort of why I'm here. I still need to run the analysis on the hair found in the window at your place. Didn't have time."

"It can wait."

Nodding, he said, "It'll have to. Because I'm heading to my room to shower and shave. Maybe the Turners will show enough pity to feed me. I'll be in after that."

Although he needed sleep, as well, she knew better than to argue with him. Picking up the sheaf of papers, she flipped through the pages, gratified to see he'd included copies of the images he'd shared. Then froze when she recalled something.

"What?"

She hesitated, feeling a bit like a traitor. "I'm sure it's nothing. But given the conversation you had with Wilson..." She paused, already second-guessing her intentions.

His expression was alert. "Someone else with a grudge?"

"No." She was certain of that. "But I found out today that my investigator was interested in my position."

He studied her for a minute from his seat. "But he didn't run against you?"

She shook her head. "There wasn't an election because Dad had been more than halfway through the term. The committee took applications, though. They seemed to have their mind set on me. It likely means nothing. I trust Hank Fallon, and so does Phil. Dad's death didn't benefit him in any way."

"Thanks for telling me."

The polite tone didn't make his words any less cryptic.

"You agree about the lack of motive, right?" When Finn didn't immediately reply she propped her fists on the table and leaned down. "It makes no sense."

"Probably not." He tried and failed to suppress a yawn. "But he goes on the list because we don't take anything for granted. We can't afford to."

After a moment she gave a jerky nod and straightened. She had to trust Finn to handle any further digging required with discretion. Because he was right about one thing. They couldn't afford to overlook anything. Or anyone.

———

Keira composed an inquiry to send out to the area Tribal Police concerning the identity of a missing Native American with a damaged left earlobe. After doing so, she considered for a moment before including the rest of the state and Wisconsin in her query. Then she went to the chart on the conference room wall again and studied it. All of the males on the list they'd put together had racial descriptors. As she'd told Finn, none was listed as Native American. But she knew that not everyone identified with their ethnicity, especially if they had mixed blood. She pored over the photographs of the recent missing persons, looking for a distinguishing mark like the one Finn had uncovered. When the picture wasn't clear enough to eliminate him completely, she contacted the case detective.

The work was tedious. Knowing how little time detectives spent at their desks, she elected to use email. But deep down she knew she was going through the motions. No cop worth his or her salt would have neglected an identifying mark like the one she was looking for, had he or she known about it.

Intermittently she fielded the emails she received back from Tribal Police, none of which were helpful. Once Keira finished the task, she brought up the county's digital file of mugshots and with a magnifying glass in hand, began examining the photos of the males in the pictures.

Three hours later she'd gotten as far back as 1997 and welcomed the buzz of her intercom. She straightened, rubbing her eyes. "Yes, Cal.."

"Matthews on line two."

It was too much to hope that Tobias was calling about her earlier inquiry. More than likely it was something else to do with the arrest last week of a tribal member. Since the man had initially refused to identify himself, Keira had had no way of knowing Matthews should be contacted. Their last couple of exchanges had been terse.

She reached for the phone. "Tobias. What can I do for you?"

"You can tell me if you're currently holding another of my tribe members in the Alger County Jail."

Stifling a sigh, Keira answered evenly. "No, all of my inmates provided identification. Unlike Romy Snyder."

There was silence on the other end of the line. When the Tribal Police lieutenant spoke again, the earlier edge in his tone was absent. "The query you sent out today said you were trying to identify a Native American male with a damaged left earlobe. He's not missing that I know of, but that description would fit Joseph Atwood. Had his left lobe chewed up pretty bad by a dog when he was a little kid. What's this regarding, Sheriff?"

CHAPTER 6

"When is this supposed to quit?" Finn squinted out the windshield at the snowfall, which was significantly heavier than it had been this morning.

"Next week." It was two hours from Munising to Baraga. It had taken them forty minutes longer than usual to make the trip. Keira flicked a glance at the clock on the dash. It was nearing five o'clock. She knew Tobias would wait for their arrival.

Keira slowed when the taillights winked in front of her. Michiganders were adept at driving in snow, but there were plenty of tourists on the UP, and not all of them displayed the same skill. "If the guy in front of me reduces speed any more he'll be stopped."

"You should see the first snowfall in DC." He'd spent a major portion of the trip with his head tilted back against the headrest, eyes closed and hopefully napping. Now he was alert, watching the passing scenery with interest. "First snowfall of the season every single driver promptly forgets how to drive in it. Tow trucks make a killing because they spend the whole day and night hauling people out of ditches."

"It first snowed on October fifteenth this year. Shouldn't be this driver's first rodeo. Thank God," she breathed when the car turned and trundled down a private drive. She pressed on the accelerator.

"Okay, give me a run down before we get there." Finn had shed his coat and snow boots for the trip. With his seat back as far as it could go, he had his legs outstretched as much as possible and still managed to have his knees practically knocking on the glove box. "We're going to a reservation?"

Without the driver in front of her, the road was even darker. "The L'Anse Indian Reservation has a split location on either side of Keweenaw Bay, with a smaller portion in Marquette County. The bigger parts are in L'Anse and Baraga and take up about a third of Baraga County. The reservation is the land base for the Keweenaw Bay Indian Community."

"And the Native Americans are from the Chippewa tribe you said."

"The Lake Superior Band." Her eyes were straining to see the side of the road. Plows had been through that day, but she knew well that with county budget constraints sometimes they were pulled off the road when the snow was supposed to continue for hours. It was snowing far more heavily here than it had been in Munising. "It's the oldest and largest reservation in the state. We usually don't have much contact with their Tribal Police. There are small areas in Alger County that belong to the Sault Ste. Marie Tribe of Chippewa Indians. We respond to emergencies there and maintain order until Tribal Police arrive from Manistique. Our jail isn't a federal lock up, so we can't keep a tribe member there.

But when an arrestee doesn't identify himself as such, things can get sticky." Which was at the heart of the recent disagreement she'd had with Matthews.

She fell silent then, trying to pick out the lights from Baraga in the distance. Hopefully, Atwood's mother would still be at the station by the time they reached there. The woman was the reason they'd made this trip in person.

A DNA swab could have been taken and sent to them in Munising. It would have arrived in a day or two. But at Finn's suggestion, Keira had agreed to come in person and have him do the swab so the test could be run more quickly. The man didn't just think like a cop, she thought, slanting a quick look at him and then away again. It was his compassion for the mother, left to sit and worry about her son that was equally responsible for his insistence. She knew from her experience with CPD that the two traits didn't always necessarily co-exist.

It was with a sigh of relief that she finally turned into the station lot on US 41. It hadn't been plowed either. She pulled into a spot in front of the structure that had recently been vacated and was void of the last six inches of snow. It was better than the alternative.

While Finn pulled on his coat and boots, she got out of the vehicle. Ducking her head against the wind, Keira made a hasty beeline to the entrance of the building. She fought to get the door opened against the wind resistance. Was surprised to have a hand cover hers. Finn opened it with enough ease to have her shooting him a look somewhat lacking in gratitude. "Show off."

He had the grace to fight his grin. "I haven't been battling the roads for two hours. I'm relatively rested."

"Sure. We'll go with that."

Inside the door they stomped the snow from their boots. Wiping them on the mat provided, Keira moved past the empty desks.

"Looks like everyone went home," Finn muttered in an undertone.

"Probably responding to weather-related calls." She stopped at the first desk with a uniformed policeman at it. "Sheriff Keira Saxon, Alger County." The stocky man with dark eyes and a graying crew cut slowly raised his gaze from his paperwork to her. The look on his face wasn't friendly. She heaved an inward sigh. Apparently Tobias wasn't the only one who believed she'd deliberately delayed alerting Tribal Police after picking up Romy Snyder.

"I'll see if he's busy."

She managed, barely, to avoid rolling her eyes. "I'd appreciate it."

The officer took his time rising and making his way to the closed door at the end of the room. Keira stayed where she was, aware of the interested looks from another officer nearby.

"I'm sensing a story here." Finn's voice was nearly inaudible.

"Just a misunderstanding."

The man who had disappeared into Tobias's office returned to the desk in front of them, sparing Keira barely a glance. "You can go in."

When they entered the cramped space, the lieutenant was behind his desk and didn't get up. Unlike his officer's cropped hair, Tobias kept his long and pulled back from his square face. "This is Rose Atwood, Sheriff Saxon." Only then did Keira notice the woman tucked into the corner of the room, behind the door they'd opened. "Joseph is her son."

Plump with long dark hair liberally threaded with gray, the woman had once been a beauty. Fear showed in her expression. Her gaze darted between Keira and Finn.

"Sheriff. Is my son…dead?"

Keira shot a look at Tobias, wondering how much he had told her. "I can't answer that right now, Mrs. Atwood. We have a body part from a victim who suffered trauma to his left ear- lobe some time back. We can't tell more without a DNA sample from you."

Atwood bowed her head, releasing a low, anguished moan as she clasped her arms around her middle. "Joseph is in Grand Marais. He met a girl at the casino and she has a place there. Not the kind of girl that he'd bring home to meet me. At least, he hasn't yet."

"When did you last speak to him?"

The woman didn't look at Finn when he spoke. "Two weeks ago. Maybe three. He doesn't have a cell but the girl does. He calls from hers."

Keira and Finn exchanged a glance. "Can I see your phone?"

In answer to his question, the woman dug in the large handbag she carried and brought out a smartphone. She brought up her call log and painstakingly went through it. Finally, she stopped. Showed them the screen. "This is the number he calls from. Ever since Tobias brought me here, I've been calling it. Trying to reach him. No one answers." Fear was apparent in her words. "The girl, she doesn't like me. Because I tell Joseph she's no good for him. She wouldn't answer."

Taking out her pocket-sized notebook, Keira jotted down the number, before looking at Tobias. "Did you call it?"

"Goes right to voice mail."

"Always as a boy he wanted to play with his uncle's dogs." The older woman's voice trembled. "They were for hunting, not for play, but no, Joseph wouldn't listen. One day when he was six, he got into the kennel. One of them latched onto him before we could get him out. Practically bit his earlobe off. It took many stitches, but it never looked right. It was too mangled." A fat tear rolled down her cheek. "I don't think a person could survive losing an entire ear."

"Do you have a picture of your son, Ms. Atwood?"

Instead of answering Keira, the woman looked at Tobias, who inclined his head. She reached into her bag again and withdrew two photos. One looked like it had been taken for a high school graduation. The other was a headshot someone had snapped with a camera. The damaged left earlobe was in full view. "I will want these back."

Because the woman was afraid she'd never see her son alive again. Sympathy surging, Keira assured her, "We'll return them. Ms. Atwood, we're going to track down the owner of the phone number. We'll talk to your son's girlfriend. Try to find him through her. Do you know what he was doing in Alger County? Where he was working?"

She shook her head. "He got fired from the casino when he didn't show up for work after taking off with her. He took his rifle with him. His traps. He learned from hunting and trapping from his uncle. He was good at both. I imagine that's how he's getting by, unless she has a job."

"Did Lieutenant Matthews explain that there's a test we can do to see if you are a match to the specimen we found?" Finn sank into the only other free chair next to the woman.

Rose nodded. "He said it wasn't a blood draw. That you had another way."

"We do." He opened the small cooler he'd brought in with him and took out a swab kit. "It's very easy."

As Finn was explaining the test to Rose, Keira opened the door and left the room. As she hoped, the lieutenant followed her. "You're positive the victim is dead, you said." Tobias pitched his voice low enough that it wouldn't carry into his office.

"Carstens is a forensic scientist as well as an investigator." Through the half-open door, she could see Finn swabbing the inside of the woman's cheek. "He established that the wound was post-mortem."

Matthews looked grim. "Joseph Atwood went to school with my youngest brother. He lacked direction, but he wasn't a bad sort. He hasn't been involved in any real trouble. Do you know who would do this?"

She hesitated. "We don't have a suspect at this time. But we do have reason to believe he's killed before. Another resident in my county."

The lieutenant's gaze sharpened. "There's been nothing about that on LIEN."

The Law Enforcement Information Network was Michigan's interstate computer system for the criminal justice community. "All of this is a very recent development."

Tobias's gaze traveled to his office, from which loud sobbing could be heard. "If there is an ear, somewhere there is a body. Maybe it will be found before the tests results are completed. I hate to think of Rose waiting weeks not knowing."

"It will be a matter of days, not weeks." Matthews' attention returned to her and she read the surprise in his expression. "I'll keep you informed as things unfold."

She nodded toward the woman in the room. "Does she have a way home? It's pretty wicked out there."

"She lives down the street." He pursed his lips. "It's you who should be worried. Radar says we're due for wind gusts up to forty miles an hour."

"Great." She saw Finn rise and help Ms. Atwood to her feet. "We weren't supposed to have blizzard conditions in Alger. Once I make it to Marquette, I'm sure we'll be fine."

The lieutenant's mouth twisted wryly. "I'm sure you will. But first you have to make it to Marquette."

————

Tobias's words proved prophetic. Keira and Finn didn't get ten miles out of town before she was forced to turn back. "If it's any consolation," he said, studying his cell, "now the forecast has changed for Marquette and Munising. The system Baraga is experiencing has spread across three counties."

"It's not a consolation," she said darkly, easing back into the Tribal Police parking lot. "Someday I want a career like a meteorologist where I can be wrong more than half the time and it's accepted with a shrug."

"Stakes are higher in our jobs," he murmured, and then called yet another of the town's hotels. He'd been phoning since they'd made the decision to turn around, with dismal results. Even the casino hotels were full, due to both winter tourism and stranded motorists. If push came to shove, they could take shelter in the police station. But neither of them would be getting must sleep there.

"You do?" The surprise in Finn's tone interrupted her thoughts. "We'll take two. Oh, I see. That's fine. We'll take it."

She waited for him to hang up before inquiring, "It? It is singular. It refers to one. One room?"

"Yeah." For the first time she heard the exhaustion in his voice, and was reminded that the man hadn't slept at all last night, and not much since he'd been assigned the job. "Motels are full, but there are some other bed and breakfasts on the list. You want to call the rest, I'm game."

After a moment she shook her head. "No, it'll be fine." They were both adults. This was doable. Finn was likely going to pass out once he hit the…

Comprehension struck belatedly. A bed and breakfast wasn't going to offer two beds to a room. She took a deep breath before putting the car in gear. Keira just hoped someone tracked down the meteorologist who'd bungled this forecast and beat an apology from him.

———

The room was charming if a little fussy and cramped. Its closet had been turned into a minuscule bathroom, and a coat rack sat in the corner next to a small dresser. It had been almost as difficult finding a restaurant as a room. The one brave diner that had remained open was doing a brisk business. It had taken well over an hour to get their food, which they'd eaten standing up in the packed establishment. Keira had spent most of the meal on her phone, talking to the night dispatcher, getting an update from Phil and then alerting Chase that she wouldn't be home that evening.

Once back at their lodging, Keira preceded Finn into the room, on the phone again. She moved to the one chair, a period piece that Finn wouldn't take a chance with. He placed the small cooler on the dresser. The DNA sample inside was protected until he could get it back to the lab. Then he took the opportunity to shower, which was damn refreshing, even if he did have to wear the same clothes. He padded back out into the bedroom wearing his jeans and tee shirt, carrying his holstered weapon, sweater, and socks. "All yours."

She nodded, her gaze avoiding him as she disappeared into the bathroom. Her discomfort was apparent, but she wouldn't mention it. She was too much of a professional. He was counting on that because the bed was a double and there wasn't another piece of furniture in the room that could serve for sleeping if he were inclined to be chivalrous.

He was too damn tired for chivalry.

Because there was no other option, he sat on the corner of the bed and answered his emails. Von Burg, the scientist to whom he'd sent the completed test results, had acknowledged receipt. She'd be the first of two to verify the outcomes before they could be moved out of preliminary status. But Finn was satisfied that his findings would hold up. And if he hadn't already been certain, the visit with Rose would have clinched it.

He felt a tug of empathy for the woman. Some said the not knowing was worse than the truth, but Finn didn't believe that. Uncertainty still allowed for hope and as long as hope lingered, even a fragile thread of it, the crushing agony of loss couldn't entirely settle.

Keira had set the pictures Rose had given them on the dresser and he got up to look at them now. He gave the close up the most attention, turning the magnifying app on his phone to study the left ear trauma. The wound had either been treated poorly or hadn't healed well. The ridges of scar tissue were evident even in the photo.

"So what do you think? Could he be our vic?"

Keira was framed in the bathroom doorway, drawing a comb through her tousled hair. She was in her uniform but carried her belt and weapon. The spill of light from the bathroom shot her red hair with streaks of gold. He recognized the pull in his gut for what it was. Hunger. And he tucked it away—mostly—just as easily.

"It's very possible, but the only way to be sure is to run the tests." His tone was self-deprecating. "If you haven't guessed by now, I'm more comfortable dealing with facts and data than I am with pondering the theoretical."

Her eyes widened with mock amazement. "No. Really? I'll bet you were the kind of kid who ruined Christmas by disproving the physics required for Santa to deliver all those presents."

He made a dismissive gesture. "Easily explained if one considers the five centuries of advanced science and technology evolution in the North Pole. It was the Easter Bunny myth that I took aim at. He didn't even have a sleigh and jet-propelled reindeer. It's like they didn't even try with that one."

Her expression lightened. "I'm not surprised you gave it some thought."

"I'm always thinking. For instance, right now I'm wondering if you're going to hoard that comb or share it. Or does my use of it require a borrower fee?"

"A borrower fee. I'm almost afraid to ask." But she tossed him the comb, which he caught neatly.

"I have a twin sister. Four minutes older, and she never lets me forget it. The borrower fee was her way of supplementing her allowance." The memory brought a smile as he ran the comb through his hair. "The payment was never reciprocal, as I recall."

"Something else I missed by being an only child," Keira responded drily as she went to her phone again. She checked the time before hitting redial. After a moment she spoke, her voice clipped. "This is the Alger County Sheriff. It is imperative that the owner of this phone call my office about a matter of some urgency at this number." She rattled off her contact information before adding, "This concerns Joseph Atwood."

When she turned back toward him, he got up to return her comb. "I'm guessing you don't have any cell phone detection equipment at the office."

She snorted and crossed to the chair. Sitting, she tucked the items she held beneath it. "Believe me, times like this make me long for the StingRay technology we had in Chicago. No, it's the old fashioned way for us. If it comes to that, getting a warrant won't be a problem. Judge Isaacson is pretty cooperative. Waiting for the response from the cell phone provider could take up to twenty-four hours, though." Keira stretched her feet out in front of her, crossing them at the ankles. "But it probably won't come to that. We can likely find the girlfriend faster just by checking out Grand Marais and showing Atwood's picture around."

Finn tried—and mostly succeeded—at keeping his gaze off that long length of leg. So sue him, he was a legman. And even encased in the dark brown uniform pants, hers would warrant attention from any male with a pulse. The pull in his gut was proof that he was very much alive. "So…" He lassoed his wandering thoughts. "How big is Grand Marais?"

"It's the only town in Burt Township. Five hundred residents. If Atwood was there, someone will have seen him. We'll stop on our way back tomorrow. If the roads are passable by then," she added darkly.

He smiled. She was really harboring a grudge against the hapless meteorologist who had so badly screwed up today's forecast. "Atwood is—or was—a trapper and hunter, according to Rose. And the EDL found scat tracked into your house by the intruder. We need to check that connection. Maybe that's how the killer crossed paths with his last victim."

"Both are popular pastimes on the UP. More people likely have a hunting license than not." She rubbed at a knot in her shoulder. "But yeah, we can check with DNR. They'd have records of the licenses and permits."

And then they'd cross-check the names on those lists with the one Keira had compiled on Danny Saxon's enemies. He needed to get the Atwood DNA test run as soon as possible. They didn't want to spend too much time on the tenuous hunting and trapping link without validation of their victim's identity. Putting to rest a mother's fear about her son's whereabouts was at least as important as furthering their case. One way or another, the woman would get tentative closure as soon as he could get it to her.

Bouts of tiredness had come and gone all day, but a cloak of exhaustion was settling on him now and he was ready to succumb to it. "I'm turning in." He looked around the room. "I'd tell you that you watching TV wouldn't bother me, but…"

"Right." The only electronics in the room was a digital alarm clock. Keira rose in one lithe movement. "Are you one of those guys with a weird territorial affinity to a specific side of the bed?"

"Well…I wouldn't call it weird. Or territorial."

She smirked. "Pick a side then."

Finn stood to round the bed. It was second nature to put himself between the door and the woman he'd be sleeping with. Not *sleeping with* in the figurative sense. He hastily amended the thought, because inviting those kinds of mental images would guarantee insomnia. He turned on the lamp on a fancifully carved bedside table before going to the door and double-checking the lock. Switching off the light, he returned to the bed and pulled the covers back to stretch out on it. He couldn't help wondering how much experience Keira Saxon had with men's affinity for a certain side of the bed.

The mattress gave slightly under her weight and he reached up to snap off the lamp. The room was enveloped in darkness. He silently thanked the owners who had paired the frilly curtains with room darkening shades. He and Keira laid there in silence for several minutes. Long enough for unconsciousness to begin to creep in.

"The selection of victims doesn't make sense to me." Her voice was pitched low. Quiet enough that it might not have wakened him had he been completely asleep.

"You mean a high profile kill followed by one with much less visibility?"

"Yeah." She shifted positions slightly in the bed. "Is it just opportunity? Because that doesn't seem to match with our suspicion for why he reached out to me. It means we're wrong about his game and motive. It would suggest a killer who's striking out somewhat randomly. And that doesn't seem to be our guy."

Fluidly he fell into her line of thought. "We still don't have enough to base a profile on, but I agree, choosing Atwood—if that's who the second victim turns out to be —doesn't mesh with the motivation we've settled on. Unless he was a pawn, chosen only for one purpose. To engage you. Up the ante."

She released a long breath. "That scenario works, but it sure doesn't make me feel any better."

"No." Finn tucked his hands behind his head, contemplating the darkness. "Was your father's death supposed to be his end game? And then something changed and he decided to take it further? He'd gotten away the murder." And that fact was sure to be one that burned for Keira. "He could have exulted in that, but after nine months it didn't prove to be enough for him. And that resonates with a serial offender. They can't stop, even if they want to. He has to let people know he's there and how he outwitted the investigators. That implies ego, and it might be what trips him up in the end."

"But he didn't choose to rub it in the face of the investigators, he chose me." He alerted to the underlying huskiness in her tone. With her studied dispassion, she made it easy to forget sometimes that the first victim they spoke about so often was her dad. But Finn had caught glimpses of the pain in her eyes a couple times before she'd looked away to compose herself. And he wondered at what price that dispassion came.

"Maybe because that's what offenders like him do. Exploit the suffering of others. Or perhaps whatever game he was playing started with my father and he wants it to continue."

"So let's start there. Did he challenge Danny? Seems to me if this is a contest for him, he may have. We should check unclosed cases in the county." And Finn kicked himself for not thinking of it before. "Maybe scrutinize any recently solved homicides, too."

"Alger County isn't exactly a hotbed of homicidal maniacs." Her voice was wry. "Up until now we've had a total of two murders in the last five years. The UP averages five annually."

"Which brings us full circle to victims that no one would miss." Because it just wasn't possible that Danny Saxon was the offender's first victim. Killers weren't that lucky, especially their first time. The terrain of the crime scene definitely had contributed to the erroneous cause of death, but he still wondered what the sheriff had been doing in the wilderness area to begin with, so far from his truck and fishing spot.

He had a sudden thought and it nearly brought him upright in bed. "Accidents. You mentioned something once about a fisherman going through the ice. Has that happened recently?"

"That's some memory you have, Carstens. Yeah, it was just last winter. His parka was found washed up on the shoreline about fifty miles from Munising, but his body…" Her voice trailed off. "Son of a bitch."

"It's a possibility," he cautioned, but there was a surge of excitement in his veins. "You'd have to go further back in your missing persons list. Maybe even five years or so."

"And not concentrate just on Alger." She moved again and, this time, her foot grazed his. She drew hers back as though she'd been scalded. "If he's hunting for victims he wouldn't necessarily be constrained by county lines."

Warmth lingered from where her flesh had touched his. It wouldn't do to concentrate on that now. Not with the cocoon of intimacy enveloping them as they spoke quietly in the darkness. It would be all too easy to forget that circumstances had forced them here, two people bound by a common cause who barely knew each other. He'd do well to remember that.

"It's difficult to accept that he almost got away with it." The words were uttered so quietly that he almost missed them. "My dad's death would have always been deemed an accident if the killer hadn't left that cooler on my porch. I had my doubts, but ultimately I have him to thank for not going to my grave believing Danny was eaten alive by wild animals. And knowing I owe him that is like taking a knife to the gut."

And here, finally was a sliver of herself that Keira hid from her fellow investigators. From pretty much everyone, from what Finn could tell. "There aren't many who could immerse themselves the way you have into the details of the death of a family member and stay objective." There were, as a matter of fact, plenty of excellent reasons for law enforcement entities precluding personnel from doing just that. But the emotional toll it might exact from her troubled Finn the most. He and Raiker had discussed the matter at length, and their concerns had been reflected in the service contract outlining his involvement.

As if echoing the line of his thoughts she said, "Phil was vehemently opposed to my bringing in an outside investigator. But I can't get over the fact that the cause of dad's death was missed, and the investigators responsible were MSP and my own office. I hate that I doubt them. I trust Phil and Hank as much as I did any partner I ever worked with in homicide. There are plenty of outstanding MSP agents. But...that agency had their chance. This isn't about me fearing being sidelined in the case...it's about wanting the best. Dad deserves that much."

She fell silent again. There was nothing more to say. Keira wasn't looking for platitudes about finding justice, and she wasn't seeking comfort. But his hand still went in search of hers on top of the covers. He felt her initial shock at the contact. Then slowly her fingers interlaced with his. And this time, when sleep crept in it took him under.

———

That stupid bitch. Boone slammed the kitchen door, fury nearly choking him. All the steps he'd taken recently had been with one goal in mind—getting the MSP called in to investigate Danny Saxon's death. He'd be matched with the best the state had to offer. Now Saxon's cunt daughter had ruined everything. He wanted to slice her up for the sheer pleasure of it and drop pieces of her on her fucking father's grave.

Boone wasn't a patient man, but he'd had to wait far longer than he'd wanted to start this contest. He'd been lucky not to bleed to death after Danny Saxon had shot him last summer. It wasn't like he could have sought traditional medical help for his wound. Recovery had been slow and painful. The only thing that had gotten him through was devising this plan. Dreaming of it.

And now Keira Saxon had just blown it to hell.

He wiped his boots on the rug in front of the kitchen door before crossing to pull a chair out from the table and sat. Taking the phone out of his pocket he started a search on the outfit Saxon had hired. It should have been the Michigan State Police. He'd counted on that. They were considered the premiere law enforcement agency in the state. Boone had counted on them being called in.

Leave it to a fucking woman to screw things up.

He ought to be getting to work. He had stuff to do today, and he liked to check his traplines daily. Instead, Boone spent the next hour reading stories on the web about Raiker Forensics. With each article his ire faded a bit. Finally, he pushed away from the table to pack his lunch, all the while contemplating what he had learned.

Maybe Saxon hadn't fucked things up after all. Could be she'd done him a favor.

He took out venison tenderloin and then some bread to make himself a sandwich. The online stories had made this Raiker sound like some sort of hot shit, and there was plenty on there about cases solved by his agents. After taking out some mayo, he slathered the meat before topping it with another slice of bread and slipping the entire thing into a baggie. Perhaps the people in Raiker's company were better investigators than the MSP. Maybe...just maybe...whomever the Saxon bitch had hired was exactly what he was looking for.

Didn't matter how great a cop was, though. The UP was different. The terrain made it unique.

Which gave him the advantage.

He shoved the sandwich in his pocket and headed back to his truck. Michigan hosted contests yearly for bragging rights for the best hunter or trapper. Those events were for suckers. Animals could be cunning, but they couldn't come close to the challenge of trailing the most highly evolved creatures on earth.

Humans.

And what happened when you pitted a highly trained manhunter against a hunter of men?

Satisfaction filled him as he got in the truck. Started it. It had become the burning goal in his life to discover that answer.

He gave his next step serious thought as he drove. Boone was up early, but the plows had been earlier, leaving the roads slick in spots. A car was in the ditch ahead, but he didn't slow to see if the driver was still in it. If dumbasses couldn't handle snowy roads, they shouldn't be in Michigan.

It wasn't until he pulled into the Hiawatha Forest entrance that a plan began to form. He would have liked to see Saxon's face when she opened that little present he'd left in her refrigerator. No doubt it had gotten her attention. Boone wondered what the hotshot investigator she'd hired had had to say about it.

It was time to raise the stakes. He considered another minute and then a smile spread wide over his face when he settled on his next move.

The forest was still and deserted when he pulled the pickup over to the side of the road. He flipped on the light of the miner's hat and fit it over his stocking cap before getting out. Lowering the tailgate, he took out his cross country skis, the large backpack, and the sled. All the equipment would be needed to haul his catch back to the truck.

His favorite sports had a lot in common. Didn't matter if it was fishing, trapping or the hunt, to land the biggest prize you had to use the right bait.

And he had just the bait in mind.

———

Grand Marais, Michigan wasn't much more than a blip on the map although even draped in snow its surroundings were picturesque. It boasted a Chamber of Commerce, a K-12 school, a bustling convenience gas station, three restaurants, one bar and oddly enough a pickle barrel house. Keira pulled into the gas station, parked and they both got out of the car. Nature was atoning for yesterday's storm with balmy mid-thirties temperatures.

The girl behind the register boasted four piercings in her ear, a stud in her brow and a hoop in her nose. Finn had always wondered if the metal transferred cold to flesh. Decided not to ask.

They stood at the end of a line of six people paying for gas, breakfast food or doughnuts. Since their hosts had offered light breakfast fare, Finn had no trouble turning his back on the other culinary treats in the bakery. He could feel the impatience emanating from the woman beside him, but Keira remained silent. She'd had little to say this morning, both over breakfast and on the way here. He wondered what she regretted more: opening up to him, or allowing that slight human contact. Keira Saxon seemed to be practiced at suppressing her emotions. Finn had the feeling that seeking comfort was foreign to her.

When they'd finally made their way up to the checkout, there were another five people behind them. Without looking up, the cashier inquired, "Gas at pump four?"

"No. Alger County Sheriff." Keira tapped her badge. "Wondering if you've seen this individual around." She took the photos Rose Atwood had given them yesterday and held out the most recent of them.

The girl squinted at it. "Um, yeah, maybe. I think. I don't know him or nothing, but he might have been in here before."

Keira turned around, holding the picture high and asking the others in line, "How about any of you? Have you ever seen this man?"

They all shook their heads. Someone came out of the bathroom at the back of the store and headed toward the door. Keira called out to him, "Sir. Please look at this photo and tell me if you've seen this man before."

With alacrity the older gentleman approached and squinted at the image. "Not that I recall. Sorry."

Because he was scanning the store, Finn's attention zeroed in on the one man who wasn't in line. He'd been there since they came in, loitering in the aisles, pretending interest in several items but never picking anything up. Finn detached himself from Keira's side and ambled toward the man. "Sir?"

The guy exploded into action. He dodged around the aisle and bolted toward the kitchen. Finn followed him through the narrow area, an outraged, "Hey! You can't be back here!" trailing after him as he chased the man through an exit toward a rusted burgundy pickup parked next to one of the pumps. Seeing the truck locks were secured, Finn slid to a stop in front of the truck's grill and then dove away when the driver revved the engine and the vehicle lurched toward him. His sore ribs furiously protested the sudden movement.

"In here!"

He reversed course and pulled open the passenger door of Keira's already moving SUV. She flipped on the siren and then screeched out of the lot, following the pickup as it turned a corner and sped down a snowy gravel road.

"So. Friend of yours?"

She flashed a grim smile. "I didn't get a good enough look to tell if I knew him, but something tells me his picture is gracing a warrant in my county or a neighboring one." As she gained on the old truck, she grabbed her radio and called in the license plate number. A couple minutes and several road turns later, she disconnected. "Adam Beckworth, wanted in Marquette County for burglary. Idiot. I probably wouldn't have known him even if he'd talked to me. Guilt turns people stupid." The pickup in front of them hit a patch of ice and fishtailed wildly. "That is if they weren't stupid to begin with."

While they watched, Beckham lost control of the vehicle and it did two complete circles on the road before sliding into the snow filled ditch. Keira pulled to a stop along the road nearby. "Ten to one he runs."

Finn peered into the driver's window of the truck. Beckworth's head was resting on the steering wheel, although it didn't look as if an air bag had deployed. The vehicle was old enough that it might not have them. If he'd cracked his forehead hard enough, he wouldn't be going anywhere. "You're on."

They'd no more gotten out of the SUV before Beckworth came to life, sliding across the seat of the truck to open the opposite door and dive through it. He got two steps before sinking in the snow and sprawling face downward.

"Loser has to wade in there and haul him out of the ditch."

Finn's gaze snapped to hers. "I'd rather just pay up."

A smile on her lips, Keira rocked back on her heels, clearly enjoying herself. "Winner gets to name the terms."

Looking back at the guy in the ditch, Finn saw he'd scrambled to his feet and had taken a few more steps before sinking to his waist again. With a sigh he pulled gloves out of his pocket and drew them on, then stabbed one finger in her direction. "You're mean."

"It's been said." She unclipped the cuffs on her belt and held them out. Grabbing them, he walked over to contemplate the man still struggling. "If I leave you down there I'm pretty sure they won't find you until spring." He'd take the obscenity the guy uttered as a sign of agreement. "You can start making your way over to me, or I can just wait until you tire and haul your ass out. Your choice."

Because, as Keira had noted earlier, the man wasn't blessed with superior powers of cognition, he continued to fight his way forward a few feet before falling and then dragging himself up again.

Finn made his way down the side of the ditch, in a position that would place him directly in the man's path. He promptly sank in snow to his upper thighs and the look he threw at Beckworth was baleful. "We're both going to regret this."

The man turned and tried to retrace his steps. Finn caught up with him and used one hand to give him a powerful push. Beckworth went down, and, kneeling beside him, Finn quickly got the cuffs on the man.

"Since when is it illegal for a guy to not buy anything at a gas station?"

"As far as I know the illegal part was when you turned to burglary." He searched him, finding only a thin wallet with ID matching the name on the warrant. With no little effort, he dragged the man to his feet.

"It's not breaking and entering when you're just going after your own stuff," the man protested. Finn guided him toward the incline of the ditch. "A guy took something of mine and I was just getting it back."

"Count me as disinterested." He didn't need to glance up at Keira on the road to know she was watching the whole scene with amusement. Grimly, he nudged the man forward when he halted in front of him. Something told him it was going to be a helluva lot more difficult climbing out of the ditch than it had been going down it.

———

"For the last time, I was laughing with you, not at you."

"I don't recall laughing at all." Finn brushed ineffectually at the snow that still clung to his pants. The journey up the incline had been somewhat more ignominious than his descent had been. Before he'd gotten Beckworth to the road, they'd both slipped and fallen backward. Twice. "It takes a hard woman to send a wounded man into battle."

"Wounded?"

He pointed at his stitches and then his eye, which this morning was ringed with a yellow bruise. "I might have Raiker amend the contract to include combat pay."

Her lips twitched suspiciously. "And what would be the most expensive, I wonder. The wound to your head, eye or pride?"

His tone was lofty. "It's the emotional scars that hurt the most."

A laugh burst from her. "That's not surprising. Just be glad I didn't film it. As comic relief goes, that arrest was gold."

She pulled into the parking lot of the convenience station again. She'd already radioed for Brody to meet her there so he could transport Beckworth to the jail. "I'm going to go in and show the rest of the staff the picture, and then we can decide where to go from there."

"Hey, let me see it." It was the first time their prisoner had spoken on the trip back to town. "I only saw it from a distance. I might know the guy."

With a shrug Keira pulled into the gas station lot and took the photo out of the inside pocket of her coat, holding it up to the cage that separated the front and back seats.

"Hey, that looks like Pitbull. I mean, not the rapper. But that's what I called this guy. On account of he said his ear got all messed up from a dog bite."

Finally, the man had Finn's interest. He shifted in his seat to look at Beckworth. "What's his real name?"

The arrestee shrugged as Keira got out of the car and disappeared into the building. "I don't know. I only saw him once. But we had some beers and got to talking and that's what he said."

"Where was this?"

"Crazy Horse. Only real bar in town."

"How long ago?"

The man furrowed his brow as if the act of remembering pained him. "I don't know. A couple weeks?"

"Did he say anything else?"

Beckworth settled back in his seat. "It was a long time ago. He might have said he had a girlfriend that he was shacked up with. This is helpful, right? My information could get those charges dropped?"

"You'll have to take that up with the sheriff." A second cruiser was already pulling into the lot. The deputy hadn't been far away. "I'll make sure and mention it to her."

The man had seen the other official car too and sank a little lower in his seat. "These charges blow. That stuff I took was *mine*."

The handoff of Beckworth took only a few minutes after Keira returned. Once finished, she slid behind the wheel. "The cook thought she'd seen Atwood before, but couldn't be sure where."

Finn reached up to the dash and turned the blower on the heat up. The car was plenty warm, but his clothes were wet and the faster they dried the better. "Your buddy in the back seat claims he drank with him at a place called the Crazy Horse."

"Yeah, that's a bar and grill in town. More bar than grill." She pulled out of the lot and cruised down a mostly deserted Main Street.

"Will it be open at this time?" The dash clock read barely eleven.

"If not, the owner will be around. He lives in the apartment over it." After a brief pause, she added, "He might not be that cooperative. The last time I saw him didn't end well. I responded to a fight here and he ended up getting thrown through the front window."

CHAPTER 7

"You know, they say people who hold grudges are the most likely to die of heart attacks, Randy. They've done studies." As Keira had warned Finn, Randy Tenney had not been happy to see them. He was blocking the door of his establishment as if guarding a fortress, his scrawny frame clad only in jeans and a thin tee shirt.

"Damn straight I hold a grudge! See this?" The man lowered his balding pate to point out a curved still-pink line. "Twenty-two stitches it took to close that gash. I'd almost gotten things calmed down in here before you showed up anyway. Then you walk in and it goes to shit again. You know how much that window cost to replace?"

"No." Keira surveyed him steadily. "But I know that I made sure the three who busted up your bar were charged and forced to pay reparations. You got your medical costs covered, too."

That stopped the man for a moment. Then he said truculently, "Didn't get nothing for the emotional trauma. And let me tell you, a fella my age goes sailing through a window, there's plenty of pain and suffering."

"We'll make this quick." She pulled out the photo and showed it to him. "We already know he's been in your place." They had only Beckworth's word on that, but Randy needed to be sidetracked, and this might be a way to jumpstart his cooperation. "We need a name."

He looked at the picture and she saw the recognition in his eyes. "Yeah, he's been here. Don't have a name for him. He's been in alone and with a woman." He shrugged. "Don't know her name either, not for sure. It's that gal who works out at Lakeview Cabins. Always wants to put their fliers up in my place, and gets plenty mouthy if I say no. Pushy little bi—woman," he amended.

Keira and Finn exchanged a glance. "You're sure?"

"Nothing wrong with my memory." He stepped back, swung the door closed.

"You should take your own advice about holding grudges," Finn advised as they made their way back to the car. At her questioning look, he added, "The meteorologist?"

"I can be excused for only handling two of the three guys at a time who were breaking up a bar. The weatherman? What kind of stress was he under?"

They got back in the vehicle and she pulled away from the curb. Finn took out his phone to look up the address of their next stop. "You know where Lakeview Cabins are?"

"I'm familiar with Grand Marais. There are far more motels than other businesses." From her side mirror, she saw a bundled up woman come out of her house to tackle the shoveling. Keira had to give her mental props. With as much snow as had gotten dumped on them last night, the woman had, at least, a couple strenuous hours work ahead of her. "Lakeview is just outside of town. I stayed there once when I was a kid." It was a good memory. "Danny and I vacationed somewhere on the peninsula every summer. There's a lot of breathtaking beauty on this slice of land." She'd always wondered why her mother hadn't been able to see it. People let their own personal unhappiness blind them to all the good in their life. For some, a new setting could bring a renewed sense of peace. In her mother's case, Lisa carried that discontent within her. She was never satisfied with anything for long.

A long buried worry worked its way to the surface. Keira and Todd had been engaged for two years and she'd been as guilty as he about putting off setting a date. She wanted to believe that thoughts of her mother's perpetual dissatisfaction were what had kept her from rushing to the altar. But in her heart, she knew it had more to do with her dad's words the first time he'd met her fiancée.

He's not the one for you, Kee-Kee.

It was the only indication he'd ever given that he didn't approve of her choice, a fellow cop. Danny wasn't the overprotective type, so his statement had resonated more than it should have. It had squirreled away in her mind and was likely the reason she'd let the engagement drift.

"I meant to ask." Finn's words were a welcome interruption from the gloomy path her thoughts had taken. "Are the pictures on the wall in your home of spots on the UP?"

Keira nodded. "The ones next to the fireplace are the Pictured Rocks National Lakeshore in Munising. I've never been able to decide if it's more beautiful in summer or winter."

"I'll have to come back sometime when you can show me some of the sights."

She slanted him a glance. His expression was sincere. The thought of seeing Finn Carstens after the case ended was more intriguing than it should have been. Keira was cautious by nature. It was his layers, she decided, turning down the road that would lead them out of town before it swooped closer to the lake's edge. It would take a while to discover all the facets of the man.

Finn shifted in his seat as she slowed before the motel's lane. He was still wet past his knees. Keira reached over to turn the blower up another notch. "Have you ever been married?" She wheeled the SUV along the narrow freshly plowed drive to pull to a stop in front of the cabin office.

He was looking at the motel sign. "No." He got out and slammed the door, waiting for her to join him before walking toward the business. A slight breeze had come up, just enough to tease the tops of the hills of snow and scatter random flakes in the air. A few landed in his thick brown hair. "I'd like to think if I ever had been I still would be." His mouth quirked. "I have a streak of idealism that life has attempted to hammer out of me, but hasn't quite succeeded."

"I hope it doesn't. Succeed," she added, when he cocked a brow. She shrugged, oddly embarrassed, and continued toward the bright red door of the office. "God knows in this line of work, a few ideals are all that get us through some days."

———

"Oh, yeah, that's Joey." The twenty-something girl at the front desk nodded emphatically as she looked at the photo. "He works here." A frown marred her forehead.

"At least, he used to. He might have gotten fired. I haven't seen him around."

"Is the assistant manager here?"

The girl rolled her eyes theatrically. "Sylvie Baxter? Oh, yeah, she's here. Been on the warpath all week. She's probably the one who fired him."

"Britta! Have you finished..." A woman at least a decade the girl's senior burst through the cracked door behind the desk that led to what Keira could now see was an office of sorts. She stopped short, taking in Keira's uniform and badge before arranging her features into a polite mask. "Deputy. Is Britta helping you?"

Keira heard Finn's strangled cough, but her focus was on the newcomer. Holding up Atwood's photo, she said, "Sheriff Saxon. I understand that you know this man."

The assistant manager pushed back her long dark hair and gave a cursory look at the picture. "That's Joseph. He worked here for a short time, but doesn't any longer."

"Why don't we discuss this matter privately?"

The woman's unwillingness was written in her expression, but finally she stepped aside and motioned for them to join her behind the counter. When they followed her into the postage stamp sized office, she shut the door behind them and said briskly, "I'm afraid I can't give you much more information. Joseph was employed here for a few weeks but stopped coming to work several..." She halted when a phone rang. Keira glanced at Finn, who had his cell in his hand, his eyes on the assistant manager.

"I thought it might save time," he said in an aside before returning his gaze to the other woman. "You might want to answer that. Could be important."

The woman's mouth twisted. "Are we done playing games? So you have my number. So what?"

"So your name is Sylvie Baxter. You met Joseph Atwood at a casino a couple months ago. He quit his job and came back here with you." Frustration flickered through Keira. "You could have saved us a lot of time and effort if you'd answered your phone messages."

Baxter sat behind the desk. "My phone was dead. I haven't had time to check them."

"Where is he?"

"That's why you're here?" The assistant manager snorted. "Why, what's he done? I'm not getting tangled up in any mess he might have gotten himself into. He took off a couple weeks ago and hasn't been back since. That's all I know."

Studying the other woman Keira figured that she wasn't one to give up all she knew without a struggle. Although likely shy of forty, the years had etched cynicism into a face that that would have been pretty if not for the hardness in her blue eyes. This was a woman who'd backed more than one losing proposition in her life. It was clear she'd already written off the one she'd made on Atwood.

Slowly and painfully Keira led Baxter through the events from the couple's first meet to their time here. "I got him this job, you know." The woman opened the desk drawer and pulled out a pack of cigarettes and a lighter. Lighting up, she drew deeply on the cigarette and blew the smoke out in a long stream. "He could have shown a little gratitude for that, at least, the bastard."

"You say he's been gone nearly two weeks? But you didn't report him as missing?"

The assistant manager gave a hoot at Finn's question. "Missing? Probably went running home to his mommy.

The apron strings were long for that one. Or more likely someone else caught his fancy and he's shacked up somewhere with her." She took several more quick puffs before grinding the cigarette out in a black plastic ashtray emblazoned with the Lakeview logo. "Thought he was different, but turns out he's the same as every other guy who's screwed me over."

"You said he might have gotten himself into a mess. What kind of trouble were you thinking of?"

"Well, I've got the law here asking about him so what else am I supposed to think?"

Keira chose her words carefully. "It's possible Atwood was the victim of a crime. That's the only reason we're trying to find him. Anything you can tell us may be beneficial. Was he having problems with someone? If so, do you have a name?"

Concern crept into the woman's expression. Her gaze darted from Keira to Finn and back again. "You're freaking me out here. What kind of crime? I mean Joseph…he was a pretty sweet guy. You think someone hurt him?"

"Do you know anyone who would do that?" Finn put in quietly.

"No!" Baxter fumbled for another cigarette. "The only people around here he knew were his co-workers. I don't ever remember him mentioning any type of trouble except for some jerk who was hassling him over his traplines."

Keira stilled. "His mother said he brought his traps and gun with him. He was trapping here?" DNR would require a different permit for each county.

It took the woman a couple tries to get the cigarette lit. "Yeah. We had some fights because he made such a damn mess cleaning his catch in my garage."

"Did he give a name of the man he argued with? A description?"

"No and no. Some asshole, that's all he said. Accused Joseph of poaching his traps or something." She shook her head, sending a strand of hair dangerously close to the ash on the cigarette she was holding. "I don't know anything about that. Wish I didn't know about any of this." She pointed the lit cigarette at Keira, a sheen glistening in her eyes. "Right now I'd give a lot to believe he went home or ran off with some other woman. It'd be better than thinking about him out there somewhere, injured."

———

They finished interviewing the rest of the employees on site. A suddenly cooperative Sylvie Baxter had provided them with a list of the off-duty staff, complete with their phone numbers. But after all the interviews, Keira and Finn had little more to go on. None of the co-workers seemed to have known the man well. Certainly not well enough to recall someone who'd wished him harm.

"Trapping gives us a similar angle. Your father was approached outdoors. Maybe Atwood was, too."

His words mirrored her thoughts. "The DNA test is a priority." She needed to be sure about the second victim's identity before looking for links between him and Danny. The fact that a growing certainty had taken root inside her wasn't enough.

But it fit. It fit too well. Keira's foot pressed more firmly on the accelerator, anxious to get back to Munising. In a sad twist of fate, if it was Atwood who'd been murdered by her dad's killer, the other man's death might provide their first real clue.

———

Neither of them went home to change. A feeling of urgency had settled, and Keira knew Finn was experiencing it, too. She dropped him off at the county garage, perhaps lingering a moment too long watching him walk away. Some men were made to wear jeans. Finn Carstens just happened to be one of them.

She pulled into the courthouse parking lot, which seemed more cramped than usual. The mountains of snow around it grew each time it snowed, encroaching further into the slots. Unfortunately, there was enough room for the dark green Malibu with license plate ALG HRD. Keira gave one fleeting thought to driving out again. Decided she'd have to deal with the Alger Herald reporter at some point.

After speaking briefly with Cal, she walked straight to the open door of Hank Fallon's office. His face lit up with an almost desperate gratitude. "Afternoon, Sheriff."

Stella Cummings turned her head and, spotting Keira, whirled from her stance at the investigator's desk to send her a brilliant smile. "Sheriff Saxon. Just the person I was looking for."

Hank stood.. "I was explaining to Ms. Cummings why her planned headline in tomorrow's paper wouldn't be a good idea."

Keira caught the warning in the deputy's words. "Why don't you come to my office and tell me about it, Stella."

The woman looked shocked at the invitation, as well she should. It had never been tendered before. Quickly she recovered and hurried to follow in Keira's steps. Cal handed her a few notes for missed phone calls, and she flipped through them as she walked. Reaching the door to her office, she pushed it open and ushered the reporter inside, stealing a glance at the clock. Five minutes, she promised herself. And knew she'd be lucky to get rid of the woman in twice that amount of time.

Showing Cummings to a seat, Keira hitched a hip on the corner of her desk and tried for a smile. "So. What can I help you with, Stella?" She tried—and failed—to suppress a memory of Phil's description of the woman. Although unkind, it held a kernel of truth. At least sixty, the reporter's hair was died to an improbable shade of platinum and worn long and straight to her shoulders. Her eyes beneath her bangs were heavily made up and narrowed at Keira assessingly.

"You can corroborate a source who told me that this office is investigating your father's death as a homicide."

Keira schooled her features to remain impassive. She'd had plenty of practice. As a detective with CPD she'd faced more than her share of reporters anxious for a new byline in a murder case. "My job isn't to substantiate rumors you're following up on, Stella. It sounds to me like you need to check your source."

"So you deny it." The woman dug in her fur-trimmed purse to pull out a pen and small tablet.

"All I'm prepared to say at this point was included in the press release." Keira folded her hands in her lap.

"Your office recently hired an outside consultant." Pen poised over a fresh page, the reporter waited expectantly. "What was that for?"

"To provide specialized expertise in a homicide under investigation." She held up a hand when the woman opened her mouth. "I'm waiting for positive ID on the victim."

"And how does that case constitute a conflict of interest for your office?"

Keira schooled her features to impassivity. The inquiry was expected. They had more questions than answers at this point. She'd require far more information before she was willing to divulge her father's connection to their investigation. "No comment."

Stella's foundation had settled into the wrinkles creasing her angular face, accentuating them. They doubled when she smiled, which she did now, her red-slicked lips curving slyly. "I heard there was some sort of mobile laboratory taking up space at the county garage. From the picture I saw it was plastered with signs about dangerous chemicals on board."

Plastered was an overstatement, Keira noted silently. She recalled one in each window. Irritation filtered through her. Right now Finn and Wilson should have the only two keys to the bay where the lab was located. The picture could have been snapped as it was making its way through town. She gave a mental shrug. It was locked and alarmed, whether Finn was inside it or not.

"Chemicals mean forensic tests, which would require evidence. That suggests your department has collected items from the scene of a crime. If this case is high profile enough to warrant an outside agent, it's critical enough to share with the media, especially if it means there is a serious threat."

She felt a stir of uneasiness. Balancing citizens' safety with the privacy necessary on an investigation could be a seesaw of conflicting priorities. There were a few instances when going public about a crime could be advantageous, especially to urge witnesses to come forward. The flip side was creating unnecessary alarm, which usually meant a flood of worthless 'tips' being called in, which then had to be checked out.

With no suspect and no motive, there really was little more to reveal to the woman unless they got a match on Atwood's DNA. She could keep the real cause of Danny's death secret, for now, but a positive ID on another victim meant releasing a second statement. She'd wait until that was necessary. "When there's something to report, you'll be notified."

The woman's bright red lips thinned. "You're not going to fob me off with this, sheriff. It can't be a coincidence that the lab arrived the evening after your house was broken into."

"It can't?" Her brows skimmed upward. "Again, I feel you're reaching for conclusions where there may not be a logical cause and effect. But for the record, I can't corroborate your assumption."

"Meaning you won't." Smoothly the reporter switched tactics. "Was the break-in connected with the rash of burglaries we had last November?"

"I think that's doubtful." She snuck a look at the clock. "Those perpetrators are behind bars."

"Do you think you were targeted as an individual, then?"

Stella was becoming visibly annoyed. Keira stood, deciding to end the meeting while things were still civil. "I can't say. If there's nothing else, I have work to do."

The reporter didn't move. "Can I at least get a reaction on the change of attorney on record for three of the four accused in that drug bust that went down recently?"
Keira stilled. "I don't have a reaction because I didn't know. But that has nothing to do with our office."

"I think it does." Finally, Stella clutched her purse and stood. "Obviously, the three are going to give testimony about the other one. I would think that might have some sort of bearing on the case you're building." Her mouth tightened in irritation. "As I told your

172 | KYLIE BRANT

deputy, if you cannot verify my information about your father's death, I'll be forced to rely only on my sources."

It was an old interview tactic; veering from subject to subject, waiting until the interviewee lowered his or her guard before striking again on the most sensitive topic. Keira had used it herself in interrogations, with far more success than she was going to give Stella. "We both know you value your paper's reputation too much to print what is no more than unsubstantiated gossip." When the woman bristled, she continued calmly. "When we have another publicity release we'll call you."

Temper stiffened the woman's ramrod figure as she left the Keira's office and made her way toward the door. She used the intercom on her desk to summon Hank, and the man joined her, humor and relief mingled in his expression. "Gotta say, I've never been so glad to see you walk through that door. Talking to that woman is like crawling through a pit of rattlers."

"She's got an interesting style," Keira agreed. "What all did she have to say?"

Fallon rubbed his shaven jaw. "Smoke, mostly. But she told me if she didn't get information from us that her next headline was going to read former sheriff's death ruled murder." He shook his head. "I don't see an upside to showing our cards publicly this early in the game."

"Me either." She hadn't been flattering the reporter. Stella was justifiably proud of the county paper she put out. "You're right, that headline was made up to shake you." If all she had were unsubstantiated supposition, she wouldn't run it.

"You think she got this from the meeting minutes?" Hank folded his arms over his chest.

"No." Last night she'd read through them. They'd been brief and factual, reporting only that the sheriff's office was paying for an outside investigator and private funds for the expense would be run through the county budget. "She could have jumped to the same conclusion that Arnie did." And had she contacted the commissioners, Hassert would be the one most willing to share his opinions with her. Keira gave a mental shrug. She'd known the act of hiring an outside investigator would garner interest. As long as her office remained silent on the matter, it would remain the subject of conjecture. That couldn't be helped.

"What do you know about there being a different attorney of record on three of our drug bust suspects?"

"Burke Landau out of Marquette is going to represent Bielefeld, Chrissy Larson, and Tom Payne."

"Landau was Bruce Yembley's lawyer for his assault trial." She remembered because the defense attorney had spent a lot of time trying to discredit her dad on the stand. Nor had that been their first meeting. Landau had an aggressive attitude that cast a wide net of blame on others to create reasonable doubt. Law enforcement personnel were often the targets of his attempts at misdirection.

"Not surprising. He's considered one of the best on the peninsula."

And the cost for his services reflected that reputation. "Outside the money found in the safe in Bielefeld's shed, I didn't see anything in his financials that suggests he has the cash for an attorney of Landau's stature."

"I've been trailing that." Fallon leaned a shoulder against the doorjamb. "He may have dummy accounts under other names. Can't see that he'd be sharp enough to manage anything overseas, but maybe he has someone smarter doing it for him. Or someone else is financing him. Someone who isn't helping Abernathy."

"Maybe Charlie is thinking about turning evidence against the other three." If he were, the prosecutor would be the one to determine whether a deal was on the table. And it would hinge on how damning Abernathy's testimony might turn out to be. "However Bielefeld is paying for his legal services, he's as to be able to pay for them. He's hiding money somewhere. Keep me posted."

"Ok." He started toward the door and then faced her again. "Hey, did you know that your dad once beat Bruce Yembley out of the UP marksmanship title?"

The news was a surprise. She vaguely remembered the trophy from her childhood. It used to sit in her dad's home office. Keira hadn't seen it for a long time, and it hadn't been among his things when she'd gone through them after his death. Danny had given up those sorts of contests a long time ago as unseemly for someone in his position. "I recall the trophy. I wouldn't have known who he was up against."

"Just caught my attention, because Finn asked me to do a thorough check on Yembley and Roger Wilson." With a wry twist of his lips, Fallon added, "Something tells me Yembley's history is going to be a whole lot more interesting than Wilson's."

She stared at his retreating back, her earlier unease about the situation returning. While he was checking out those names and others on the list of people who might have a grudge against Danny, Finn would no doubt be delving into Hank's background for the same reason. With any luck, her deputy would never have to know.

Next she summoned Mary and Brody, turning on her computer while she waited for the two deputies. When they entered, Brody was trailing the woman, steam rolling off the coffee in the foam cup he carried. "I'm going to fine-tune your assignment a bit," Keira told them.

The younger deputy blew on the brew before cautiously taking a sip. "Think Atwood's our guy?"

"We can't be sure yet. But I'd say it's likely. Mary, I want you to concentrate on cases on either side of the peninsula that might have been closed, but the victims were never found. Like that case last year with the ice fisherman."

The female deputy looked intrigued. "You think he could have been a victim of this killer, too?"

"It's a long shot," Keira admitted. "But I can recall Dad mentioning some cases on the peninsula where there were people lost and a body was never recovered. Get me all those details, complete with the contact information for each case officer." When the woman nodded, she switched her attention to Brody. "We're going to change the focus on the missing person's compilation. Now I'm interested in cases as far back as seven years. Narrow in on those with notes indicating some sort of outdoor activity as a hobby. Fishing, hiking, hunting, trapping, snowmobiling…anything that might have the individual in an isolated area, possibly alone."

Brody's eyes were alert with interest over the brim of his cup. "I recall a couple where something like that was in the description."

"I want an update before you leave for the day."

The two nodded. When they'd left, Keira went out and got herself some coffee before sitting down to access the state's DNR files.

The Department of Natural Resources had law enforcement duties included in their mission to preserve and protect the state's natural resources. Incidents that happened on state or federal land would fall under their jurisdiction, regardless of county lines. The list of Alger County fishing license holders had several thousand names. Tourists would be included as well as county residents. She'd bought one herself each year she'd visited in the summer.

Switching her attention to the register for hunting licenses, she perused it even more carefully, looking for familiar names. The compilation numbered in the thousands, although it was significantly shorter than the one for fishing licenses.

She didn't find Joseph Atwood's name, so she quickly brought up the trapping permits. He was absent from that record, as well.

Switching to Baraga County, she found Atwood listed as holding hunting, fishing and trapping licenses there. Keira's knowledge about the regulations for each was vague, but she did know that Native Americans enjoyed higher limits for fish and animals caught and trapped than did the general population. She wondered if Atwood's failure to apply for a license in his new county of residence indicated that he hadn't expected to live here long. Or maybe he had applications that were pending.

The stranger Baxter had talked about had accused the man of poaching. If Atwood had ever been caught at that, it would be on the DNR list of violations. That was the next database she turned to. After studying it for several minutes, she could see that Atwood had no infringements for either Alger or Baraga Counties.

Deciding the coffee had cooled enough, she reached out and brought the cup to her lips, sipping as she returned to Alger County records. Keira paused to take a legal pad and pen out of her drawer to make notes. For the next few hours, in between juggling phone calls and interruptions from staff, she pored over the registers.

She wasn't done—not by a long shot—when she dropped the pen on the notepad and leaned back in her chair to rub the heel of her palms against her eyes. Another hour and surely blindness would strike. Keira reached for the cup next to the computer, found it empty. Turning her attention to the notes she'd made, some familiar names leaped off the page at her.

All of her deputies except for Mary were hunters, and all fished. Hardly surprising, given their surroundings. Only Brody and Hank held trapping permits. Bruce Yembley and Pete Bielefeld had licenses for trapping and fishing. As felons, they couldn't possess guns for hunting. Two of the commissioners held all three licenses, as did Roger Wilson. She recalled a long ago occasion when one of their awkward conversations had been about fishing.

Keira scanned the rest of the names, frustration mounting as she did so. There were people on it that would also appear on the list Hank and Phil were checking for those with reason to dislike Danny. She'd need to cross-check them when her deputies were finished with them.

Somewhere, on one of these records, might be the killer they were tracing.

Leaning back in the chair, she closed her burning eyes. Her father had been found in a wilderness area, which would have been protected and squarely in DNR territory. But there was no way to know where the second victim had been killed. She reached out a hand toward the phone, letting it hover in the air a moment before withdrawing it. The nearest DNR service center was Marquette and the officers were frequently in the field.

Keira rose. She knew someone who had as much practical experience in outdoor activities as a DNR officer would. And he was only a handful of miles away.

She checked in with Mary and Brody for a progress report and then told Cal where she was heading before collecting her coat and going out the door.

———————

Fuck that. Why was she leaving so soon?

He watched from across the street from the courthouse as the SUV pulled out of the lot and drove away. Not even four o'clock. Bitch probably didn't even work a complete workday. He'd be doing the fine citizens of Alger County a favor by taking her out. Save 'em some money. .

After a minute he fired up his truck and followed her, heading west out of town. Just outside Christmas, he slowed when she turned into a private drive. Where the hell was she going?

He considered his next step as he drove slowly by. Already four-fifteen. It wasn't as cold today, although it'd be dark in another forty-five minutes, and temperatures would be dropping. Unless she was planning a very short visit, Saxon might head home after this stop.

Slowing, he waited for the cars ahead of him and behind to go by before pulling a 'U' turn. The sheriff hadn't returned home at all last night, so it might just be some more worthless hours hiding in the trees with the rifle, freezing his nuts off for nothing.

But he was feeling lucky. She'd go home tonight. And when she did, he'd be waiting.

———————

"Hey, Keira." Doug O'Shea came out of his metal machine shed to greet her as she pulled up. "Not every day that I get a text from my favorite sheriff."

She smiled. She'd known the man since she'd played Little League with his daughter when they were both eight. He'd been their coach for two consecutive summers. "I don't get to see you around much. How's your mom?"

"Ninety-three years old and running laps around the other folks in the assisted living facility. I hope she passed those genes down to me. Come up to the house. Let's get out of this cold." They walked side by side toward the blue ranch-style house back-dropped against a densely wooded lot. "I have to admit, I'm thinking strongly about retiring soon."

She cut a look toward him. "Can you keep yourself busy? That's the question. I recently heard that Danny had been contemplating the same thing. Can't really imagine him not going to the office every day."

"Spoken like someone in her thirties." There was a twinkle in his eye as they stepped up to the front door and kicked the snow off their boots. "There comes a time in your life when you dream of leaving behind the hassle and the commute, and spending more time with your family and hobbies."

She wiped her feet on the rug just inside the home, remembering how particular his wife had once been about her house. But Nancy O'Shea was gone now, killed in a car accident nearly seven years earlier. Looking around, Keira realized that Doug still kept it as tidy as his wife had.

Accepting a mug of coffee she took a seat at the kitchen table and used the cup to warm her hands.

"I suppose the drive to Negaunee every day does get tiresome." The town was an hour away in Marquette County. The last she knew the man had worked in the office as the company's accountant.

"More every year." He pulled the off his hat and sat across from her. Doug was a little balder than she remembered. A little older. But the warm blue eyes and friendly smile were the same. "Got off a bit early today because I got stuck there last night. I only drove a couple miles out of town before realizing it was stupid to take chances in that storm. So." He shrugged his flannel-clad shoulders. "Went in early, left sooner than usual. I'm working more flexible hours these days. They don't care when I'm there as long as I put my eight hours in. Gives me some time to check my trap lines or just sleep in."

She brought the mug to her lips. "So you're still trapping."

"In my blood. Of course, the fur market went to hell a couple years ago. Fewer of us out there these days."

"Why is that?"

"Not as much demand in the US anymore. Animal rights organizations have money and a platform. They reach consumers and lobbyists." He took a drink from his cup. "It's the nature of markets to rise and fall. It'll rebound. Some day. Greece was one of our biggest buyers, but their economy has affected demand. Demand in China and Turkey is still strong, though. So." He sent her a crooked smile. "Tell me why you ask."

"There may be a trapping element to a case I'm investigating." She felt her way carefully. Although she trusted Doug O'Shea's confidentiality far more than she did Stella's, it was still a department matter.

"You're investigating? Not DNR?"

Keira gave him a brief smile. "It's a bit complicated. A crime victim did some trapping, and I'm considering the possibility of whether that brought him to the attention of his attacker."

To the man's credit, he looked intrigued but didn't inquire further. "So how can I help?"

"It's a solitary pastime, for the most part, right? How often do you see someone else when you're checking your lines?"

"More than you might think, especially on state and federal lands. There are a lot of outdoor enthusiasts on the UP, and sports that keep them outdoors all year round. Right now I see the occasional cross-country skier and snowmobiler. I'm usually out there too early or late, though."

"How about other trappers and hunters?" she pressed.

He took a slurp of coffee. "I see more hunters for the most part. Deer and turkey season you can't turn around without running into another orange vest. But trappers try to avoid areas that already have traps and snares and find fresh territory. Sometimes we pay for exclusive rights to a landowner's property, so you better not see anyone else there. But on public lands I run into others more frequently."

"Have you ever encountered poachers?"

His mouth flattened. "Every now and then. I report the bastards to DNR, too. Not just because they're breaking the law. But because they have no ethics. They don't care about leaving the habitat in a good condition so the animals can repopulate. All they're thinking about is themselves." Doug paused to drink before continuing. "Of course it's a bit different with trapping. Hunting poachers might bag more than their share, or hunt out of season. With trappers, you get the guys who will set their traps on top of yours, or take the catch right out of your snares. The biggest jerks will steal both the animal and trap."

"So if someone came upon an individual they caught poaching, there'd be some animosity." That might explain why the second victim was killed, but it wouldn't apply to her father.

Doug gave a slow nod before raising his mug to his lips again. After a moment he set it down and said, "Some people don't need a reason to be aggressive. There's a lot of competition in the field. And even more ways to game the system."

Interested, Keira sipped from her cup. "Tell me about that."

"Well, the easiest is to buy licenses and permits for every family member, when only one is actually trapping. That can quadruple his limit on each animal or even better. Gives him a helluva edge over the guys like me following the rules."

"Anything else that would anger other trappers?"

His expression turned bemused. "Some people are easily antagonized. I know people who carry a real grudge against Native Americans because they're given special privileges when it comes to seasonal limits on animals. I figure life deals us enough unhappiness to go around looking for more."

The truth in his words arrowed deep. "You're right about that."

"Anyway." He cleared his throat. "Doesn't take long to get dark around here this time of year." Giving her a wink he added, "If you want some firsthand experience you can ride along with me while I inspect my lines."

Laughing, she shook her head. "You've given me a lot of information already. I think I'll pass. After getting snowed in last night, I'm anxious to get home."

CHAPTER 8

Keira reminded herself to call Chase as soon as she got back to the cabin. The deputy had had more than his share of surveillance time, given her unplanned stay in Baraga. He deserved a break. As her headlights cut through the darkness on her plowed drive, she felt a sense of homecoming. She could access the DNR database from her home computer. All it took was the law enforcement code. The thought of a hot bowl of soup in front of the fire, while she worked, was even more enticing.

She pulled around the curve and the cabin came into sight. The security lights were on all around the house, each emitting a soft pool of light. First she'd change into sweats and a tee, she planned, reaching up to the garage opener on her visor. It'd be a relief to get out of this uniform.

"Dammit," she muttered as the opener came loose and fell to the floor. Slowing the vehicle, she bent to retrieve it.

CRACK!

The window shattered. Tiny shards of glass rained down on her. Shocked, she stayed crouched down, switching off the ignition. Comprehension filtered through her numbed mind. Someone was shooting at her.

Instinct took over. Staying low, she opened her door and dove out the side, rolling toward the front of the SUV. Another shot kicked up snow and gravel inches away. She scrambled over to the tire and took out her weapon and radio.

The silence after the two shots was eerie. "10-0 requesting assistance. Shots fired." She reeled off her address and the code for immediate backup. The call would have any law enforcement personnel in the vicinity responding.

Hopefully, one of them would arrive soon.

Another shot came whizzing only inches above her head. The shooter knew exactly where she was. Of course, he did. And he'd have to realize that he had her penned here, with no place to move.

She snuck a glance up at her door and her stomach hollowed out when she saw the fist size hole in her window. A matter of clumsiness. That's all that had saved her. A few brief seconds had been the difference between life and death.

She wasn't home free yet. Keira considered the odds. The shot had been fired from the front of the property, through the woods where they'd seen the moose. Given the damage to the window, he was close. Maybe hiding in the trees and brush that lined her driveway.

She drew up just enough to be able to see over the hood and sprayed bullets along the area bordering the drive before ducking down again. There was no return fire. Sirens screamed in the distance, but silence shrouded the immediate vicinity. .

Whoever had shot at her was already gone.

———————

It wasn't difficult to find the shooter's station. His footprints disclosed his position. He'd been well hidden in a copse of trees and had stepped away from the fir providing him cover each time he'd taken a shot. He'd had a prime view of the front of her house.

A chill worked over Keira's skin as she joined the other officers walking the grid they'd established, Maglites sweeping the snow for evidence. Periodically the floodlights were moved to provide more illumination. The shooter's trail had been easy enough to pick up. He'd parked on the side of the road a mile away and made his way through the wooded property to where he'd chosen to lay in wait.

"Got another clear boot print here."

"Cast it."

The radio on her belt crackled. "Finn wants to see you at the cabin."

Finn.

Keira turned on her heel and made her way back toward the house. She'd managed only a brief text to him before she was surrounded by the responding law enforcement. Two of the city officers were there, as well as half of her department and some troopers who had been in the area. As grateful as she was for their assistance, she found herself hoping that most of them would be gone upon her return to the cabin. Other than evidence collection, there wasn't much to be done.

She found Finn standing in front of her vehicle, bare-headed, hands jammed deep into the pockets of his coat as he stared at the driver's window. Slowing as she rounded the car, she stopped beside him. "Hey."

His gaze swept her from head to toe. Back up again. "You're bleeding." The words were dispassionate, belying the intensity in his eyes.

"Oh." She wiped at her forehead and cheek. "Just nicks from the glass. Amazingly enough, I'm unhurt."

There was a tightness in his jaw that was new. A lethal tension emanated from him. "Helpful text. 'Trouble my place. Fine.'" He nodded toward her car window. "I think you took wide latitude with the word 'fine', but that's me."

Keira felt like she was tiptoeing through a minefield without knowing exactly why. The sensation was annoying. "Excuse my semantics. It would have taken too long to text 'homicidal shooter trying to kill me. I think he's gone.'"

"Keira!" Mary stood in the doorway of the cabin. "If we can finish this report I'll take it back to the office and get it typed up tonight."

She took a step toward the house. Paused to look at Finn. "Did you complete the tests?"

He stepped forward and with a hand at the small of her back, guided her toward the porch. "I did. We can now be sure that Joseph Atwood was the second victim."

————

"Well, you sure as hell aren't staying here by yourself."

Keira scanned the faces of Brody, Hank, and Phil. They looked like a row of pugnacious linemen. "He's gone. I don't need a bodyguard." Bad enough that the law enforcement entities had already worked out a schedule for constant patrols of her property. Worse still was knowing she wasn't going to be allowed a moment alone for the foreseeable future.

Finn was propped against the family room wall nearby, arms crossed over his chest. After insisting on tending to her scratches himself, he'd gotten progressively more reticent while she dictated her statement to Mary.

"We can take turns staying here. For back up," Brody stammered when Keira's narrowed gaze met his.

"It's stupid to take chances." As always, Phil cut to the chase. There was an expression of concern on his face. She could read his thoughts. First his best friend, and tonight nearly his best friend's daughter. Looking away, she took a breath. "You have your own lives. Families." Glancing at Fallon, she added, "Hank, your wife would skin you if she had to take care of your toddler every night by herself. And you other two…"

"I'm staying." They were the first words Finn had spoken in the last several minutes and his tone brooked no opposition. The three men turned to look at him as he pushed away from the wall, dropping his arms to his sides. "I agree that someone needs to, even if Keira doesn't. And it makes the most sense for it to be me." His smile was grim. "No one's inconvenienced that way."

No one, she thought darkly, except her. It was more than a little maddening to have decisions made for her by four thick-headed males, she decided twenty minutes later after the last of her deputies had trailed through the door, and she'd re-secured the locks. But it was the lone man standing a few feet away, silently contemplating her that she focused on.

"This is stupid." Now that everyone was gone, there was a welter of emotion churning in her. It was easiest to pluck out anger and ride that. She stalked toward the kitchen. "I don't know what you guys think having another person around here will…"

There was a thud behind her and she whirled in a crouch, weapon drawn. Finn froze in the act of removing his other boot. She blinked, embarrassment surging. Straightening, she re-holstered her gun. "I guess I might be a little jumpy."

His gaze was sober. "You have reason to be."

It would have been easier to settle her nerves had she been alone. A hot bath with about a gallon of wine would do the trick. But instead, she went to the kitchen, pulling out two cans of soup. Opening them, she dumped the contents into a pan, got a spoon and turned the burner on. Then stood there for a minute and tried to draw a deep breath through lungs that seemed suddenly strangled.

Adrenaline had long since faded. She was left with the shaky aftermath and seized on routine and procedure to fill her mind and stave off further reaction. When her knees wanted to go a little weak, she straightened them. But it was all she could do to keep her hands from trembling.

In the next moment, two strong arms snuck around her waist and destroyed her efforts. She was pressed against the muscled wall of his chest. Keira stiffened in Finn's embrace.

"One of the reasons I wanted a break from pathology was because I was tired of people I cared about ending up in my autopsy suite." His voice was a rumble in her ear. She was no longer certain whether the muscle weakness creeping through her was due solely to adrenaline crash. "I was just ready to call you with the test results when I got your text." His arms tightened a fraction. "It took seventeen minutes to get from the lab to your cabin. Seventeen. Minutes."

Her body ignored the dictates of her brain, and she let herself lean on him. Just a bit. "I know. Everything happened so fast. He was probably gone by the time I returned fire. Or at least leaving. Even seconds can feel like…" The rest of her words were lost as he reached around her to switch off the burner. Then she was turned in his arms. His mouth settled over hers and all thought spun away.

The initial softness of his kiss was not unexpected. The hint of urgency was. His lips moved against hers comfortingly at first, but there was more here than comfort. One arm remained at her waist and the fingers of his other hand speared in her hair, cupping the back of her head.

Keira was motionless, surprise and pleasure coursing through her. When Finn used the tip of his tongue to trace the seam of her lips, press them open, her arms twined around his neck and she gave herself over to the moment. The taste of him was heady. Unfamiliar. It would have been natural to rely on her innate caution to call a stop to this if she didn't recognize the harnessed control in his touch. If she wanted to, she could return his kiss, glide her tongue along his and revel in the knowledge that it'd go no further. And she discovered at that moment that she did want to. Quite desperately.

She drew up to fit her mouth more firmly against his. In heels they'd be nearly eye to eye, but stocking footed his height topped hers by a few inches. As their lips moved together for the first time, she interpreted the whisper of demand in his touch and wondered what else lingered beneath it. Because she'd learned enough about Finn Carstens to know there was far more to the man than met the eye.

His hand stroked up her spine and down again, the simple movement imbued with sensuality. She caught his bottom lip in hers and scored it gently. It had been a long time since she'd been in a man's arms. It shouldn't be a near stranger's embrace that felt like coming home.

But Finn Carstens didn't seem like a stranger. And that realization would have had a more rational woman running far and fast.

His mouth went to the area beneath her ear, and her throat arched to give him access. Keira didn't know when her hand had gone to his hair, but the feel of the strands tangled in her fingers, the sensation of his lips on her flesh had her pulse rollicking in a way that made distant inner alarms shrill.

She wasn't given the chance to respond to them. She could feel the stillness coming over him and knew reason had filtered through him, as well. And she was honest enough with herself to recognize that a part of her mourned the change.

He straightened, creating a barely perceptible distance between them. "Ah...." It was gratifying to see the effort it took for him to collect his thoughts. "You've mentioned your dislike for bossy men, so consider this a suggestion. Go up and change. Maybe soak a while and I'll take care of dinner."

She gave herself another second to enjoy the warmth of his body against hers, the sound of his thudding heart before stepping out of his loosened arms. "There isn't a whole lot more than the soup, I'm afraid." The idea of a bath was tempting. She'd been planning exactly that on her way home, before... Her mind skittered away from completing the thought. *Before.*

"I don't lack imagination. I'll figure something out."

Because she was having trouble tearing her attention away from his mouth, Keira took the opportunity he offered and beat an almost too hasty retreat from the kitchen.

By the time Keira returned downstairs clad in a Chicago Police Department sweatshirt and flannel pajama bottoms and thick socks, Finn had regained his composure. Her absence had given him time to recover a control that had threatened to slip its leash the moment he'd tasted her. For a man who had long ago mastered the art of restraint, that moment of near desperation was unnerving.

Keira Saxon had fascinated him from their first meeting. Tough and beautiful. Poised, yet vulnerable. Casual sex held no interest for him, but in those brief moments he'd had her in his arms, there had been nothing casual about the surging in his blood. His gut had been in knots over her near death experience, but it hadn't been concern that had fueled his kiss. That realization was more than a little troubling.

"You must have raided the deep freeze in the garage."

"I did." He set a bowl of soup and a cheeseburger in front of her along with a glass of the wine he'd found in the fridge. "Plenty of meat. No bread, though. We'll have to make do." It didn't escape his notice that she reached for the wine before the silverware. He could have used something stronger than beer himself.

He sat down beside her. "I almost nabbed the leftover Chinese in there. Figured maybe you were saving it."

Shaking her head, she set the glass down and picked up her spoon. "Tiff was here a couple nights ago. She brought Chinese and wine."

Finn cut into the cheeseburger. If he were going to be staying here for any length of time, he'd get some groceries himself. He hadn't even been able to find ketchup. He wasn't a fussy eater, but he did require the basic necessities. Who didn't stock ketchup? "Do you need to call her?"

Swallowing, Keira shook her head. "I sent her a quick text an hour ago. With the law enforcement presence here tonight it'll be a wonder if she doesn't hear something at Dizzy's." Reaching for her wine again, she added, "I didn't have much to share even if I'd been free to give her the details. I've been over and over this and can't figure it. Why would the killer try to engage me in this game of cat and mouse, ensuring that I knew about Danny and Atwood's deaths…and then attempt to kill me? Where's the payoff in that for him?" She drank and resumed talking as she lowered her glass. "Unless… Maybe he didn't mean to kill me. Maybe it was just a scare tactic."

His jaw clenched, making it impossible to continue eating. "If so, I'd say mission accomplished." And Keira hadn't been the only one scared. "But it wasn't. If you hadn't ducked at that precise moment, you'd be dead right now. A head shot. In the dark." He saw her almost imperceptible wince, and mentally throttled back the words that had been bottled up inside him, fueled by fear. "Did you find any brass out there?"

She shook her head, scooped up some soup. "Hank will rent some metal detectors tomorrow. They will be our best chance of retrieving anything. There were three shots and fresh snow on the ground. It would have been difficult for the shooter to find anything in the dark."

Three shots. Finn took a long swig from the beer. Which made her three times lucky. It was impossible not to wonder if and when Keira's luck was going to run out.

He put the bottle down. Picked up his fork and tried to tamp the fear the thought brought. It could fog thinking. Cloud objectivity. And it was imperative that it be allowed to do neither.

"Tonight took a specific skill set. One hundred yards out, in the dark, through the trees. And he was able to put a hole directly through the center of the passenger window." Savagely he stabbed at another piece of hamburger. "Not a spectacular shot, but well above average. We'll take another look at the list of names with grudges against your dad. Start digging to see which have marksmanship skills. It's natural to assume this is linked to your dad's killer, but we can't be sure it is. Not yet."

Keira reached for the bottle to tip more wine into her glass. He didn't object. Finn knew few women who demonstrated nerves as reliably steady as hers. But they would be understandably frayed now. "I realize that. I just have trouble believing that all of a sudden we have two crazed killers in Alger County."

"Has Bielefeld been released yet?" The man was facing a stiff prison term based on their findings on his property, and once the drug investigation was completed might even be charged under federal drug laws. Revenge could be a powerful motive for a man looking at the possibility of a thirty-year sentence.

She shook her head. "No, and he won't be. The judge denied him bail. The prosecutor successfully argued that he was a flight risk, plus he was slapped with multiple parole violations. His buddies haven't been able to pay the bail yet. Given the amount it was set at, maybe they won't."

Finn nodded. "Doesn't mean none of them were involved, just that they weren't the ones to pull the trigger." And what better alibi than to be in jail when someone tried to take out the sheriff who arrested you?

Keira sat back, her fingers toying with the stem of her wine glass. "Hank Fallon dug into his portion of the list you gave him. He discovered Bruce Yembley lost a long ago marksmanship contest to my dad."

"Interesting." He got up and carried his dishes to the sink. "Fallon has some skills in that area, as well. So does Milestone." He turned in time to catch the shock on her features. "Hank has taken part in law enforcement sponsored contests all over the upper Midwest, from what I was able to discover today."

"You were busy." Her flat tone told him more than her words how unappreciative she was of his efforts. "Cops have to re-qualify on weapons regularly. Hank has placed at some National Police Shooting Championships. Just like Phil did in his time. And my dad. I recognize we need to look at everyone, but I find it hard to believe any of my deputies is capable of this."

Because she seemed to be finished eating, he cleared her dishes, as well. He realized how difficult it would be to suspect co-workers in a case like this. But it didn't matter if Keira was able to be objective about it. That's what he was here for. He started to rinse and load the dishes in the dishwasher. It was a measure of her distraction that she didn't object.

"I began combing the DNR records for those with hunting, fur harvesting and fishing licenses. Figured we'd cross-reference them with the list of Danny's enemies."

"We will." Finished with his task, Finn shut the dishwasher and grabbed the dishrag to wipe the stovetop and table. Then he poured the last of the bottle into her glass and picked it up with his beer. "Let's finish these in the family room."

For the first time, she seemed to realize that he'd cleaned up. A small smile curved her lips. "You're a handy guy to have around, Carstens."

That smile punched into his chest like a rocketing right jab. It took a moment to summon a response. Another before he had the breath to utter it. "Glad you've changed your mind." He moved out of the room, feeling a sudden need for distance. For the first time he questioned the wisdom of being the one to spend the night—and all nights in the foreseeable future—under the same roof as Keira Saxon.

The curtains had been kept drawn since the first break in. He put the drinks on the coffee table and busied himself switching on the fireplace. When he turned, he saw her on the couch, powering up the computer. He realized she'd be reviewing the security footage at the front of her property. And he knew it would be futile. "You've been in contact with your deputy who's been monitoring the cameras?"

"Chase called in the shooting as it was going down. Probably sped up response time by at least a minute." She glanced up from the screen as he sat next to her. "I told him he could knock off for the evening, but I know him better than that. He's likely been over this feed three or four times by now."

She had no more brought up camera one, however, than she bounced up off the couch, reaching for her phone. "Rose Atwood," she said, seeing his quizzical look, and again he realized what she was about. He didn't pretend not to listen as she placed the call to Matthews, who in turn would inform Joseph Atwood's mother that her son was indeed dead. The single thread of hope the woman no doubt harbored would be snapped. Her life would be forever altered.

Just as Atwood's life had irrevocably changed the moment he came into contact with his killer.

Keira's face was grim when she rejoined him. "We need to comb through the victim's life," she said flatly, her gaze trained on the monitor. "See if we can find any more intersections besides the outdoors one that would link him even remotely to my father."

"We definitely will." Maybe this wasn't the first time the man had lived—or trapped—in the county. Finn reached for her wine, handed it to her. "I also ran the tests on the hair we collected at your break-in. I'm over ninety percent certain that it came from a beaver."

Her head jerked around to stare at him. "It was on the intruder's clothes. His gloves maybe."

He nodded. "So we have scat and an animal hair left behind at the scene. I looked it up. Beaver is in season right now."

"It could have been shed from a fur hat or a vest of some type." But he heard the thread of excitement in her cautionary words. He'd felt a similar surge of interest at the finding until her text had shattered all thoughts except getting to her side, as fast as humanly possible.

"You say you're only ninety percent certain?"

He lifted a shoulder, flicked a glance at the screen. There was nothing but stillness showing. "There's no law enforcement database of mammalian hair, but Raiker does have a contract with a forensic biologist to compile one. It's still going through the verification process. Hence I can't be one hundred percent certain. And I considered fur clothing. But there was a tiny amount of animal blood on the hair shaft. And no evidence that dyes or chemicals had been used to treat it."

She brought the glass to her lips. Drained the rest of the wine before leaning forward to set the glass on the table. "So we have an indisputable link to trapping. Which connects again to his second victim, but not to Danny. That narrows our focus for tomorrow, cross-checking individuals with fur harvesting licenses and those who resented him for some reason."

"The prints we collected after the break-in were a bust." He supposed it had been too much to expect otherwise. "I didn't find one on the ear, but I had sent the clear ones from the window frame, counter, fridge and plate in to a fingerprint examiner at Raiker's lab. I received the results tonight. Because you and Danny are law enforcement, your latents were in the system and both popped up. There were other prints found, but they had no hits."

Her cell rang and she brought it up to check the screen. Her shoulders slumped a bit. "My mother."

Finn looked at the time on the computer. "At this hour?"

Keira was already getting up from the couch. "She's in LA for a couple weeks. She can never seem to keep the time zones straight." She strode a few paces away. "Hey, Mom, what's up?"

Tuning out the rest of the conversation, Finn turned his attention to shutting down the computer. Screening the feed was useless. The cameras probably had a range of up to forty feet. Unless the shooter had actually been in the drive, he wouldn't have been caught on screen. He froze in the next moment as the image on the computer showed headlights approaching the house. But they didn't belong to the shooter. The time stamp on the feed told him that much. Finn sat transfixed as Keira's vehicle drew closer.

A sense of fascinated inevitability filled him. The SUV slowed. Because he knew where to look, he saw the muzzle flash and then the shattered window. A fist squeezed his heart as the vehicle stopped and the door opened. Keira hurtled through it. The next shot was inches away from her.

"Okay, I'll talk to you later."

He pressed the power key and shut the lid of the computer when he heard her sign off. Forced a smile when she crossed back over to him. "That was short."

"She's off to a party. She'll call tomorrow to give me a detailed rundown on what everyone wore, their hair and a hundred other details that I have zero interest in." A corner of her mouth kicked up as she sat down again. "But I'll listen because it gives us something to talk about, and with my career off limits, those topics are in short supply."

"I take it she doesn't approve." His own parents had a bit of difficulty adjusting to the fact that he wouldn't be using his medical degree anymore, at least not full-time.

"That would be a polite way to state it." Keira eyed the laptop. "You shut it off?"

"Pointless to watch it." Somehow he'd find a way to forget the images captured there. "He was too far away to be caught on camera."

Her gaze went to his face. "You saw the scene on screen?"

His lips tightened. But all he said was, "And there's no point in watching that either."

"Not if I expect to sleep tonight, I suppose." She didn't move, falling silent for several minutes as she gazed into the fire. He imagined she was pondering the near-death experience. But her next words proved it wasn't her death she'd been contemplating.

"What did you mean, earlier? About autopsying bodies of people you cared about?"

He folded his arms, aware of the tension creeping through his muscles. Sorting through possible answers, he offered her a slice of the truth. But not all. "I was with DGR, which is a DC organization for doctors providing global relief in needy spots internationally. Did one mission annually for about five years running. The last was in an Afghan hospital a couple of years ago. A terrorist ran into the ER area with explosives strapped to his chest. He detonated them." Her hand crept up to rest on his arm. Finn stared at it unseeingly. "Thirty medical personnel were in that clinic. At least triple that number of patients. Twenty were killed, half of them staff. The victims had to be identified." The thread of desolation that worked through him was all too familiar. "For some I could only do that by matching DNA with body parts."

Her fingers squeezed his arm. Long and slender, they'd look right at home poised over the keyboard of a baby grand. But they appeared equally proficient holding a Sig Sauer pistol.

"I'm sorry."

He recognized the sincerity tracing through the simple phrase. For an instant it summoned the rest that he couldn't—wouldn't—bring himself to tell.

"Yeah." A long slow breath escaped him. He turned to look at Keira, who seemed closer than he'd remembered. "Sometimes what we do sucks."

"And sometimes it makes a difference."

And those were the moments they worked for. He wondered if that was the source of the connection he felt between them. One that had nothing to do with familiarity or long friendship, and everything to do with the recognition of a kindred spirit.

Her cell pinged, and she straightened, removing her hand from his arm to read the incoming text.

"Tiffany?" Finn was a bit surprised the woman hadn't called and demanded a full explanation for the message she'd received. From their only meeting she hadn't seemed the type to be put off.

"Chase. He just wanted me to know he's watched the feed a couple more times and can't make out anything. He suggested sending it in for enhancement, but that's a long shot, with the cover the shooter was using as a screen."

"He was too far away to be picked up by the cameras," Finn agreed.

There was a slight frown between her brows as she scrolled through her messages. "Now that you mention it, I am a bit surprised that I haven't heard from Tiffany. It's Friday night. The restaurant is probably packed and she hasn't had a free minute to check her phone. Which is fine with me." Rising, Keira stretched tiredly. "Further explanations can wait until morning."

"Further everything can wait until morning." He rose, as well. "And for the record, this time I won't be sleeping on the couch." There was an intriguing hint of shock in her gaze when it met his. He added, "Something tells me the bed in one of the spare rooms is far more comfortable."

"You're about to find out." She double-checked the lock on the doors while he turned off the fireplace. Then he followed her to the stairway. Up the steps. Finn had the errant thought that after the day they'd had, he was going to feel closer to Keira lying down the hallway from her than lying in bed with her last night.

————————

Fuck Diz, and fuck this place. Tiffany Andrews locked and slammed the back door after she went through it and bee-lined for her car. As miserable as the owner's stomach flu allegedly was, it couldn't come close to the misery Tiffany had gone through having to run the entire damn place on a Friday night with only one cook, one bartender and herself.

A single security bulb above the door threw off weak light as she huddled into her jacket and stomped toward her car through what was more like an alley than a parking lot. She dodged the crammed Dumpster and rounded the trunk of her 2004 Ford Escape. Keira was right. It was time to move out and move on, and Tiff wasn't going to wait until summer. Whatever her future held, there had to be something better than going home every night smelling like grease and having bruises on her ass from the creeps who got too handsy.

None of them ever grabbed her twice. She made damn sure of that.

If she stayed in Munising one more day…week… month…she might just end up like her mom. Bemoaning her lot in life and never lifting a finger to better it. That wasn't going to be Tiffany, and if it took a shitty night at work to force her to make a life decision, maybe it was high time.

The keyless entry on her vehicle hadn't worked since she'd owned it, so she stuck the key in the lock, then stopped, surprised to find it unlocked. She paused, frowning. She always locked her car. Always.

She was too far from the light to see much of anything, but she peered into the window. Could barely make out the latte she'd left in the cup holder. She'd been in a mad dash to respond to Eldon Diznoff's desperate call for help on what was supposed to have been her first weekend off in months. She'd forgotten all about her Creamy Caramel Latte Supreme.

Yanking open the door, she climbed inside and stuck the key in the ignition. Turned it on. Diz was going to have to figure something else out tomorrow. Tiff tried the engine three times before it turned over, then roared to life. Because first thing in the morning she was heading to Powderhorn, and taking the rest of the weekend for some skiing while strategizing her future.

She pulled away from the building, nosing her small SUV through the narrow tunnel made by the towering snow banks on either side of the cleared passageway. Tiffany didn't have a moment's regret for the paying customers she'd shoved out the door at midnight. After the night she'd had, there'd been no way in hell she was sticking around until four in the morning. And if Diz wanted to bitch about it, she'd have plenty to say about unreliable help who didn't show up and left her short-handed.

There was a small sound in the back of the vehicle. Of course, there were always noises. The damn thing was held together with duct tape and baling wire. Tiffany looked in the rearview mirror and caught a flash of movement.

A moment later a large hand had something shoved in her face, holding tight when the stench of a drenched rag filled her nose. Her lungs. Eyes burning, she bucked and fought, but a second arm snaked around her neck to hold her fast. As consciousness ebbed out of reach, she had a last distant thought that that her worst fear was coming true.

She was going to die in this damn town.

———

Dorie Hassert giggled as she checked the peephole and hurriedly unlocked the back door. He crowded inside and pressed her against the counter, his hard mouth coming down on hers. The edge of the Formica dug into her ample behind, but she didn't murmur a peep of protest. This was exactly like the romance novels she devoured by the stacks. The thought of having her own secret lover who couldn't get enough of her made her absolutely giddy. One who called hours before dawn and demanded to see her. Claimed he just couldn't wait another minute.

She was a little dizzy when he lifted his mouth from hers and finally kicked the door shut with one booted foot. Reaching out a shaky hand, she fluffed the hair she'd quickly curled, and wished she'd thought to light a candle. A woman was supposed to look her best in candlelight.

He grabbed her again, one hand sliding inside her newly purchased mint green bathrobe to squeeze her breast. "Is this a booty call?" she tittered.

"It's an I'm gonna fuck you call," he muttered in her ear. Turning her around, he bent her over the table with enough force to send the vase of fake sunflowers teetering.

The unfamiliar position had a sudden flicker of unease surfacing. "Here? Like this?" Then she moaned when his fingers tweaked her nipple a little roughly.

"Here." She heard the scrape of a zipper. His hips shimmied a bit against hers before her robe was flipped up in the back and she felt him, hard and pulsing against her. "Like this."

His apparent hunger ignited her own and when he surged inside her, she was more than ready.

Minutes later she lay limp, his weight heavy on top of her, and tried to draw a breath. Maybe he didn't have the smooth words and moves of the heroes she read about, but his cock worked the same way and damn if it wasn't satisfying.

She giggled at that, and he withdrew from her, then pinched her on the ass. "What the hell you laughing at?"

"Just thinking how good you are."

He grunted at that, and when she would have turned over, he put a hand on the back of her neck to hold her in place. "I like the view from here." He slapped one of her butt cheeks hard enough to sting, and she felt a stir of excitement all over again.

"You have to let me up some time." But she wiggled her hips enticingly, hoping he wouldn't. Like a gentleman he used a condom every time, and she'd never found one in her trash, although she wouldn't have minded the visual reminder. He must flush them before he left.

"Maybe I won't." His hands were rough from the woodworking he'd told her he did in his spare time, and when he stroked her flanks, she felt a shiver that shot clear to her womb. "Maybe we'll stay like this all night."

Just the thought of it got her hot. "Let's do it again."

"Gimme some time here." But his hands went to her breasts and began to rub and knead them. She could feel him hardening behind her. "I was busy all day and didn't get into town. What's new in Munising, anything?"

CHAPTER 9

"I'm about to make Stella Cummings a very happy woman." Keira glanced around the table in the conference room. "I've prepared two press releases, one about last night's shooting and the other stating the victim has been identified. Atwood's name, of course, was withheld pending notification of the family. I've sent copies to all of you. Familiarize yourself with them. No other details will be released by this office."

"But we're not revealing Danny's death as a homicide yet." Phil's words were more a statement than a question. She knew from the brief talk they'd had when he'd picked her and Finn up that he agreed with her decision.

"Not publicly, no. It would lead to more inquiries, and there are details I don't want released. It was, however, included in the briefing I sent out on LIEN. Those people were Danny's friends. And they'll want to offer assistance in any way they can." There were sober nods of agreement from her deputies. City police, county sheriffs, and troopers in the area crossed paths constantly. The response last night epitomized how interconnected they were when one of their own was threatened.

Another example was this department. It was Saturday; normally the day they ran their smallest crew. And yet most people were here on their own time. Hank was likely at her place with the metal detectors. The budget didn't run to overtime expenses, but that meant nothing to those who had once worked for Danny Saxon.

"Stella Cummings might stroke out with all the news heading her way."

Phil's reminder had Keira suppressing a wince. Less than twenty-four hours after Keira had stonewalled her, the reporter was going to have juicy headlines for days to come. Just not one mentioning Danny Saxon. At least not yet. "She'll publish the number for the tipline. Someone might have seen something last night. Maybe even the truck the shooter left along the side of the road." And sifting through reliable and useless tips would suck man hours that she didn't have to spare, Keira thought grimly, but it couldn't be helped. "Mary and Brody have a list of four persons so far who have gone missing from somewhere on the UP in the last five years. All were involved in some sort of outdoor activity when they disappeared." The door opened, and Finn slipped inside the room. "I'll let them tell you about them."

As the two passed out the information they'd compiled, Keira and Finn exchanged a glance, and she was shaken by a feeling of déjà vu. Only a few short days ago he'd walked in on a meeting much like this one, and she'd wondered at the time what a scientist would have to offer this investigation. She could admit when she was wrong, and she'd been all wrong about Finn Carstens. He was as fine an investigator as she'd ever worked with, and there was no denying his dual role in the lab had fast-tracked this case in a way conventional procedures wouldn't have done.

But she'd been dead on when she'd guessed there was more, far more to the man than what showed on the surface. He'd given her a glimpse of it last night, and she'd thought about what he'd revealed long after she should have been asleep. And wondered how some people had the resiliency to continue when faced with the results of man's darkest brutality. In that way they were alike. Somehow that connection was just as strong, just as compelling, as the one established in the short moments she'd been in his arms.

"The missing persons might be from the mainland or surrounding states, but they were last seen in one of the fifteen counties of the western Upper Peninsula." Mary was unrolling a map of the UP and attaching it to the wall with tacks. "Stan Vila," she touched a spot on Gogebic County. "His relatives said he'd gone hiking on some of the abandoned logging roads three years ago and never returned. Brian Sanchez," her finger traced over to the Keweenaw Peninsula. "Disappeared four years ago, and had no immediate family. But his friends reported the man had been spending his free time exploring the ghost towns and copper country in Keweenaw County. Emmett Ford." She stabbed at a point in Chippewa County. "Was supposed to be on his way to a sportsman contest in St. Ignace. Registered but never showed." The last spot she indicated was on Alger County's Lake Superior shore. "Harley Grayson. In conjunction with the DNR investigation last year, our office ruled his death accidental. Although no body was recovered, it was presumed he slipped inside the hole cut in the ice, which was a great deal larger than the eight inches usually recommended."

"We're following up on a few more," Brody put in when Mary finished. "Some had incomplete details so we're reaching out to case officers who will have to contact the families and ask specifically about outdoor hobbies. The weekend will slow down the responses some."

"After last night I want to look hard at people in the area who are considered marksmen." Finn spoke for the first time since entering the room. "Not just going through archives for old sportsmen or shooting contest awards, but finding the names of people around here with a reputation as a good shot. Any individuals that come up get cross-referenced with the list of those with a grudge against Danny Saxon." He leveled a glance at Keira. "We'll need to make another compilation of those with reason to dislike the current sheriff, as well."

"Hopefully, there will be fewer names on it," she said drily. "I've only been on the job a matter of months."

"Plenty of time to lock up some scumbags," Phil noted. "As evidenced by the four in our jail right now."

"The fact that they're still behind bars takes them out of the suspect pool for the incident last night." Keira suppressed the mental flash of the shooting before it could replay on an endless reel in her mind. "We can't assume that the shots taken at me are linked to Danny's and Atwood's deaths. At least not until we look at the evidence collected last night."

"True. But given what Hank discovered about Yembley's shooting ability, his place will be the first Keira and I stop this morning."

"I started going through the DNR databases yesterday and cross-referencing holders of trapping or hunting licenses with names on the list of those who have reason to resent Danny." Keira passed a copy of the page

210 | KYLIE BRANT

she'd made to her deputies. "They can be further triangulated with any names we acquire of marksmen in the area if we decide the shooting is connected to the two previous homicides. I didn't get very far into the DNR violation and infringement registry. Not quite sure what I'm looking for there yet, but the poaching accusation Baxter claims was leveled at Atwood triggered something for me."

"We'll check into it further," Phil promised, and the others murmured in agreement.

"One thing struck me when I was poring over those DNR lists," Keira said soberly. "There were a lot of familiar names. Friends. Neighbors. Probably three-quarters of the people you know hold outdoor Sportsman licenses of one type or another. The offender we're tracking might not be a stranger to us, and I don't necessarily mean only those with a criminal record. With two members of this office targeted, we can't be certain the department itself isn't the focus for the killer, and it was Atwood who was the anomaly. I guess what I'm saying is to be careful out there."

———

Bruce Yembley's address was nearly twenty-five miles away, near Deerton. According to the tax rolls the man didn't own the place, which, Keira thought, as she turned into the overgrown drive, meant he couldn't be held totally responsible for the condition of the property.

The outbuildings all had a definite lean to them, and the house itself was ten years past its last coat of paint. Both of the windows on the front upper story were boarded over. Somehow Keira wasn't surprised to find the man living in a shit hole. He didn't seem to care overmuch about appearances.

It had snowed overnight. She could see fresh tire tracks in the rutted drive, and boot prints going back and forth between the house and detached garage. However, nothing had been shoveled, including the porch where the blowing snow had drifted against the house. They climbed the steps toward the front door, and she felt the give of rotting lumber beneath her feet.

"Somehow these seem like fitting surroundings for a guy like Yembley," Finn said as he stepped gingerly on the stairs next to her.

"Not as fitting as a federal prison, but guess we don't have any way of making that happen in the near future."

"At least not yet." There was no storm door so Finn pounded on the metal front door. They waited for a minute before he repeated the action.

"Open up, Yembley. Sheriff." Keira called out. She peered at the window, which had old-fashioned rubber backed draperies lining it. She could see no lights at the seams, but that didn't mean much. The man could still be sleeping. It was barely seven-thirty.

But if he was inside he wasn't answering the door. They knocked for another few minutes before heading around to the side entrance and tried again. There were footprints leading to and away from it, both sets fairly fresh. They weren't yet filled in although flakes of snow were still drifting out of the sky. "We could save ourselves a lot of time by casting one of these boot prints and comparing it to the ones Hank took last night." But legalities prohibited it. They had no proof Yembley had anything to do with the shooting and no warrant to collect evidence trying to prove it.

Finn crouched down next to one print and took a small tape measurer from his pocket. Drew it out to take the dimensions of the track. "No one's going to know if we make a few notes for our own purposes." He used his phone to record the measurements before dropping the tape and cell back in his pocket and rose. Squinting, he looked toward the garage. "Looks like fresh tire tracks leaving the property."

"Yeah. Maybe he really isn't here."

They descended the cracked cement steps to approach it. Its sliding horizontal wooden doors were ancient. By pressing on one Finn created a large enough gap for them to look into the shadowy interior. Empty.

Keira blew out a breath, which instantly condensed. She had a sudden memory of Tiffany and her spending far too many hours one day over Christmas break blowing ice kisses and timing how long the vapor hung in the air. They'd been ten maybe. A lifetime ago.

The memory summoned another, and she made a mental note to check her phone to see if she'd missed a message from her friend once they were back in the car. She scanned the rickety outbuildings. None of them had tracks of any sort leading to or away from them, which meant they hadn't been accessed at least since the last snow.

"Well, this trip was a bust." Keira turned back toward the cruiser. They were driving the one left unused while Chase was on medical leave. Phil had driven it out to pick them up this morning and then Finn had taken it to Turners to collect his things and check out before rejoining them at the courthouse. "But the deputies have his plate number. If he's sighted, he'll be stopped."

"He could be on the run already," Finn pointed out as they made their way back to the cruiser. "Have you alerted surrounding counties?"

They parted as they reached the car, and she rounded the front hood. "I'll put out a BOLO." Yembley was by no means the only marksman in the region with a grudge against her department. But at the very least he should be hauled in for questioning.

Because it would have been certain death last night had she not dropped the automatic garage door opener. A matter of seconds had been all that had saved her. As Keira got into the car, she decided that discovering Yembley's whereabouts yesterday evening would go a long way toward answering one important question. She still wasn't all too sure what he thought he'd gain by killing her.

Keira couldn't allow herself to get tripped up trying to second-guess possible motives. It was always a mistake to try to ascribe rational thinking to people who committed irrational acts.

She had no sooner finished issuing a BOLO alert on Yembley's vehicle for UP law enforcement than Phil contacted her.

"Any luck at Yembley's place?"

Sending one last glance at the dilapidated house in her rearview mirror, she turned out onto the main road. "He wasn't there, but he had been. I just radioed a Be On the Lookout on his truck for the surrounding counties."

"Probably not a bad idea. I got another name for you and it's in the approximate area, so thought you might check it out on your way back. Burt Kasim." Phil rattled off the address, which Keira mentally placed about seven miles from here. The name sounded familiar but she wasn't able to place it. "Don't know that I'd say he had a grudge against Danny so much as he was constantly calling a couple of years ago. A crackpot I'd guess you'd say. Vandalism and noise complaints. Used to count how many times he saw a patrol unit go by and then claimed his area wasn't getting its fair share of department protection. Raised a stink about it at some commissioner meetings about three years back."

"Sounds like what I was told about Arnie Hassert's problem with my dad," she said. "Mostly nuisance stuff."

"Yeah. The difference is he's on both the list you made and on the one we've been working on for Finn. He's got a trapper's license, *and* he won the 2009 UP National Sportsman championship. We're finding a few names that hit all areas we're triangulating. He's worth checking out."

After promising to do so, she looked at Finn. "This is starting to feel like searching for a splinter in a snow bank."

He shifted to a more comfortable position in the seat. The vehicle didn't have as much room as the SUV she usually drove. Given the damage from last night's shooting, it was going to be a while before she'd have her vehicle back. "Is that Michigan speak for finding the needle in the haystack?"

"It's Michigan speak for what's likely to be a huge waste of time."

"Not totally," he disputed mildly. While she was already frustrated by what she was certain was going to be a long fruitless day, his expression was impassive. "Even though we don't know if the shooter and the killer are one and the same, we're still working through possible offenders with a grudge and a trapper's license. We'll hit on one or both of those eventually."

"Can I quote you on that?" She slowed for a buck with an impressive rack to leap out of the ditch and bound across the blacktop, making its way to an abandoned logging road.

"You can quote me on one thing. I'm not leaving the UP before your shooter and your father's killer are brought to justice." He settled back in his seat and turned his face toward the window. "You've already noted my stubbornness before. Whatever game this offender is playing, I have no intention of letting him win."

Boone hung around the house later than usual, because he was expecting the call. Hearing Dorie Hassert blather on about the bitch sheriff almost getting herself blown away last night had been a shock. The old cow had a way of running on long past the time he'd gotten tired of listening, but she was a fountain of information about the subjects he was interested in. He'd let her talk, a hot arrow of rage lodging inside him as she spewed forth gossip.

Saxon was alive. That was the important thing to focus on.

The call came earlier than he would have expected. It was light outside, but just barely. "Yeah."

"I'm in your drive. Go out and open your shed. I don't want anyone seeing me here."

He thought about what was in his shed and gave a hard smile. That wouldn't figure into his plans at all. "I'll back out of the garage. You can keep your truck in there."

The response wasn't long in coming. "Goddammit. Just do what I tell…" Boone disconnected the call and pulled on his boots. Shrugged into his coat, but didn't fasten it before heading to the attached garage. He raised the overhead door and backed out, arcing around to allow the pickup to drive inside. Turning off the engine, he got out and let himself in the house again, unsurprised to find Bruce Yembley already standing in his kitchen, Boone's borrowed rifle in his hand.

"Give me the keys to your truck." The bastard didn't ask. Didn't think he needed to. He was used to people being too damn afraid of him to refuse him anything. He took a mug out of the cupboard and helped himself to the coffee that brewed automatically every day at four AM. "Mine's leaking oil and I gotta take a trip."

"How'd the rifle work?" Boone resisted the urge to plow his fist into the other man's face. But that wouldn't be wise, and it was always the end game that mattered. Bruce Yembley was dangerous. But so were some wild animals, until you outsmarted them. Moving to the counter, he picked up the coffee he'd been drinking while waiting for the phone to ring. "Did you get the coyotes on your property?"

Pests, that's what the other man had claimed. Had to get rid of them before his dog showed up missing some day. Asshole probably didn't even own a dog.

"Oh, yeah, I got the bastard." The other man grinned broadly, as if to a secret punch line. "Don't have to worry about being bothered anymore. No one needs to know that I'm driving your vehicle either. Keep your mouth shut about it."

"I won't say a word." He took the rifle from Yembley and with a practiced move unloaded it, shoving the unspent ammo into a drawer. Son of a bitch had probably been too dumb to pick up his fucking brass, too, not that it mattered. Nothing about the weapon was going to lead them to Boone

"You in a hurry?" He leaned against the counter like he had all the time in the world. "Got something out in the shed you might be interested in."

Yembley snorted, took a gulp of coffee. "I don't want to see any of your damn furs if that's what you're talking about. Got my own. Plus, I've got better things to do.

I'm sort of in a hurry to get moving. I've got an appointment to get to."

He hid his smile by raising the mug to his lips. His mother had been right, all those years ago. Brains really did win out against brawn. "Oh, I think you're going to find this interesting. I can promise it's one of a kind."

The other man looked at the old kitchen clock on the wall and then lifted a shoulder. "Fine. But if it's another one of those damn animals you got stuffed, you're gonna give me your keys *and* some cash. You haven't paid me for the last time I patched you up after you got winged with a bullet. Never thought my short stint working with a veterinarian would come in so handy." He trudged after Boone out the front door and down the steps, following the path to the shed. It had snowed a couple more inches last night. Time to shovel again. Boone made a mental note as he walked up and punched in the code to the keypad lock he had on the overhead door.

"Since when do you keep this place heated?" Yembley ducked inside ahead of him as the door descended again. The man walked by the weapon bench and gazed around impatiently. Boone set the rifle on the bench and knew the exact moment the other man saw the woman.

"What. The. Fuck." He stalked toward the blond waitress Boone had hanging from her cuffs fastened around the overhead pipe. "That's Tiffany Whatsherface. From the bar."

He turned back to him, a nasty smile on his face. "You fuck her yet? Because I ain't leaving here until I take my turn. Bitch has been giving me grief for months."

He gestured expansively, the knife he'd grabbed from the bench hidden up his sleeve. "I have plans for her.

But if you want a piece, be my guest." As if Yembley would have asked permission. The woman hadn't fully regained consciousness. Boone must have used more chloroform last night than he'd thought.

He waited until the other man had both hands on the woman before closing the distance between them and thrusting the knife between his ribs. Then he twisted the weapon viciously.

Yembley screamed, a surprisingly shrill sound. "What the…" The man staggered forward into the woman's listless body, sending it swaying. He tried to reach a hand behind him, fingers grappling for the handle. "You fuck…you…kill…you…"

"I don't think so." Boone shot a foot out and shoved the larger man over it. Yembley fell hard, smashing his face against the metal grate that ran through the center of the building. "You stupid fucker." Pent up hatred propelled the kick he aimed at the man's wound. The howl Yembley let out would rival any emitted by the coyotes the man had purported to be hunting. Boone stomped on the back of his thigh, gratified to hear the femur crack. "Your problem has always been forgetting that you don't make a move without my okay. Ever. You could have ruined everything. If you had, I would have gutted you like the animal you are. As it is…" He reached down to lift the man's head with a hand to his hair. "You're still gonna die. But not before we have some fun once it gets dark."

———

As it turned out, Burt Kasim did know his way around a rifle. Keira and Finn discovered that for themselves since the man was aiming one at them when he swung open the front door of his ranch-style home.

"Whoa, buddy." Finn raised his hands placatingly.

Keira wasn't in the mood to talk the man down from whatever might be igniting his temper. "You are going to want to put that weapon away, Mr. Kasim before I haul your ass to jail for threatening a law enforcement officer with deadly force."

"I haven't threatened anybody. Yet." The man lowered the barrel. "You here about my complaint?"

Making a split second decision, Keira nodded. "But we're not having this conversation while you're armed. Put that rifle down and unload it." The man surveyed them balefully from beneath bushy brows just long enough for Keira's hand to creep up to the weapon strapped at her side. Finally, he obeyed.

"You give a lot of orders, but just remember, I pay your salary." He nodded toward Finn, likely mistaking him for a deputy. "Yours, too. You both work for me. And it's about time county employees started listening to the taxpayers, instead of the other way around."

"We're here to listen." Keira scanned the room behind him. "Are you alone? Do you have anyone else in there with you?"

"'Course I'm alone," the man snapped. "It's my house. Live here by myself." He raised a shaking finger and pointed it toward the road in front of the drive. "But that don't matter. What matters is what your county folks did for the second time this winter. Happens damn near every year and I'm sick and tired of it."

Keira followed the direction he indicated and understood the source of his fury. His mailbox at the side of the road had been knocked off its post and laid in the snow next to it.

"I've called the courthouse a dozen times. Tried finding that little weasel Wilson at the county garage, too.

He's ducking my calls, the bastard. His plows did that, early this morning. Fucking snowplow drivers must be blind. They go too damn fast and don't give a shit about the damage they do to private property."

She looked at the man again. "It's Saturday, Mr. Kasim." When he screwed up his face uncomprehendingly, she added, "Most county offices are closed. The county engineer isn't ignoring your calls, he's home for the weekend. But if you agree to answer a couple questions for me, I will call Mr. Wilson myself and have him personally phone you, if you give me your number." She wasn't entirely sure she could get Roger to do that. And she was reluctant to ask for another favor from a man who made her even more uncomfortable now that she knew about him and her mother decades ago.

Her words seemed to work some sort of magic on Kasim. He recited his cell number as he pulled up the suspender that had started sliding down one bony shoulder. "Well, that's all I want. What any citizen wants really. For their elected officials to show some sort of accountability to the public." Keira didn't bother pointing out that the county engineer was not an elected position. "What questions did you want to ask?"

"Have you heard about the shooting that took place near Hancock Road in Munising about five-thirty last night?"

Kasim puffed out his bottom lip, shook his head. "Nope. Don't have a TV and haven't had the radio on today. You talking a hunter or did someone get shot?"

"Multiple shots were fired at the sheriff last night." Finn took over the conversation. "We're questioning county residents to find out whether anyone might have seen or heard something."

"How the hell would I hear anything clear out here? Shit, I'm at least twenty miles from there." He looked at the two of them suspiciously. "What are you really asking?"

"Maybe you were in town and saw something. We think the shooter was parked on the side of a public road. Anyone going by…"

Burt shook his head. "Didn't go by because I wasn't out. I haven't been near Munising in days. I mostly only go in to stop by the sporting goods store or to get groceries."

"Good night to stay in." Keira offered him an insincere smile. "You were home alone?"

Clearly tiring of the conversation the man huffed, "Already said I lived by myself, didn't I?"

"You did." She nodded and sent Finn a glance. This trip had been as big a waste of time as she'd predicted.

"That rifle you were holding…is it the one you won the 2009 Sportsman Championship with?"

"Damn straight." The man puffed out his non-existent chest, clad in a dingy white tee shirt. "Competition was stiff that year, but I beat them all. Some of the best hunters around entered that contest, but I took home the gold. Not your father, of course," he added to Keira. "He must have taken a look at the registrants and figured he couldn't compete."

"That must have been it."

"Heard the DNR shot that bear they thought mighta attacked him. Guess there're different rules for when the government takes down animals out of season." The man was getting agitated again. "The conservation officers sure seem to think so. Always sneaking up on folks going about their business. Telling them they're doing this thing wrong or that. I'm just saying, this damn country is to the point where there's a cop breathing down our neck every time we turn around. It's time for real Americans to…"

"I'll be sure and pass on your message to the county engineer." Keira broke in before he could work himself back up to a full-fledged rant. He was wrong about the bear; it had only been sedated and released, but Kasim would believe whatever fit his views. He'd never see the irony of wanting to be free of government interference at the same time he enjoyed having his road plowed and his property protected. His type never did.

"Okay," Finn said as he fastened his seatbelt when they got back to the car. "That might have been wasted effort. I have a hard time imagining that pipsqueak hiding in the trees waiting to squeeze a shot off at you. Especially since he didn't seem to have any particular beef with you, per se."

"Not me, just anyone wearing a uniform." Keira started the engine, pointed the vehicle down the drive. "His mindset is shared by plenty of people in the state, many far more dangerous than he is. Michigan has the second largest militia group presence outside of Texas, and some of the groups are active on the UP." At his quick look, she added, "Most are just fervent gun enthusiasts. Survivalists. At any rate, I'm willing to admit that Kasim, as annoying as he was, might have given me one idea."

"I'm all ears." He had his phone out and was texting as he spoke.

"It was when he starting going on about the DNR." Keira waited for two cars to go by, which passed for heavy traffic in the area before pulling out of the drive onto the road. "Conservation officers are spread pretty thin, and the UP has lots of state and national forests, not to mention major waterways to patrol. Nearest DNR office is Marquette, and officers handle multiple counties. Chandler is one I know." She couldn't recall now whether he'd been among those who had responded to the search for her father. That scene was all a bit of a blur now. She shoved the memory aside before it could take root and bloom. "He's someone who's out in the field a lot, as Kasim noted, because of his enforcement duties. If he's around, I'd like to pick his brain."

"He lives in Munising?"

"No, Marquette." She hit an icy area on the road and the cruiser fishtailed slightly before she righted it again. "But he grew up in Au Train, and his dad still lives there. The man's disabled and Beau spends a lot of time with him."

"I take it Au Train is close."

She shot him a grin. "Everything's relatively close in Alger County. It's on our way. I just hope he's around. A conversation with him might end up being the most helpful one of the day."

Beau Chandler was not only in Au Train, he was outside splitting wood when they drove up toward his father's house. Seeing the cruiser, he set down the ax on the stump he was using as a base and headed toward them. "Keira." His features wreathed in a broad smile when she got out of the vehicle. "This is an unexpected surprise. You working Saturdays now?"

"When it's called for. How you doing, Beau?"

After the conversation she and Tiffany had had about the man, it took more effort than it should have to keep her eyes off his Adam's apple. Okay, it *was* large, she admitted silently, but nothing like Tiff had made out. And the guy was genuinely nice if a bit on the quiet side.

Beau turned to look at Finn quizzically. "New deputy?"

"Finn Carstens, Beau Chandler. Finn is consulting with the department on a special project." She felt a little mean spirited not telling the man more. DNR district law enforcement supervisors would have gotten the memo she sent out today. But it was up to each agency to determine how far down the ladder to share it. "How's your dad doing?"

The man's angular shoulders bobbed up then down. "Same. Once winter sets in his rheumatoid arthritis gets worse. It's hard for him to get around much. I'm trying to get him an appointment at the Mayo Clinic. Maybe they'll have more ideas."

Keira nodded sympathetically although from the stories she'd heard over the years, Mike Chandler didn't deserve anyone's empathy. He'd been emotionally and verbally abusive to his wife and son. Once Beau had gotten a job in Marquette, his mother had joined him there. The man was disabled now. She hadn't seen him since she'd returned.

"Sounds like he's lucky to have you."

Beau jerked a thumb toward the house. "You want to go in and say hi? He doesn't get many visitors. He was napping when I came out, but…"

"No, that's okay. I was hoping you'd be here. I just left one of your fans." She told him about her visit with Kasim. Chandler rolled his eyes. "Yeah, he's a case, that one. The guy shouldn't even have a license. He's a chronic violator. Caught him using an illegal artificial light with his rifle while hunting. He paid a fine and lost his privileges for the rest of the year. Should have done jail time. Wish he had. Our office has gotten several complaints about him."

"The more serious violators do sometimes end up as guests of the county," she said for Finn's benefit.

Beau nodded. "It's the habitual ones usually. I'd bet my left arm that Kasim is a chronic violator, he just hasn't been caught often enough at it." He gave a shoulder jerk again. "There's a lot of land for the DNR officers to cover. We're not going to catch everyone."

This evening, Keira vowed, she'd take a closer look at the DNR database for license revocations and violations. "You know many of the hunters in the area. Are you familiar with any sharp shooters? Better than average shots?"

"Know more who claim to be." A wide grin split his face. "But sure, there's Al Siegel on Grand Island. I can say for a fact that he's everything he claims. I've been hunting with him. Doug O'Shea in Christmas. Helluva good tracker, and a great shot to boot." She pulled out a notebook to write down the names as he rattled off a half a dozen more. When he'd wound down, she asked, "What about Bruce Yembley? You know him?"

He made a face. "Ran across him a time or two in the Hiawatha Forest. Rough customer, that one. I have my doubts about whether he obeys the rules and regulations, but can't say I ever caught him at anything."

"Your office takes a lot of calls, people reporting on others for poaching, trapping and hunting violations. Do you have any names of individuals who seem to have problems with one particular person?"

He bobbed his head. "We get some complainers, sure, pissed that they're following the rules and the guy down the road isn't. The thing is, without proof, there's not much we can do to follow up, other than talk to the people. I can't say I recall the same names popping up, though, at least not in Alger. That sort of thing is more common in Marquette and Baraga. A lot more land to cover there."

Though he didn't say a word, Keira could feel Finn getting restless. "I appreciate your time, Beau. I'll let you get back to your work." She looked toward the house. "You have a wood burner inside?"

"We discovered that it helps dad's arthritis some. It's a drier heat. 'Course so is Arizona." His voice was amused. "But he'll never leave this place."

"Thanks for your help."

He raised a hand. "Good seeing you, Keira."

It wasn't until they got back in the car that she realized what had caused Finn's disquiet.

"Fallon found some brass. I checked an incoming text."

"I didn't notice." He must have been discreet.

"There's more. Whoever the shooter is, he's not the same man who broke into your cabin."

She took her foot off the accelerator to look at him, mind racing. "You sent him the measurements you took at Yembley's house, didn't you?"

Finn nodded. "I did. Even though I haven't examined the casts from last night yet, Fallon compared the dimensions to prints at your place that had been marked as belonging to the shooter. They match the ones I took of Yembley's. But they're about a size too small to belong to the intruder. I accessed the email I had that information in to make sure."

She pressed her foot on the accelerator again, but it was instinct that had her turning toward Munising. "That doesn't prove he's the shooter."

Finn gave one slow nod. "But now we know Yembley isn't the man who left that cooler on your porch, or the ear in your refrigerator. He could have fired those shots last night, but he isn't likely to be the killer we're tracking."

———

By mid-afternoon, Keira took pity on Finn and stopped by the sandwich shop before returning to the office. Hank still wasn't back, but she gave Phil the names of the marksmen they'd gotten from Chandler to add to the list of shooters they'd been compiling. After making short work of his lunch Finn left for the lab. Keira talked to Mary and Brody and the two brought her up to date on the four missing persons they'd been following up on. Since law enforcement responses today were as slow as they'd expected, she sent everyone home, not without some argument.

Before she did anything else, she looked up Roger Wilson's number from the county employee list and called him to pass on Burt Kasim's information.

She'd been counting on the man to be away from his phone. Had hoped to leave a message. Her heart sank when she heard his voice on the other end. "Roger. This is Keira Saxon."

"Keira! My God, are you all right? Of course, you are, you're calling, but…were you hurt? The news is all over town. Everyone was talking about it at Claire's today." His torrent of words came in a flood, one tumbling after the other until they were hardly recognizable. "This is horrible. Absolutely horrible. You could have been killed!"

"I'm fine, thank you for your concern." After speaking to people all day outside of Munising, she was unused to having to answer questions about last night.

For the first time, she took a look at the stack of phone messages on her desk. That reprieve was likely over.

"I hate to ask you for another favor, Roger…"

"Anything. Absolutely anything. You should know by now that there's very little I wouldn't do for you, Keira."

Taking a deep breath she barreled on. "I was questioning someone today and the only way I could enlist his cooperation was to promise you'd call him about a complaint he had. I'm sorry to use you that way. I have his number here if you want it." The silence on the other end had her searching for a graceful way to finish the conversation. "I'm afraid he's burned up the phone lines and you'll probably have plenty of messages from him when you get back to work on Monday."

"No, no, that's fine. Anything for you. My God, you could have been…"

"I really appreciate it." Hastily she gave him Kasim's complaint and his number. "Again, I'm sorry about this, but the situation started out volatile and this was a way to defuse it."

"Of course, of course." Wilson's voice held a forced heartiness. "That's the nature of our jobs, isn't it? Responding to the public."

"It is. You'll have to excuse me, I have another call. Thank you again."

"I'm always here to help, Keira."

With a desperate sort of relief, she hung up the phone, her breath releasing in one steady stream. Talking to the man was made worse knowing what she did about his history with her mother. Things had always been oddly strained between them but now…she moved her shoulders as if to dislodge the uncomfortable feeling. It was just weird.

Weirdness was a step up from being shot at, she thought with dark humor. She supposed she should be grateful for that.

She flipped through the stack of notes, sorting them into piles according to what she intended to respond to and what could be handed off to someone else Monday. Minutes later a foreign sound reached her ears. Keira was familiar with the normal office noises. Given the age of the building that housed it, there were plenty. But the faint swish swish heading toward her door wasn't a usual one. She was halfway out of her chair when a knock sounded, and it opened to frame Pammy.

At least—Keira blinked—she thought it was Pammy. Gone were the dyed black hair and dark clothing. Her gaze traveled lower. Absent were the clunky platform shoes with stacked heels. The woman was wearing ballet flats, rainbow colored tights, a sparkly tulle skirt and bedazzled turquoise leotard. Her hair was a color of platinum remarkably similar to that of Stella Cummings, worn with much better effect.

"Saw all the cars and thought, what the hell. If everyone else can come in on a Saturday and lend a hand, I can, too." The hands the woman offered, Keira saw now were encased in stretchy baby blue gloves. She'd done something to her eyes, too. False eyelashes perhaps, encrusted with crystals. "Put me to work. Please."

"Ah…" She swallowed the suggestion of tasking the woman with changing her wardrobe and blindly scooped up a stack of messages. Held them out. "Any notes from the paper can be placed in the circular file. The rest of these are tips that were called in about last night's shooting. You can follow up with the ones who left numbers and get more information."

"Excellent." The woman glided—literally glided—over to Keira's desk to take the notes. "Do you like my new outfit?"

"I...can't say."

"It's a work in progress."

Keira nodded. "Aren't we all?"

Pammy continued to the door, tossing the messages Keira had indicated into the trashcan on her way by. Before she left the office, she looked over her shoulder. "Keira." She stopped for a moment, before swallowing hard. "I'm glad you're not dead."

"Yeah." She watched the woman sashay out the door. "Me, too."

Her cell phone rang then, distracting her. It was Finn, but she was reminded of Tiffany again, mentally chastising herself for not following up with her friend the way she'd meant to earlier today. "Hi."

"Keira." His low tones had a frisson of awareness pulsing through her veins. The sensation was as unwelcome as it was unfamiliar. "I sent Fallon out to Yembley's house a couple hours ago."

"Had he returned?" Certainly she'd gotten no word of sightings of the man or his vehicle.

"It didn't look like it. I had him cast the boot prints around Yembley's mailbox on the road. No reasonable expectation of privacy there, right?"

She shook her head, belatedly realizing he couldn't see the action. "No."

"Perfect footwear match to those taken yesterday evening at your place." The words reverberated through her. "You can issue a warrant for Bruce Yembley's arrest. He's the one who tried to kill you last night."

CHAPTER 10

Finn stepped into the conference room, feeling more than a bit bemused. "There's a woman out there at Cal's desk…"

Keira didn't look up from whatever she was engrossed in. "Pammy. She's following up on some tips."

"That's…ah. She looks…different."

"You'll get used to it. I always do." Finally, she pulled her gaze away from what he could now see were spreadsheets covering every inch of the conference room table. "I issued the warrant. Had to get Judge Isaacson off a snowmobile trail to get it done. It just went out over the law enforcement alert system. That and the BOLO should be enough to scoop Yembley up from whatever rock he's hiding under. I also have deputies doing frequent passes by his house. We'll find him."

"Let's hope so." Although it would be much more satisfying for Finn to happen upon the man himself, in a secluded spot minus witnesses. He indulged himself by fantasizing about it for a brief moment. Last night's concern for Keira had coalesced once he'd discovered the

232 | KYLIE BRANT

identity of the shooter. The white-hot ball of rage that had lodged in his chest now had a focus. They had a name for the man who'd tried to murder her.

But they still hadn't found the killer they'd been tracking all week. That fact had him shoving aside thoughts of retribution and refocusing his concentration.

"Along with the brass, Fallon also recovered one of the slugs fired. It was buried in the snowbank in front of your porch."

She nodded. "The third one went wild. Over my head."

The words summoned an image, one he'd had trouble dislodging since yesterday evening. Finn would give a great deal to have not seen the video of the shooting. "I spent the afternoon photographing the markings, magnifying the images and sharing them along with the documented measurements with a colleague at Raiker's main lab. I'll FedEx the physical evidence for validation purposes, of course, but for now..."

"You mean you can't do it?"

The question stopped him. "I'm not a ballistics expert."

"Okay. I didn't know. I spent a lot of time talking to various experts while in CPD, but never gave much thought to forensic scientists' specializing." Her smile looked a bit strained around the edges. "It's your fault for being so supremely competent in a multitude of fields."

"I strive for better than competent," he responded drily, "so I'm going to focus on the adverb and ignore the adjective. Because the slug Hank discovered didn't suffer much impact damage, it also yielded enough markings to run through some ballistics databases, along with the brass. We found a match."

Keira's eyes went wide and she aimed a not so playful punch at his bicep. "Way to bury the lead, Carstens! You traced the rifle to another crime?"

He caught her hand as she was withdrawing it. Held it tightly in his. "The rifle used was your father's personal weapon."

She stared at him, but her gaze was faraway. "That case. Ten, eleven years ago. I don't quite remember all of the details…"

"Closer to ten. There was a rash of break-ins in the county. Only weapons were being taken. Your father had his hunting rifle stolen."

"Kent Little." Her fingers curled in his. "Nineteen years old. Dad's department tracked him down and there was a standoff. The kid had been selling most of the guns, but he was shooting at them with Danny's rifle. He was outmatched."

Finn had read the reports hours earlier. Some of the guns had been recovered. The boy hadn't lived to see prison. When Keira tugged at her hand, he let her go. She bounced out of her chair, to pace halfway to the door before swinging around again.

"It doesn't make sense." She was captivating to watch. He could all but see the inner gears turning in her head. "We know Yembley didn't kill dad because he hadn't been released from prison yet. He wasn't the one to break into my house. Not only was there not enough time, the footwear impression doesn't match. But he shot at me last night…and his motivation is still unclear. The offender had dad's cooler so it would follow that he took his rifle, as well. Which connects Yembley to the killer…"

"Because that's likely who he got the rifle from," Finn finished. "Yeah, I think so, too. Any other explanation relies on far too much coincidence. He's a felon…he couldn't get a firearm by legal means."

"So maybe he borrowed one." There was a look of stunned realization on her face. Coupled with a renewed sense of purpose. "We trace Yembley, and he can lead us to the murderer."

She turned on her heel, throwing over her shoulder, "All of a sudden I'm in a hurry to execute that search warrant the judge signed for Yembley's address."

———————

Hours later, Finn was willing to admit that whatever association Bruce Yembley might have to the killer wasn't going to be found inside the place he was renting. Keira had summoned all of her deputies to help with the search and given the size of the home it hadn't taken much time to cover every square inch of it.

The man had left in a hurry. That fact had been apparent by the mess they'd encountered when they'd entered the place. Drawers were standing open, and a box of black garbage bags was on the chipped laminate counter.

"Whatever he took with him, it wasn't his trash." Mary sat on the edge of a rickety wooden chair with gloved hands going through the contents of the wastebasket. There were empty food containers sitting all over the house, even in the bathroom. Finn imagined that in the summer months, habits like that led to a bug infestation.

They'd lifted the old carpet from the rooms, looking for hiding spots beneath floorboards. But cracked linoleum with a floral pattern covered the area and hadn't been disturbed. Vents were taken apart, and the low false ceiling removed, but neither revealed more than dust and cobwebs. The furniture, what there was of it, had been systematically dismantled. Even the toilet and appliances had been thoroughly searched. Finn was willing to bet the operation was going to be a bust. All it was going to prove was that the man had lived one step above an animal. Big surprise.

"There are still clothes in the closets and dresser." Keira came up to stand next to him. "He might have swept some of his belongings into one of those garbage bags and took them with him. But he left enough behind to make me think he's planning to come back."

"Maybe he belatedly thought of the need for an alibi and went off to try to manufacture one."

"Or perhaps he went to return the rifle." They exchanged a look. Just the thought burned. They'd missed the man by no more than a couple hours, from the looks of the tire treads out front this morning. Finn consoled himself with the thought that had they found Yembley at home, they couldn't have held him. Not then.

"Let's finish up." He heard the note of weariness in Keira's tone. Looked at the clock on the stove and noted that it was nearly ten o'clock. She took her cell out of her pocket and checked it.

"Expecting to hear from someone?"

She shook her head. Then shrugged. "Thought I might hear from Tiff. She never responded to the message I sent her last night and I followed up with a couple phone calls earlier today. Goes right to voicemail."

He studied her carefully. "You're worried about her?"

After a brief hesitation, she said, "No. She might be out of range. I know it was her weekend off, and she'd mentioned going skiing. I'm not sure if she worked last night or not. If she didn't, she might even have left yesterday." Seamlessly she looped back to the investigation. "I need to get back to the department. Compile a complete list of Yembley's known associates." She smiled grimly. "Got one of them locked up right now, but it's a sure bet Pete Bielefeld isn't going to be talking to me."

"Time enough to do that in the morning."

Finn was unsurprised when she shook her head stubbornly. "I'll send everyone else home, but I can work a few more hours. Somewhere on that list of associates might be the name of the person he's holed up with right now."

"You can't go knocking on doors tonight. It can wait until tomorrow." Her look was pointed enough to draw blood, but he withstood it with masterful stoicism. "First thing. Nothing's gained if we're exhausted. We stand to miss something important if we're not refreshed."

Her hands in her pockets, she watched her people finish up. "I can't figure all the angles. Not yet. Hard to think about sleeping with all these questions rattling around in my mind."

He understood what she was saying and guessed at what she left unsaid. It was harder still to rest when they didn't know when—or if—the killer would strike again.

———

Boone untied Yembley's feet and took the gag from his mouth. "Get up."

"You fucking son of a bitch." But the words lacked strength, delivered as they were on a moan. "I need a doctor."

"You need some balls," he said unsympathetically. "You want to get out of this alive, you have to earn the privilege." The blond was watching them with wide eyes.

She'd recognize him…of course she would. So after that first time walking in with Yembley this morning he hadn't made the mistake of coming in with his face uncovered again. He had plans for her. But Yembley had proven an unforeseen complication. One that needed to be taken care of first.

"What the fuck." The bigger man changed tactics. Grimaced in what was probably supposed to be a smile. "We're partners. I did you a favor. Saxon can't testify about Pete now. They'll have to release him. I saved the operation. You should be grateful."

Boone dropped to one knee, grabbing a handful of hair to turn Yembley's face up to his. "No, you dumb fuck, that's not how it works. And we aren't partners. You're just brainless muscle. You didn't kill Saxon last night. And that's the only reason you're still alive. I have other plans for her."

"You don't got an operation without me and Pete."

Boone shrugged, although there was enough truth to the words for a sliver of worry to work through him. "Pete was a small-timer when I caught him pissing around with portable meth labs in the forest. If it weren't for me, he'd still be selling half grams to high schoolers. And you…you're expendable. Always were." Boone had supplied the brains to the outfit. He was the moneyman. There were plenty of levels between him and the likes of Bielefeld and Yembley. He'd made sure of that. "Get in the truck."

He watched the man's gaze flicker to the pickup. Knew what he was thinking. That he had a chance. That escape was possible. Because Boone wanted him to believe just that, he said nothing, waiting patiently for Yembley to obey.

He didn't move. "You owe me. I patched you up just a few days ago. Who's going to help you if you get shot again?"

"Not your problem." He kicked him ungently. "I've got a cattle prod under the bench. Get up or I'll use it on you."

The knife wound had been tended to, but you wouldn't know it by the way the man bitched and moaned as he struggled to his feet then walked slowly to the passenger side of the vehicle, hands bound behind him. Boone's weapons were in a locked case in the bed of the pickup. No help there. And none at all if he were planning to dive out of the moving truck because he'd had jammed the lock. Once secured, it wouldn't open from the inside at all.

He blew a kiss to the blond. "Don't worry. I'll be back for you." Then slammed the door after Yembley and rounded the hood of the vehicle to get in the driver's side. Already the anticipation was crashing and churning through his veins. Better than sex. Way better. He started up the pickup and pulled away, shutting the overhead door behind him with the opener he dropped back into his pocket. And on the drive he concentrated on the building excitement from the one thing that made his life worth living.

The hunt.

———

"Yembley doesn't have a hunting license, obviously, but he has one for trapping. So that's another connection." Keira rubbed her forehead as she and Finn walked into the family room of the cabin. "Eating made my thinking fuzzy."

"That would be exhaustion," he countered. Which was exactly why he hadn't suggested opening up a bottle of the wine he'd bought when he'd insisted on stopping for groceries. Dropping down on the couch, he patted the seat next to him. Groceries might be too kind a word for shopping at a convenience store, but, at least, they had something to eat for the next few days, although he had given into Keira's repeated pleas for pizza tonight. "Our minds replenish after we empty them. Sleep works marvelously to that end."

She sat, crossing a foot to her knee and rubbing it. "It's emptying my mind enough first that's the problem," she countered. "All these loose threads are tangled up in there and I can't figure out how they all tie together."

He reached over and gave her foot a slight tug to straighten it and took over the task of massaging. "Yembley is a new lead. We focus on how he ties in tomorrow." In the next moment, he had both her feet on his lap, his thumb working her arches and the purr of pleasure she emitted shot straight to his groin. Maybe this wasn't a good idea. Definitely wasn't, he amended a moment later. She was facing him now, resting her head against the couch, eyes heavy. A strand of hair curved along her jaw and the flickering fire painted it more gold than red. Hers was a femininity that was impossible to hide, but the uniform usually did a good job of masking it. It said she was a cop first, and he knew that was true. But she was more than that—much more.

Because he was wandering down a dangerous path he cast about for something to break the spell of intimacy that he'd started. Then grinned, oddly charmed. "You have a hole in your sock."

She smiled, a feline curve of the lips that made his jeans feel uncomfortably tight. "I need a personal shopper. Groceries. Socks. Do you know how long it's been since I've had a pedicure? I'm not even sure, but my mother actually keeps track of those types of things. According to her, it's been a lifetime. When this is over, I just might take a weekend to remember what it's like to not wear a gun and a badge."

To focus on the woman, instead of the cop. There was no reason, none whatsoever, for his mind to spin a vivid mental image of all that might entail.

She went silent for several minutes, staring into the gas flames as if hypnotized. "I was engaged once." He wondered if she felt the jolt of surprise that worked through him at the words. But then in the next moment he decided the real shock was that a woman like her was still single. "He was a great guy. Funny. Brave. A little too cocky, maybe, but he was a cop for the right reasons. We had that in common. It should have been enough to start a life together."

"But it wasn't." He knew better than most that you couldn't force yourself to feel something you didn't.

"No." She sounded a little melancholy. "The engagement drifted along for two years before it occurred to me that neither of us were in a hurry to take that next step. Sometimes there's not enough there. No matter how much you might want there to be."

"And sometimes you're not allowed to know what all is there."

Keira didn't seem to hear him. That was probably just as well. "He was on a SWAT unit. They had a domestic situation and a breach was ordered. He was on the entry team. The guy had the place booby-trapped." Her voice trailed off. He didn't need to hear more. He'd spent more time than he'd ever imagined matching and identifying body parts from a very similar scene.

Keira straightened to swing her legs off his lap. "I don't regret my time with Todd, even knowing now that marrying him would have been a mistake. It's never the path not taken that haunts me. It's being faced with a fork in the road and being too paralyzed to make a choice at all." Her eyes were clear when she slid over to him. Close enough to transfer the heat from her body to his side. And then in a quick and sneaky move she was straddling his hips, and looking supremely satisfied. "This is me," she said huskily, her mouth lowering to his, "making a choice."

He cupped her nape in his hand, returning her kiss hungrily despite it only being a matter of hours since he'd last tasted her. And he knew that in this one area they were in complete accord. Missed opportunities could be mourned. Whatever the future brought, he'd never regret taking a chance with Keira Saxon.

He took the kiss deeper, blindly reaching for a silky strand of her hair and wrapping it around his index finger. In doing so his knuckle brushed her jaw. Her skin would feel that soft all over, as smooth and fragile as the petals on his mother's prize orchids. But there was nothing delicate about the woman above him. And he found her strength an enticing contrast to her femininity.

There would be countless other silky spots on her body, and he had to fight a sudden urge to discover them all. To explore the places that made her sigh, and ravage the areas that made her moan. He released her hair as he changed the angle of the kiss, his tongue going in search of hers. And battled the temptation for hard and fast and furious. There was far more satisfaction to be had in taking it slow.

Obeying an unconscious urge that had been simmering longer than he'd admit, he tugged her uniform top out of her waistband and worked the buttons loose one at a time. With a hand on his to still them, she murmured, "We'll be more comfortable upstairs."

He drew back a fraction to look at her. Found himself distracted by the pulse pounding in her throat. "Right now I'm plenty comfortable here." He closed his teeth on the cord in her neck, scoring it gently. When he inhaled the scent of her soap or lotion, something subtle and inviting, he felt his senses fray. No, he wasn't going to hurry this. Wasn't going to race toward the inevitable conclusion. He returned to her lips and let the kiss spin out long and as achy as the throb of a sax vibrato while they both quivered.

When he released her mouth, it was only to part her uniform shirt and drag it a bit over her shoulders. Leaning forward, he tasted the skin he'd bared and felt a kick in his pulse. His hand stroked her back, feeling the tense set of muscles, the rigidity of her spine. His fingers worked at the tightness there slow and soothing as he trailed a lazy path of kisses along her jaw. After a few moments, he was rewarded when he heard her issue a slight sound and sag against him.

She slid her hand into his hair and brought his mouth back to hers. Her kiss was direct, much like her personality. No subterfuge, just an unvarnished longing that was a match for his own. He liked that about her. Too much. Each facet she shared, every layer he uncovered fascinated. Their breath mingled as he sank into the flavor of her. Mouths mated, tongues tangled, first quick and darting then a slower, more languid glide. He gathered her closer to deepen the kiss and demand edged in, fierce and sharp as a blade.

As if she recognized the change in him she pulled away, her gaze never leaving his. She shrugged out of the shirt and tossed it aside. Finn threaded his fingers through her hair, pushing it away from her face. Her profile was as regal as a mythical goddess, and her perch above him like a female deity showing pity on a mere mortal. He reached behind her to undo the clasp of her bra before drawing it down her arms to bare her breasts. High and round, they were made to fit his palms. With her torso bared, her hair shimmering fire around her shoulders, she took his breath away. She was flesh and blood and bone, pulsing with life. Tempting him to join her in descent to wicked pleasure. It was a journey he was anxious to share.

Shifting position, he pressed her against the arm of the couch and drew one of her tightly beaded nipples between his lips. He laved it with his tongue, quick teasing strokes before sucking more fiercely on it. She gave a little gasp and pressed closer to him, forcing a deeper contact. He complied, covering her other breast with his hand kneading lightly and felt all his other senses dim.

There was the taste of her, exquisitely feminine and the feel, curves gilded with heat. Everything inside him was focused on diving into those flames and allowing desire to scorch them both.

Finn lifted his mouth to rub his shadowed jaw against the wet swollen nipple he'd released. Then swallowed her murmur of pleasure. Keira's hands tugged at his shirt, but he wasn't in the mood at the moment to help her. There was something too gut-wrenchingly sexy about holding her half naked body in his lap, savoring first one breast and then the other and feeling her twist against him.

He was a patient man. He'd had to be to work his way through a constant series of accreditations and medical school. So the impatience he felt now was more than a little disconcerting. It was both heaven and hell to take things slow. Especially with a woman who'd ignited a fever in him that just might prove incurable.

Keira reached down and dragged his shirt from his jeans. Her hands slid beneath its hem, trailing fire in their wake as her fingers stroked his sides before moving to his back, gliding over the muscles there. Her touch torched his blood. He could feel it surging through his veins like a thoroughbred straining toward the finish line. And thought abruptly receded.

He undid the buttons of his shirt in quick, savage movements and when it was open, he splayed his hand against her spine and brought her closer. That first blessed contact of flesh kissing flesh seared through his system. Skin to skin. Curves to angles. Heat to heat. Her breasts flattened against his chest, he went in search of her lips, fighting an inner battle against the hunger she ignited in him.

It was moments…or hours later when her hands pressed between them. Reluctantly he released her mouth. Her palms skated over his torso, slowing when she found the indentation where they'd dug shrapnel out of him in Afghanistan. He'd been one of the lucky ones that day. He'd never taken that good fortune for granted. Just like he was unable to forget the luck that had saved Keira last night.

He didn't want to think about that now, not any of it. Not when he felt more alive than he had in years. The beat of his blood throbbed to a single synchronized rhythm. Every breath he took had to be battled out of clogged lungs. And all his senses were awash in her.

She leaned forward, dragging the tips of her breasts across his chest and with each sensual stroke a corresponding bolt of lust tightened low in his belly. She nipped at his shoulder, the tiny sting of pain honing his desire to a razor edge. Finn's hands settled on her hips pressing her closer to his straining length. He wanted to be buried inside her to the hilt. Wanted to plunge into her velvety dampness until the need exploded for them both, leaving only pleasure in its wake. And he wanted, quite desperately, for that to be enough.

He'd been balanced on a sword of his own making. Eschewing casual relationships, skirting serious ones. Keira's earlier words took on new meaning. Avoiding making a choice at all was a coward's way out.

Acknowledging the thought had caution stirring. One taste of her wasn't going to be enough to quench the fire in his blood. One night, however pleasurable, was never going to sate a desire that surfaced whenever he was near her.

Her fingers went to his zipper. Finn mustered his tattered control and gathered her in his arms. Stood. Then pretended to stagger under her weight as he headed toward the stairway.

"Smart guy." She looped her arm around one of his shoulders and grazed the other with her teeth in an ungentle caress. "Maybe you should save us both broken necks and let me walk."

"And risk ruining my best Rhett Butler move?" He paused, one foot on the first landing as he leaned down to take her mouth with his again.

When their lips parted, he saw humor dancing in her eyes. And wondered if he'd ever seen her look so carefree. "I'm afraid this staircase isn't made to showcase your re-enactment of Gone with the Wind."

"When Rhett Butler fails…" He set her on her feet for an instant before hoisting her over his shoulder in a fireman's carry and resumed climbing. "I always fall back on John Wayne."

Her helpless laughter was every bit as seductive as her position was. It would be difficult to walk away from a woman who made his blood churn like a teenager's. Harder by far to leave one he could laugh with at the same time.

When they were at the top of the stairs, he let her slide down in his embrace until they were eye to eye. "Do you have any more unexpected moves in your repertoire?"

Against her lips he whispered, "As a matter of fact…"

Scooping her up in his arms again, he turned unerringly toward her bedroom. He'd been in it once, fleetingly, the night the intruder had broken in. He hadn't noticed the skylight that first time, though, or the way the bed was positioned in the center of the room directly beneath it, surrounded by walls of glass. Right now curtains blocked out the night on the windows, but the moon hung low in the sky overhead, a jewel pinned to velvet. Moonlight dappled the rumpled covers, and he had a brief mental image of her sprawled on the mattress, her pale limbs painted with starlight. And then it melded into a vision of him joining her on the bed, stretched out atop her, buried in her.

He set her down and, hooking his thumbs in the sides of her pants, dragged them over her hips. And when Keira pushed them down her long slender thighs to the floor, stepping out of them revealing only a scrap of panties, he felt his mouth dry.

She swayed toward him. Her gaze was direct, her eyes smoky with desire as she worked to release the button of his jeans. He splayed a hand over her bottom to urge her closer and smoothed his lips over the side of her throat before taking the lobe of her ear in his teeth, worrying it gently.

His hands molded her curves, tracing the edge of the elastic where it met the tops of her thighs, before cupping her lace-covered mound. Covering her mouth with his, their tongues dueled in rhythm with the brushing movements of his fingers. He could feel the damp heat of her behind the thin fabric. Could imagine that slick wet softness opening. Surrounding him.

Then her hands were freeing him, stroking with a firm movement that threatened to send restraint careening away. He withstood her teasing as long as he could until the breath was strangling in his chest, and his vision began to haze. Then Finn stepped back, his last functioning brain cell reminding him to retrieve the condom from his jeans pocket before kicking out of his remaining clothes and reaching for her again.

He tumbled her onto the bed, pausing to appreciate the way the moonlight sheened her skin to alabaster. Her hands were greedy, her mouth demanding as she drew him down to her. But he wasn't ready for this to be over. Not yet. Not until he'd tasted every inch of her. Explored all the curves and hollows where her scent lingered, her pulse throbbed.

He moved his lips over the satiny skin of her belly, pausing to dip his tongue in the delicate whorls of her navel. Her muscles quivered as she guessed his intent. He felt the bite of her nails on his shoulders when he swept away the scrap of lace and slid his hand up her thighs to part them.

He sensed her protest, but it remained unuttered. He explored her delicate folds with the tip of his tongue just once before parting them to feast, relishing the low moan she released. Her fingers clenched in his hair. The taste of her was liquid fire and it called to something primal in him. When he found her sensitive clitoris, her hips arched off the bed.

The long broken cry she made had his last remnant of civility slipping its leash. This was what he'd wanted. The scent of her in his system. Intoxicating his senses. He wanted to strip away every vestige of control she might cling to. Wanted to lose his own. To shatter every defense until she was a mass of sensation, a creature driven only by need.

He entered her with one finger, exploring her inner softness as she twisted against him. His name on her lips fulfilled one need; summoned a hundred more. Her body bucked beneath his touch, her urgency signaling her imminent release. And when it came, ripping a cry from her, need slashed through him, dark and edgy.

Lifting his head from her sated body, he searched blindly on the rumpled covers beside him. Found the condom in the folds of the comforter and attempted to rip it open, his movements made awkward by pent-up hunger.

Then Keira's hands were pushing his aside to roll the latex over his straining penis. Finn closed his eyes, trying to summon a sliver of control. Any thoughts he might have had of

finesse were beyond him now. He pressed her back on the bed, meaning to make a place for himself between her thighs, but she had other plans. Suddenly it was Keira pinning him to the mattress and straddling him. Her torso arched languorously above him. And at that moment he would have given everything he had to freeze the sensual picture of her.

She reached between their bodies and guided him inside her. The words on his lips were desperate. The hands on her hips more so. As if sensing his unraveling restraint, sharing it, she sheathed herself fully. He surged up against her in helpless demand, focusing on her face.

Her eyes were at half-mast. Color rode high in her cheekbones. He wanted to commit every change of expression to memory as they moved together in a sensual battle. But his climax was rushing in, making thought impossible. His hips hammered against hers following the pace she set, fighting to get air into his lungs.

Their rhythm quickened, each movement driving him deeper inside her until his release rocketed through him, wiping his mind clean.

———

It was the heat that awakened her, a furnace-like seal pressed against her back. Then she noticed the weight. An anchor over her waist. Another pinning her ankles to the mattress. Keira dragged open her eyes and struggled to make sense of her world.

Her bed. Her room. Not her jeans on the floor.

A smile settled on her lips as memory filtered in. Finn Carstens was the cause of the heat and the weight. As well as the soreness in her muscles. She couldn't muster a single regret for any of them.

The sky overhead had lightened. The urgency of the day was already pressing in, but she was going to allow herself the next little while to simply be.

It was only a few minutes before a quiet alert sounded, followed by Finn's sleepy murmur. "Is that your phone or mine?"

With some difficulty, she turned over to face him. His eyes weren't open yet, but his arm tightened around her, pulled her closer. She rested her head against his chest, lulled by the slow, steady beat there. "Yours."

"Can you hand it to me? I think I've gone blind."

"Your eyes are closed," she observed amusedly. But levered herself up and over him to get the cell, which at some time during the night he'd retrieved from the pocket of his jeans to set on the table next to him. Unerringly one of his hands went up to cup her breast. She stifled a laugh, shoving the phone in his questing fingers instead. "Apparently you don't need sight for some things."

His lips curved as he freed his other hand to rub at his eyes even as he swiped in the security code with a thumb. The calendar reminder was easy enough for her to see.

Cady's memorial.

She stilled against him. "Who's Cady?"

The change that came over his expression was immediate. He stared at the cell for a moment and she knew that he was suddenly irrevocably awake. He shifted in bed to prop himself against the headboard. "I'll never be certain. A little girl who died."

He didn't have to tell her. She wouldn't push. Keira had experienced enough loss to respect the space of others who'd suffered the same. "She'd be six by now. Today's the anniversary of her death. She and her mother died three years ago." His expression was impassive when he turned to face her, but his eyes...the haunting pain there was palpable. "Cynthia...her mother and I...we dated for a while, but it was never serious. I was preparing for my first DGA trip and we were both seeing other people. After I left, I never saw her again. Until she and her daughter showed up in my autopsy suite."

The awfulness of what he was telling her carved a hole through her gut. "God, Finn."

"It's standard procedure to excuse ourselves if we know the victims, but I didn't recognize Cynthia's last name. She'd married. Some idiot with a gun started shooting up a mall and she and her daughter were just in the wrong place at the wrong time."

A minute passed, stretching interminably. "I told you I was a twin. My sister's name is Fiona." His smile flickered, there and gone again. "There's this dopey picture of us on my parents' mantel wearing matching sailor outfits. And Cady...that beautiful little girl on my table...I swear to God she looked so much like my sister in that photo...I had to wonder."

A sigh rattled out of him. "I got someone in there to relieve me. Made an excuse." He shook his head as if to dislodge the memory. "I never knew Cynthia was pregnant. I've run a hundred different scenarios through my head. I wasn't ever unavailable, even when I was out of the country. I didn't hear from her again. But the girl...her age was right. She could have belonged to someone else Cynthia was seeing. She just looked so damn much like that picture..." He turned his face toward hers. She could see the ghosts that lingered in his eyes. "I'll never be certain."

Her chest was tight with empathy. Keira's hand reached out for his. Squeezed hard. "Not knowing must be torturous."

"There was something in the paper with the obituary. A suggestion for where to send memorials. That's what the note on the phone was for. I make a donation every year. It's important that she be remembered. No matter..."

No matter who the girl's father was. Keira completed the thought silently. Her heart ached for a child cut down before she'd had a chance to live. It hurt equally for the man beside her.

"When Raiker approached me about a job I jumped at the opportunity to get out of the ME's office." He skated his thumb along the side of her hand where their fingers were laced together. "I still do pathology when it's called for, but I can't practice it on a continual basis anymore."

Her throat tight, she shook her head. "No one could blame you." There was nothing more to say so they fell silent, her hand gliding rhythmically over his arm as if she could soothe away the pain. Ghosts. They all had them. Sometimes they haunted for a lifetime.

They stayed that way long enough for a pre-dawn glow to appear at the edge of the curtains. When her cell rang, she reached for it with her free hand. She checked the screen. Six forty-two. "It's Phil," she said to Finn as she answered it.

"Took a call fifteen minutes ago from Doug O'Shea." By the noises in the background, it sounded as though the man were already in his car. "He was out checking his traplines and found a body in the Hiawatha Forest."

She was out of the bed in seconds, heading to her closet for a fresh uniform. "Male or female?"

"It's male. Haven't made it there yet myself but Doug seemed to think it could be Bruce Yembley."

CHAPTER 11

Tiffany was glad he kept his face covered. Not because it hid the man's identity. She'd already recognized his voice when he and Yembley were talking. No, wearing the facemask meant that maybe he planned to let her go. At least, that's what she told herself.

But when he'd forced Yembley into the pickup she knew in her heart that even if she was allowed to leave this building alive, she wasn't going to stay that way. Because the man had come back alone. And it was at that moment that she realized that whatever he'd done with Yembley, he had something even worse in store for her.

"You do any hunting?" He seemed in a fine mood right now, his voice echoing a bit in the building as he approached her. "Trapping?"

She shook her head and tried to keep herself from shrinking away when he stopped in front of her.

"Too sensitive? Don't like the mess? Or don't like taking trophies?" When she remained silent, he reached

254 | KYLIE BRANT

out one gloved hand with a vicious swipe that snapped her head back. "Answer me, bitch."

The blow accomplished what hours of terror-filled solitary couldn't. A hot ball of fury formed in the pit of her stomach. Tiffany welcomed it. Embraced it. This wasn't a man who'd be swayed by tears or pleading. She needed brains to get out of here.

Brains and the devil's own luck. She spit the blood that pooled in her mouth at the man's feet. "No. I don't think I'd like it."

"Doesn't matter. I don't need you to make the delivery. Just to write the message." He reached up to unlock the cuffs that kept her wrists secured to the pipe running over her head. Her arms dropped down numbly. She'd lost feeling in them hours ago.

Frowning, she watched him take a piece of glossy white paper out of the bag he carried, followed by a black Sharpie.

"Go ahead," he said impatiently. "Get the circulation back in your hands. You're going to need one of them to write with."

Awkwardly she rubbed her hands and arms until needles of sensation could be felt stabbing through them. "Okay, enough." He shoved the marker at her. "You're going to send a message to your bitch friend. Saxon."

Tiffany stilled. "Like hell I am."

The fist he plowed into her stomach had her doubling over, gagging and retching as she struggled for breath. "I can hurt you. Bad. I will, eventually, although women aren't near as much fun as men." He wrapped his hand in her hair to pull her head back painfully until his masked face with its slits for eyes and mouth filled her entire vision. "You're nothing but bait, get that? Either you write the note, or I cut off a body part and send that along to Saxon because all I care about is letting her know I've got you. To find you she'll have to come through me." He released her and shoved the Sharpie at her again.

She didn't understand this. Not any of it. But she knew he was planning to hurt Keira, and he was going to use Tiffany to do it. Thinking rapidly, she said in a weak voice, "She hasn't seen my handwriting for years. But I can write like we did when we were kids. She'll recognize that."

It was a struggle to hold the Sharpie. When it slipped from her hand once he punched her again, this time with enough strength to have pain singing through her jaw. "Jesus, it's simple enough. Just say, 'Come and get me.' Can you fucking do that, or should I just slice off your tit and send that along?"

"What makes you think she'd recognize that, asshole?"

He smiled as she bent down painfully to prop the paper he handed her on her thigh to start writing. "You always were a smartass."

She had no idea what he was trying to accomplish, but she knew this might be the one and only time she would have a chance to warn her friend. She wrote the words, adding flourishes as clues. He grabbed the paper away from her, stared at it. "What the hell is that supposed to be?"

"Half hearts," she lied, bracing herself for another blow. If her feet weren't bound, she'd kick him square in the balls, regardless of what the action would cost her. "We were half-hearted. It's a joke from when we were kids."

"Lame." He took the paper and set it next to a cardboard box. When he stood again, he snapped the cuffs on her wrists, but this time threaded a chain through both that he looped to the overhead pipe. It would allow her to move a short distance. More importantly, she could lower her arms.

Her gratitude was short-lived. He pulled a knife out of the back of his waistband and approached her, seeming amused by her efforts to scramble away from him. "Count yourself lucky." He stopped her with one hand in her hair. She felt a sawing motion, pulling and snapping until she was free again. When she opened her eyes, she saw him holding a long hank of hair. "I could have removed it like Yembley's." He flipped open the carton with one foot, and her horrified gaze followed his. And for the first time since he'd taken her, Tiffany Andrews began to scream.

————

"He was lying right next to my trap." Doug O'Shea's voice was shaky, and he took another gulp from the thermos he held. "Face up. I didn't touch him. I didn't touch anything. It was still dark. At first, I thought a large animal was feeding on my catch. Then the flashlight beam caught him. I contacted Phil right away." He tried for a smile. Couldn't quite pull it off. "We golf sometimes in the summer, so I had his number. Probably should have called 911. To tell you the truth, I wasn't thinking clearly."

"That's understandable." Keira looked over his shoulder at the body. She'd called for the ME, but the man would be coming out of Manistique. Finn was serving in that capacity at the moment, and he likely had a great deal more experience than did the general practitioner that served as ME for four counties.

But after last night, she felt more than a little guilty about asking Finn to assume the duty.

Turning her attention back to O'Shea, she asked, "You knew Yembley?"

He nodded. Took another sip. "I've seen him checking his traps now and again. I give him a pretty wide berth usually."

"Have you had trouble with him in the past?"

"Not really." He rolled the thermos between his gloved hands. "I'm referring more to his reputation, I guess. He always has something to say when I run into him out here. I ignore him when I can, but sometimes he makes that hard." As if realizing how that sounded, his head jerked up. "Not that there was bad blood between us. I barely knew him."

"Okay. At least you don't have to worry about going in to work today." She patted him on the shoulder.

"I was planning on church later. Not sure that's such a great idea now."

"Why don't you get the statement out of the way then? Mary's right here, and she'll walk you through it."

He nodded, and she left him sitting in the back seat of her cruiser, and beckoned Mary over. Phil appeared at her side. "Hank will try to get here later. They were in the hospital all last night with his son. Double ear infection or something."

They walked toward the approaching newcomers. She recognized Sergeant Gomez, the U.S. Forest Service's special agent who served several local counties. Gil Stevens, the investigator for the National Park Service, flanked him. Both men had been on the scene when her dad's body had been found. They were accompanied by Gary Paulus, a district forester and DNR Conservation Officer Beau Chandler.

"Hell of a thing, Sheriff. Have you identified the victim?"

She nodded at Gomez's question. He was a short, stout man and looked rounder today in his down jacket and stocking hat. Although it wasn't snowing at the moment, the breeze was dislodging flakes from the branches from overhead trees and a few adorned his bushy black mustache.

"Bruce Yembley. An ex-con who lived in Deerton."

"Saw the BOLO on him yesterday." The sergeant's dark eyes were shrewd. "Guess we know why you never caught up with him."

Keira looked toward where Finn was crouched down beside the body. "If we had, he'd still be alive. We had just identified him as the shooter at my place the other night."

Stevens followed the direction of her gaze. "Was he killed here or dumped?"

"The ME hasn't arrived, but I have a special consultant working with the department who has the same background." Keira had drawn her own conclusions when she'd first seen the area, but she'd wait for corroboration. "He'll be able to give us some answers."

Chandler asked, "How'd they get in, do you know yet?"

Nodding, Keira said, "They must have used the skid path a couple of miles north of here. There are two sets of prints leading away from the vehicle. One set returning." She saw Gomez's gaze go to the logging road they were standing beside. "The treads here were made by the person who found him. You would have seen his car back where you parked. We'll put out a media alert, but he was discovered at about five-thirty this morning. Finding more witnesses is doubtful."

They'd take a cast of the tire tread, but discovering the vehicle that had made it seemed a long shot. It wouldn't be difficult to match the footprints leading into the forest. Yembley's had been identified yesterday. There wasn't a doubt in her mind that the other set would be the same as the tracks of the man who'd broken into her home. She led the group toward where Finn was working. He looked up at their approach.

"Jesus." Beau slapped a hand over his mouth, but his eyes remained fixated on the bloody body. "Is that…was he…?"

"For lack of a better word, the victim was scalped."

The forester looked once, then swallowed and averted his gaze. Even Gomez was looking a bit green, Keira noted. Which made her feel less embarrassed about the queasiness that had reappeared in her stomach.

"Rather an expert job done of it, too." Finn stood, placing himself between them and the body. She knew intuitively that he was protecting the scene. Regardless of the distance he'd put between him and his former career, the man was still a forensic pathologist at heart. "That act occurred post-mortem. I suspect the cause of death will be attributed to a bullet in his back."

"He was killed here."

Although she hadn't phrased it as a question, Finn nodded. "There's a large blood spill beneath the body. The bullet would have damaged his spinal cord, making further movement impossible. I found a blood-soaked bandage on his right side with another wound, covering a puncture mark. It would have required medical attention, but didn't receive any. That occurred perimortem, but probably only a matter of hours before he died. That's about all I can tell without getting him to a morgue."

"Any idea of time of death?"

He looked pained at her question. "I don't have a body thermometer, and I'd need to do calculations taking into consideration outside temps, humidity, precipitation…plus the snow would lower body temperature quickly. Without undressing him, I can't fully assess the stage of rigor. And we don't know how long he was outdoors prior to being killed. But best guess…maybe sometime between ten pm and four am this morning."

Gomez caught Keira's eye, and they turned to walk several feet away. Stevens followed. "Is this victim related to the murder investigation being run out of your office?" the sergeant asked.

The men would have received the law enforcement memo she'd sent out yesterday, given their positions in local criminal justice agencies. "He's connected, but I'm just not quite sure how yet. Not only was he the shooter from the other night, but he used Danny's weapon."

Shock flickered in Stevens' expression. "The one that was missing from your father's crime scene?" He mulled that over for a moment. "Maybe this victim ended up on the wrong side of the killer you're hunting."

Keira's voice was grim. "That seems certain."

Gomez blew out a breath. It hung in the air like a dragon's expelled smoke. "This kill site means your case just became the subject of a multi-agency task force. We'll need to be brought up to speed quickly. A full summary of your investigation so far would be helpful."

After promising to get copies to both men, she walked back for a private word with Finn. He was photographing the body with a camera he must have gotten from the evidence van.

"The knife marks on the scalp…" she started.

"...and the one in his side, yes." He lowered the camera to look at her. "There should be comparisons made to the weapon marks on the second victim's ear."

"The ME doesn't have that sort of experience. He's a general practitioner that works for the Department of Health." She paused, thinking furiously. "I can probably figure out a way to get you invited to the autopsy." Being employed by Raiker's agency should throw a lot of weight in Finn's favor, but there were always territorial factors to consider. "Having Yembley killed on federal property complicates things. But I'd really like you to do the comparison examination."

He nodded. "There's something I didn't mention in front of the others." At her look he shrugged. "This may be a fact you don't want generally known. In addition to the scalping, there's another injury the victim suffered post-mortem. He was castrated."

Keira gave a low whistle. "He really pissed someone off."

"And I think we can guess whom, even before we cast those footprints. I can even hazard a prediction as to why."

A shiver worked down her spine. One that had nothing to do with the outdoor temperature. "Maybe Yembley trying to kill me threatened whatever game the offender is playing."

Finn's expression was fierce. "Which means the killer will try to engage you again in some way. Sooner, rather than later. You go nowhere alone, understood? If I'm not with you, someone else is. Every minute."

The words would have annoyed her even a day earlier. But last night changed things. She could understand the more personal concern underlying the professional because she felt the same way about him.

But the reality was, manpower was limited. Finally, she conceded, "No unnecessary risks. For either of us."

He would have liked to say more. She could see it in his expression, but her radio went off.

"Did a drive by of your property, Sheriff." There was a slight shakiness to Brody's tone that had her senses heightening. "Saw the lid to your mailbox was open and something hanging out of it. Got up close enough to take a look. You're going to want to come and check this out yourself. At first, I thought it was a dead animal, but..."

She raised her gaze. Met Finn's. And knew they'd both reached the same conclusion. The killer had wasted no time making his next move.

————

"What the hell is it, Sheriff?"

Keira didn't look up from her task. "Brody, I'm not going to think any less of you if you puke. But if you hurl in the evidence room I will do you serious bodily harm."

"I'm not. I won't."

"Good." She used tweezers to pick up the note that had been lying on top of the box, before utilizing the sterile forceps to grip the bloody object with her other hand and lift it far enough out of the carton to look beneath it. Satisfied that there was nothing else inside, she gently replaced the item and carried the note to a clean sheet of paper. Rules of evidence collection would say a paper item could be enclosed in plastic, but she couldn't be sure whether the blood smearing it was transfer stains or a bloodstain. Hence, she'd play it safe.

"That looks...human."

She glanced at the young deputy who appeared a bit sick. His work for the department was primarily patrol and the sight in the box would be enough to turn anyone's stomach. "The victim they found in the forest today? Yembley? He'd been scalped. I think we'll discover that this came from his body."

Placing the carton in the refrigerator, Keira returned her attention to the note.

Come and get me.

Four words, and those written in a rounded, girlish handwriting. Some sort of flourish was used above the d and the t. Two humps over each, like unfinished m's. She and Finn had both expected the offender to reach out again. This was the most direct method yet.

The paper was thick and glossy, like the type for running off pictures. The writing was done with a black fine point marker. And, Keira peered closer, there was a hair stuck to the note. Not from Yembley's scalp. This was so light she hadn't noticed it at first. Picking up the tweezers again, she attempted to grasp it but it didn't loosen. Instead, she turned the note over and stared, comprehension slamming into her with the force of a truck.

Strands of blond hair were twisted into a tight curl and taped to the back of the sheet. Although there might be others with hair that shade, mostly small children, Keira's mind sprang immediately to one. She turned the paper over again. The writing didn't look male. But could her friend have written it? A bit frantically, Keira had to admit she didn't know. The only handwriting she'd seen of Tiffany's in recent years was on an order pad at the restaurant, and that wasn't enough for her to be sure.

She reached for her phone even as Colton, her part-time weekend dispatcher, poked his head in. "Everyone else is still out at the forest. I've got a burglary report in Chatham. Do you want me to radio Mary or Hank?"

"No, Brody will take it." The deputy looked reluctant, but headed out of the room, speaking with Colton as they walked away together. Keira called Tiffany's phone again. It went right to voice mail. She hung up and stared at the note.

It was a leap to think that somehow her friend had gotten drawn into this. The victims so far had all had some sort of connection, at least loosely, to outdoor sports. Tiff skied, but otherwise considered the outdoors a necessary evil to be traversed only when she was moving from one heated structure to the next. And she was a woman. She didn't fit the killer's profile.

Keira quickly folded the sheet of paper over the note and placed it in a large envelope, before securing it in the evidence locker. And then she headed toward the front door of the offices for her coat and boots. She had to find Tiffany. That was the only way she could lay to rest the fear coursing through her that her friend was in the hands of a madman.

———

"But this was her weekend off." Keira stared at Eldon Diznoff, who she'd awakened at his home. It was barely eight am and the man looked like he felt every bit as bad as he'd claimed.

"There's nothing I could do; I had to call her in." He wore a ratty bathrobe over his flannel pajama bottoms and a tee shirt. The robe wouldn't have fastened over his protruding belly. "She knows I wouldn't do that if there was any other way. But some of the other workers had the same bug I did. I heard she closed early Friday night. Midnight, Lonny said." Lonny was a bartender, Keira recalled. "I figured maybe she got sick, too. 'Cuz she never answered the phone all day yesterday when I wanted her to go in again. We didn't open at all. Without her, I didn't have enough people to run it. She's not answering today. We'll have to stay closed."

"Did she give Lonny a reason for shutting down Friday?"

He shrugged and coughed into a ham-sized fist. "He says not. That loser probably wanted to get out of there to go bang his girlfriend. He claims it wasn't busy. I call BS. It's always crazy on Fridays."

Turning back toward her car, Keira strove to keep her earlier trepidation from blooming into full-blown panic. Diz's place had been on the way, which was the only reason she'd stopped there first. Tiffany lived in a walk up over a quilting shop near the clinic. That was her next stop.

No one responded to her knock. As far as she knew, she was the only one with a spare key to Tiffany's apartment. The woman didn't trust her mother with one. Rhonda Andrews had taking ways and if she could find something to sell she would.

The place was quiet. Eerily so. And cold. Tiff kept it toasty when she was home, but each time she left she turned the heat way down. Keira walked to the wall-mounted thermostat in the tiny living room. Sixty-two.

It was an odd experience to be in her friend's home when she wasn't there. She checked the bedroom. The bed looked undisturbed. She crossed to the closet and opened it. And her stomach plummeted.

Tiffany's large pink striped overnight bag was sitting on a shelf. So was her black suitcase. Keira scanned the hangers and saw no spaces that looked like clothes had been removed. Turning, she went to the minuscule hallway closet and yanked the door open. Tiff's ski boots sat inside. Her ski jacket and pants were hung neatly on hooks lining the back wall. Wherever the woman had gone, it hadn't been Powderhorn, unless she'd planned to rent her equipment.

And leave without packing a bag.

———

"Probably shacked up with some loser." Since Keira didn't think Rhonda Andrews could be drunk this early in the morning, she decided the effects contributing to the woman's sway and slurred words were a leftover from last night. Tiffany's mother took a deep drag from her cigarette and squinted at Keira through the smoke. "She does that, you know. Finds some bum and goes off with him until he dumps her and she has to come crawling back."

"No," she said pointedly, wanting to reach for the woman's saggy neck. "She doesn't. And Tiff's responsible about her job. She wouldn't just take off knowing Diz was having trouble. At least not without telling him."

"You think you know her so well." Rhonda pointed the cigarette at Keira. "You don't know shit. She went somewhere to have a good time and she doesn't give a damn that we're all worried about her."

With a tight smile, she said, "You do look worried. If you hear from her, please call the office." She turned and went down the listing porch steps.

"Think I don't care about my kid?" the woman hollered through the torn screen door. "Think I don't know her? I know her better than you could. Nosy bitch. You're just like your old man. He was always poking his nose in." The woman was loud enough to have people peeking out the windows of the neighboring trailers. Keira ignored them and the words Rhonda hurled after her. She'd go back to Tiff's place. Talk to the neighbors. Call the owner of the quilt shop beneath the apartment.

But the knot in her chest came from the growing certainty that her efforts would be in vain. She didn't know where Tiffany was. But she was becoming more and more afraid that the woman hadn't left of her own volition.

———

"But you can't be sure whether this is her handwriting." Finn had retrieved his glasses to look over the evidence. Despite his words, the curl taped to the back of the paper was damning, indeed. He'd only seen Keira's friend the one time, but her pale blond hair was unmistakable.

"No. I could get a DNA sample from her house. Her toothbrush." Because that, too, had still been in the apartment. "You could compare the sample to one taken from her hair."

"Right now I'd rather have her toothbrush or other item only she would have used, for elimination fingerprints. See this?" He held a magnifying glass she'd found for him in the evidence room over the note.

"Looks like a thumbprint."

"Likely is." He picked up a sheet of printer paper and mimed handing it to her, his thumb near a top corner, his index finger crooked beneath. "There are other prints on the paper, too. This surface is perfect for pictures or markers, and great for latents. The tape on the message should also be checked. I'd recommend prints as a first test."

"Tiff has a handheld mirror with a mother of pearl back that belonged to her grandmother. She probably uses it daily."

He nodded. "Bring that to the lab. But Keira…" Finn could see the hope bloom on her face. Hated that it was mingled with worry. She'd face danger herself with far greater equanimity than she would consider a threat to her friend. "At the risk of eliciting another less than enthusiastic outburst like yesterday, I need to make it clear that I'm not a fingerprint examiner." Once prints were taken, they could be inputted into databases, but the process was nothing like TV routinely showed. The systems came up with several possible matches, which often then had to be examined by a qualified expert for a more detailed analysis.

"But you ran the latents taken from my house."

"I submitted them to an examiner at Raiker's lab facility. It's Sunday. I can't make any promises about how quickly I can get results."

She hauled in a breath. "That thumbprint might belong to the killer."

"Let's hope. AFIT is a lot more inclusive than IAFIS. Faster, too." The FBI's replacement for IAFIS, the national fingerprint database, would have criminal, military, and millions of civilian prints on record. He was confident he could have possible sets of matching prints an hour and a half after submission. He was less certain that the results wouldn't require verification.

"AFIT not only has improved accuracy, it supposedly reduces the number of manual fingerprint reviews required." Despite his trying to temper her expectations, hope was evident in her tone. "Maybe we'll get lucky."

His gaze fell to the blond hair fastened to the note. If Tiffany Andrews was in the hands of the killer, the woman was going to need far more than luck on her side.

———

After checking with every one of Tiffany's friends that she knew, Keira's next move was to call the Big Powderhorn Resort and the neighboring motels and lodges. The ski resort was in Gogebic County, between Bessemer and Ironwood. It was one of the last places Tiff had mentioned to her. And Keira still harbored a fragile hope the woman had taken an impulsive ski trip.

Logic had a way of shredding that possibility. Tiff had left her belongings and ski clothes at home. More tellingly, her phone charger hadn't been in her apartment, because it was her habit to carry it in her purse. Stoically, Keira went through the motions the same way she did with any missing persons case. By checking all leads.

Two hours later she admitted defeat. There were plenty of places to stay in the Big Powderhorn area, especially with the resort as full as it was now. But none of those she called reported having a Tiffany Andrews registered. If the woman was there, she was staying with someone else under his or her name.

Worry nagged at her, but there wasn't more she could do right now. Keira went back to her spreadsheets. When Finn had come in yesterday, she'd finished a painstaking construction of DNR hunting and fishing violations, going back five years. Hank and Finn had started the process; she'd just completed it. She'd highlighted names that also appeared on the list of people with a grudge against Danny. And now she began eliminating those on both lists who'd been locked up during Danny's murder, or Atwood's. The record was still depressingly long, but far shorter than the one she'd made after her dad's death. She prioritized the other names and decided tomorrow their next step would be to divvy them up and interview the individuals included.

She turned her attention then to establishing a victimology report. Danny. Atwood. And now Yembley. Keira added the four missing persons Mary and Brody had zeroed in on as possibly having an outdoors link. Every detail she knew about each of the victims was listed below their name. People they knew. Places they'd been. Hobbies and occupations. They all shared two connections—a leisure activity that took them outside and a random meeting with a killer. There had to be more.

She paused to make a call to Tobias Matthews, jotting down the additional details the man could provide about Atwood's life. His family. His friends. And then when she hung up she added those facts to the list beneath the second victim's name.

Finally, she put down her pen, drawing lines to the few—very few—links she'd found. Keira needed more information. Now that she had a direction, she'd follow up with the families of the missing persons herself.

Staring at the chart, she wondered about Yembley's portion. If they relied solely on a victim profile that consisted of someone involved with the outdoors, Yembley fit. But she and Finn were convinced the man had been killed because he'd tried to shoot Keira, which would interfere with the plans the killer had for her.

If the offender had kidnapped Tiffany, it had everything to do with her relationship to Keira. She had the thought, struggled to push it aside. She didn't have proof that Tiff was involved. Not yet. Regardless of what the leaden feeling in the pit of her belly was telling her.

They knew the offender was adaptable. She tapped the capped highlighter against her teeth, considering. He likely killed for both necessity and enjoyment. A hot ball of emotion lodged in her throat as she wondered which one her father's death would qualify as.

The buzzer on the door to the department offices sounded. Usually Cal handled visitors. Frowning, Keira got up and went out to check the door. Her step slowed when she drew close enough to recognize Hassert. Letting him in, she said, "Arnie. What brings you here on a Sunday?"

"Oh, I was on my way home after taking Dorie to brunch." He was looking as uncomfortable as she'd ever seen him. His gaze touched on everything in the vicinity but her. "I heard about the shooting the other night. Thought I'd check and see how things turned out."

She tried to hide her surprise. She'd fielded a few calls of concern yesterday, but she'd never thought to hear him voice a similar interest in her wellbeing. "I'm fine. We identified the shooter." She didn't tell him that the man was now dead.

"Well." He put a hand in his coat pocket, jingled some keys he had in it. "That's great then. Great." He was sporting a red plaid hunting hat today, with the earflaps snapped above his ears. "You and I might disagree on occasion, but I never wished you ill."

"I know." It occurred to her then that he hadn't known she was at the office at all. She rarely was on a Sunday. With her SUV in the shop, he couldn't have realized that one of the cruisers in the parking lot belonged to her.

He cleared his throat, his gaze landing on her before skating away again. "Dorie said she heard at church that there was some sort of commotion in the forest this morning."

At church. Of course. Some went to worship. Others to gossip. Keira wondered whom he'd hoped to find to pump for information when he stopped in here. Normally there would only have been a couple of jailers present. "We found a homicide victim. I can't release the individual's name yet, but we believe he's linked to our case."

The man's reaction was immediate. "Was he killed there?"

Ordinarily Keira didn't share those types of details outside of this office, but she was intrigued enough by his response to answer, "We think so, yes."

"I knew it." He slapped his hand against the wall for emphasis. "I've been telling people for years that there are odd goings-on in the forest. I filled out several complaints with your father and the district forester's office about the same thing."

"What were the details of the complaints?"

"Screams. Cries for help." A trickle of foreboding worked down her spine at his words. "I used to do some night hunting in season. Not anymore. Twice there was a person screaming in the distance. And now someone has come to a bad end." He nodded decisively. "I wonder if anyone heard him scream."

"How long ago was this?"

The man pursed his lips. "It's been two years since I stopped night hunting. That would have been about the date of my last complaint to this office about it. But it happened the season before that, too." Apparently what he saw in her expression wasn't reassuring. "I suppose you think the same thing your father did. That I was imagining things. Or that I only heard the normal sounds of predator meeting prey. I was never convinced. Especially now."

She stared at him long enough to have the man fidgeting. "You know what, Arnie? I may check into that myself."

His face remained dour. "Well, Danny sure never gave it any credence. But if you want me to show you sometime whereabouts I heard the sounds, I could retrace my steps. I usually kept to a very precise location when I was out at night."

"I appreciate the offer. Thanks for stopping by."

He didn't seem to know what to do with the pleasantry. In the end, he just turned and walked out as abruptly as he'd appeared.

Keira went to the computer in her office and sat down, bringing up the archived record of incident reports. Criminal complaints filed were kept separate from more routine matters. She brought up the one he'd cited and read it. It had Arnie's name, date, and her dad's initials, which meant that he'd taken the complaint himself. There was a brief description of the encounter, along with the acronym NAT. No Action Taken. A routine note when a call was received that had no actionable response for the department. It took longer to look for the earlier report Arnie had mentioned. It was nearly identical to the one she'd just read.

She rose to pace. Keira doubted that she'd have treated the matter any differently than her father had, and there was nothing in the reports that came close to proof. Or evidence. But they got her thinking, and she was still formulating her thoughts when Finn appeared in the doorway.

For a moment, she forgot the urgency of the tests he'd been doing and pointed a finger at him. "Arnie Hassert was here…doesn't matter." She waved away further explanation of the man's visit. "It just gave me an idea. Maybe we're thinking too small when we just look at how the victims came to the killer's attention. What if he not only uses the outdoors to select them, but also to kill them? He kept Atwood for a while, but we don't know how he died."

She was rambling, and took a moment to haul in a breath and arrange her thoughts. "The outdoors, whether it's forests, wilderness area, wherever…it's his hunting grounds. *His.* He thinks about it as such, at least I believe he does. And the victims…they're tests, maybe. Of his skill. Or his ingenuity."

"Your mind at work is fascinating." He came further into the room as he spoke. "And yes, the scenario you describe makes sense. Does he hunt them? Is that part of his game? Track them down before killing them? I suppose that's something only the dead would know. But as a theory, it's sound."

The dead. There was a quick stabbing pain in her heart. That included Danny. She couldn't prevent the thought that her father would have put the clues together faster. Arrived at conclusions more quickly. Whatever he'd known at the end had died with him.

Her mind belatedly switched gears. "You have results?"

"Yes." He came further into the room as he spoke. "All evidence collected in the forest this morning has been logged, with duplicate copies given to Gomez and Stevens. I did an examination of the footwear tracks." Her stomach did a nasty slow roll in anticipation of his next words. "We've matched them to Yembley and the intruder at your house."

There was a dampness to her palms. Keira resisted the urge to wipe them on the front of her uniform pants. "And the latents?"

"I haven't gotten verification."

She ignored the cautionary note in his voice while her system went straight to panic. "You found Tiffany's prints on the paper." Her eyes slid closed briefly when he inclined his head.

"Rather, I found prints on the note that *seem* to be a close match to those on the hairbrush of hers you brought me. I'm unused to making these announcements without corroboration, but I think we should conclude that the killer has her."

She nodded because she'd known. A niggling fear had taken root inside her as soon as she'd noticed her friend hadn't returned her text. And it had gotten stronger with every failed effort she'd made today to find her. "He took her because of me."

"We don't know enough about him to predict…"

"Yeah, we do." Her voice reflected the bleakness she felt. "She figures in his end game. A pawn. That handwriting was hers, and I didn't even recognize it. We'd never gone to school together…I'd never seen…"

He came to her side and slipped an arm around her shoulders, and for just a moment she allowed herself to take strength from the feel of him beside her.

"We also have a lead on the killer." When she frowned, he said, "That thumbprint? The AFIT system is so much more precise than IAFIS. I'll still want expert validation to be completely certain, but I got a hit from the military database. It belongs to Doug O'Shea. The so-called witness from this morning."

CHAPTER 12

The longer he stayed away, the better Tiffany liked it. Despite the fact that it was too damn cold in the shed even with the heater. And she'd had to pee herself. Several times now. He hadn't been back with food, although he'd given her a drink of water before he'd gone away last time. Taking the note she'd written and that bloody piece of skin and hair with him.

Her stomach hollowed out all over again just thinking about what she'd seen in that box. He'd do the same to her. In a heartbeat. She'd thought he was going to when he'd chopped off her hair with the knife. He'd left shortly after that, and knowing he was going to use what she wrote to lure Keira into a trap was as bad as thinking about what he had planned for Tiffany.

She'd been glad that he'd linked the cuffs around her wrists to the overhead pipe with the length of chain. It had meant she didn't have to have her arms in the air for hours. But she'd spent most of the day with them in that exact position. Because the pipe wasn't smooth. It was some scrap piece of metal that had once served a completely different purpose. It'd been painted several times, and the paint was cracked and peeling off.

But more importantly, it had ridges at one end. In its first lifetime, this section of pipe had screwed into another. And she'd spent hours scraping the length of chain back and forth crosswise over those threads. She'd rest when her arms got tired and lower them for a few minutes, but not for too long. Because she didn't know when the asshole would come back.

And the chain was as ancient as the pipe. There was already wear on the link where she'd been working it across the threads.

A slight sound at the door had her starting, the way she did each time the wind blew or a limb scraped the shed. She waited, muscles bunched, but the door didn't slide open. If it did, she'd quickly move back to the center of the bar, looking scared and hopeless. It wouldn't be much of a stretch. When he came to undo her cuffs again, maybe he wouldn't notice the bright silver glint where she'd worn off the chain's tarnish.

The activity gave her something to concentrate on, and she wasn't concerned when darkness crowded into the shed. Tiffany actually preferred it. She could no longer see the bench that looked like it might hold weapons she could use if she got free. But neither could she view the trophies the asshole had of things he'd killed. She shuddered and lowered her arms for a quick rest. She didn't want to be able to look at the jars that lined the shelf, and she certainly didn't want to see what from here looked like a pair of human feet.

Just the thought of that particular trophy had her raising her arms and rubbing the chain against the pipe again. She was going to make damn sure that neither she nor Keira ended up on that shelf.

It took time for Keira to put the warrant together. Even longer, apparently to convince Judge Isaacson that Doug O'Shea—who as it turned out sang in the choir with him —was guilty of killing at least three people. Of kidnapping another. Finn thought she might be having the same difficulty considering the man as a possible suspect. That came, he supposed, from living in a place where you knew almost every damn body.

"We play it low key." If Keira's deputies were surprised that the order came from him, they hid it well. Finn had argued his case in private with Keira and she'd reluctantly agreed. This was a major reason she'd brought him on board. There could be no appearance of a conflict of interest. Never was that more crucial than at the moment of arrest. "Everyone clear on their team's responsibility?" He scanned the faces in front of him. All were dressed in riot gear and armored vests. "Then let's go. We'll roll up silent."

No lights. No sirens. No notice. They filed out of the office and separated for their cars, two by two. He climbed into the cruiser with Keira. Only then did Finn give voice to the doubts plaguing him. "If he's our guy— and that thumbprint says he is—O'Shea is dangerous and unpredictable."

"And you would have preferred a surprise breach. I get it. But we didn't get a no-knock warrant. This isn't Chicago."

"Or DC," he muttered, watching the snow-draped trees flash by as they headed out of town. "But that note was issued today. He'll be on high alert."

Her face was still as stone in the shadows. He wasn't sure how familiar she was with the man, but based on their friendliness at the scene this morning, he guessed they knew each other quite well. "If he's taken by surprise he may come docilely. That message was just a taunt to let me know he has my friend. He can't realize that we found the thumbprint, or traced it to him."

Finn remained silent. That might be true enough, but in his book, having Tiffany in the man's custody put the woman in imminent danger, which should have been enough for a no-knock warrant. He pushed the thought aside. They'd work within the parameters that the judge had given them. And hope like hell there were no surprises.

Keira had briefed them on the layout of O'Shea's property. Single story home straight ahead of the drive with attached garage. Machine shed on the right, two hundred feet inside the property. Woods surrounding the space on three sides. He could already picture it in his head because it sounded like half the homes he'd seen in the county.

The moon hung full and heavy in the sky and for the briefest of moments he entertained the memory of it last night, fingers of moonbeams slanting through the skylight. Then he wiped his mind clean as she flipped off her headlights and turned into a long snow covered drive. Showtime.

Two minutes later Keira stood on one side of the front door and Finn on the other. They didn't speak at all. With his fingers, he indicated the countdown. Three. Two. One. He reached out to hammer on the door while she drilled the bell with her forefinger. He kept an eye on the garage. Mary had circled the house to cover any back entrances.

A light flicked on in the hallway and Doug O'Shea's face showed through the crack he'd made between the curtains covering the door's window. Finn threw her a cautionary look, which she couldn't see and wouldn't have needed anyway. She'd gone through more doorways than he had. She knew to be ready for a weapon.

But O'Shea didn't have anything in his hands when he pulled the door open. He blinked at Keira, sparing hardly a glance for Finn before fumbling with the lock on the storm door. "Keira. Did you have more questions about today?"

She had the warrant in her free hand. Her weapon in the other. She held out the paper. "We have a warrant to search your property, Doug. You need to show us your hands. Step away from the door."

The man was shy of sixty, but the confusion on his features, the utter lack of comprehension was like that of someone decades older.

"Step back," Keira repeated, and this time, O'Shea slowly raised his hands and moved aside. He seemed shocked when they came in and she shoved the warrant into his hand while Finn patted him down for weapons. Finding none, he radioed Mary to join them inside.

"What...I don't understand." Finn left them standing in the hallway to conduct a search of the house. Minutes later, when he'd determined it was empty, he made his way back to the dining room where a shell-shocked Doug was seated in a chair.

"There's no one here." The man raised his gaze to Finn's. "I keep telling them that. What's going on? Is this about that body today? Because I went to Critical Care afterward to get something for my nerves. The Valium they gave me knocked me out. I slept most of the day and woke up with you pounding on my door."

"We need to ask you more questions, Doug."

"And this is how you do it? Break into a man's house? What the hell, Keira, your father would never..."

Finn didn't wait to hear more. He checked the garage. Found a pair of snow boots there sitting neatly next to the step. He reached under his vest and pulled out a large evidence bag that he'd brought along for just this reason. Set the boots inside. There was a gun cabinet in the house, and he needed to get the key. He didn't know how long it would take for ballistics to be done on Yembley's body. But O'Shea's weapons would have to be compared...

The radio on his belt crackled. "The woman isn't here. But there's other stuff. Keira and Finn, you'll want to see this."

Minutes later they had O'Shea loaded in the car and left Mary with him as they strode back to the shed where Hank, Phil, and Brody met them at the door.

"Is there any sign that Tiffany's been here?" Keira's tone was tight as she moved into the building and scanned the interior. Without waiting for an answer she crossed to an area beneath the watery overhead lights and crouched. "Looks like blood."

Finn came to kneel next to her. After a minute he nodded. "We'll test the stain for hemoglobin. But this guy's a trapper, you said. It might not be human."

"We found this." They straightened and turned to join Hank, who was standing in front of a tool bench. The pegboard and tools that had hung above it had been taken down. Silently they looked at what had been uncovered.

A computer printed list with Tiffany's address and details. *Lives alone. No dog. Curb parking. Work. Park back lot. Mon. Left 1:27 am. Tues. Left 2:22 am.* There was more. Much more. He must have watched the woman for days. Keira stood there a moment longer, her jaw clenching and unclenching until Finn nudged her to get her attention. She switched her gaze to the photos scattered across the wall. They had been taken at night. Longitude and latitude were noted on each along with a big red X and a time. Three am. "What is this?" she muttered.

He wasn't sure himself. "Ideas where to hide her?"

She peered more closely. "You could get these from Google Earth. Or maybe some other sort of geospatial technology." Finn nodded at Phil. From the camera in the man's hand, he knew he'd already started a photographic log. The entire place needed to be documented before the evidence was collected.

"Found this," Hank said. When he pulled a drawer out of the workbench, Finn saw a package of photo paper and a black Sharpie. "And there are stray strands of blond hair all over this place."

"There's more," Brody put in excitedly. Keira and Finn followed the man around the woodpile stacked neatly in the far corner of the shed. Wedged between two logs in the center of the pile was a rifle.

Keira looked at it for a long time, before glancing at Finn. "You can stay to complete the search. I'm taking Doug O'Shea in for questioning."

"I want to help. I do." The man shook his head helplessly. "But I don't know what we're talking about here. Who is the 'she' you're looking for? What am I supposed to have done with her? *Why* would I do anything with her?" His expression turned pleading as he looked from a silent Mary to Keira. "Help me help you. Tell me what this is all about."

It was difficult to conduct a criminal interview of a man she'd known most of her life. One she'd liked. Admired. Respected. Harder still to Mirandize him and listen to him waive his right to legal counsel. Although a law enforcement officer's dream, that move was rarely in a suspect's best interest. Doug O'Shea was going to need a very good defense attorney.

Keira opened the file she'd carried in the room with her and placed a picture of the message she'd received today on the table in front of them. "Last night after Dizzy's closed, you kidnapped Tiffany Andrews."

O'Shea's gaze bounced from the paper to Keira's face. "Wait. What?"

"You forced her to write this note," she continued inexorably. "You cut her hair and attached some of it to the back."

"No. No. I would never..."

She pitched her voice over his. "Tell me where you've hidden her. I'm not going to play hide and go seek, you understand? The games are over."

"Games?" The man rubbed his forehead. "What games?"

"The ones you played with my father before killing him." The sound Doug made could have come from a wounded animal. "The game you played with your second victim. The one you engaged in with Bruce Yembley..."

"What the hell are you talking about?" O'Shea asked in a roar.

Satisfied to have gotten a response, Keira sat back in her chair. "We found paper that matched this in your workshop." She tapped the photo of the message between them. "A Sharpie. It will require lab testing but the paper and marker will match the note, written in

Tiffany's hand. There was a rifle concealed in your wood pile that I'm guessing will turn out to be the one used to kill Bruce Yembley." She wondered for an instant if it were the same one that had been fired at her. Her father's weapon.

She abruptly switched tactics. "It's hard…what you've gone through." He blinked at the softness in her tone. "No one else can understand the kind of pain you've experienced. No one cares. No one respects you. Look at everything you've accomplished. Played by the rules all your life, didn't you and where the hell did it ever get you?"

He frowned. "You know better than that. No. No, I don't feel that way."

"You told me yourself, everyone cheats out in the wild."

"That's not what I said."

"They bend the regulations. But not you, you follow all the guidelines, but so what? Do you get gold stars from the DNR when you play fair while trapping? Bet you don't. Everyday you see people screwing around and no one steps in. Maybe you wanted to even the score. Or perhaps you decided to teach them a lesson."

The man slumped in his chair, hands folded in front of him. Every now and then he'd give a weary shake of his head, but that was the most she got from him until she changed tacks.

"You tell us where she is right now and we're looking at a completely different situation."

"I wish I could." There was a sheen in his eyes before he blinked it away. "Tiffany…she was a good kid. I don't know where she is."

"You'd be cooperating." Keira was growing hoarse. "We'd make sure and note that. We need your assistance.

You're in charge here. You're still in control of the game. Help us find her."

O'Shea's voice, his expression, were exhausted. "I think I want a lawyer."

————

"You did well in there." Finn handed Keira a bottle of water when she returned from the interview room. He'd only caught the tail end of the interview on the closed circuit TV in the next room, but she'd come at the man from several different ways. Playing it tough, sympathetic, indifferent, then soft. He wasn't so sure he wouldn't have broken himself under the pressure.

Instead of drinking the water she held the bottle to her forehead. "I don't know. I'm not sure he's our guy."

"All evidence to the contrary." And there was evidence. A ton of it. Enough to tie O'Shea up in a bow. "If that rifle turns out to be your father's, you might be singing a different tune."

She lowered the bottle to glare at him. "I've done my share of interviews, okay? I'm not letting emotion sway me here. I get anyone in that room for as many hours as I questioned him, and he doesn't budge, I'm going to have doubts. I'm going to recheck my facts."

"Fair enough." Finn did the same when test results didn't add up. He verified and re-verified trying to discover the source of the problem. "But you can't tell me you've never come across a killer before that no one would suspect. That case I mentioned with the bodies in the South Carolina swamps? The perpetrator was a pillar of the community. Ran the local food pantry. Sunday school teacher. An officer at the bank. His neighbors are probably still shell-shocked."

Keira nodded reluctantly. "Okay, yeah. Of course, I've had my share of suspects like that, too. But this is just a little too neat. We found nothing in the house; it's all in the shed. It could have been planted. The padlock he had securing it is a joke. Everything we discovered could have been placed there to make it look like we had our guy."

"Except the thumbprint on the paper," he reminded her.

"Right. I haven't figured that out yet." She paused a moment before asking, "What about the boots?"

"They're tens," he admitted. "But..." He waylaid her next words. "It would be easy enough to wear a larger pair to disguise his size."

"Which would make perfect sense...if we'd found a second pair."

"I've never been on a case yet where every piece of evidence fits. Where we can figure out every single move an offender made and why. O'Shea could be convicted based on what was on his property. He has no alibi for any of the nights in question. Don't be too ready to dismiss him. We didn't find your friend, but maybe those photos tell us exactly where to look."

She finally twisted the cap off the water bottle. Brought it to her lips to drink. "And could be that's why we found them. Because the game can't start until the killer gets all his players in one place."

––––––––

He could label them leadership skills if he wanted, she thought later, but she preferred to call a spade a spade. And Finn Carstens didn't *lead* her toward leaving work that night. He *bullied* her into doing so.

She'd allowed it because she was ready to pitch face forward. It was well after midnight. Keira had sent her deputies home long ago. She and Finn still had to analyze those photos and pinpoint the locations and scout them. Both would take hours of work. In the meantime, they were going in circles about O'Shea's culpability. They needed to start fresh tomorrow.

Keira hoped from the bottom of her heart that Tiffany had that long.

Once she got to the cabin, she was too tired to eat. Too weary to do anything but crawl into bed. Finn slipped under the covers beside her minutes later. And the warmth of his body next to hers had a measure of her tension slipping away.

"You could have eaten." The man didn't do well skipping meals and eating on the random schedule she often kept.

"I had a PopTart."

She surprised herself by smiling. "You bought PopTarts? What are you, eight?"

"Only my palate. Actually," his arm snaked out to settle her closer against him. "I had two."

"Well, I don't want to hear any more complaints from you about food then." Her smile faded away as the urgency of their discoveries today returned. "I wonder if he's feeding her."

Finn didn't utter empty platitudes. He just swept a comforting hand down her spine. Up again. "Whatever he has in store for her, she'll need her strength." Diz said Tiffany had closed the bar at midnight. She might have been too busy at work to check her phone, but it would have been the first thing she did once she got home. *If* she'd gotten home. She'd left Dizzy's nearly forty-eight hours ago. Had she eaten in that time? Been given something to drink? Was she terrified, wondering why Keira hadn't found her yet?

"I think she was trying to send me a message on that note," she whispered. Her eyes were open in the darkness. How could she sleep knowing her friend was in danger? "I don't get it. I can't figure out what she was trying to tell me."

"You will."

But she wasn't so sure. And if she did, she didn't know if it would be in time. "Tiff didn't deserve this." The thought brought guilt, but also a flare of anger. "She wouldn't have come to his attention if it weren't for me."

"Random acts of violence can happen to anyone. Anywhere. And she has you to depend on." His voice was a husky murmur in her ear. "You're her best chance of escaping this. So you focus on that. Bringing her home. And everything that happens after."

Everything that happens after. It occurred to her that she had no idea what that involved. Certainly it meant Finn would be gone, back to DC. And she…Keira still wasn't sure what the future held for her. Not long-term anyway.

"Sometime I want you to visit Ohio." It was as if he'd plucked the thought from her head. "Meet my parents. My sister. They'll like you. Not the fact that you're from Michigan, of course. Buckeyes are equally disparaging of both the Spartans and the Wolverines."

She smiled, as he'd meant her to. "As it happens, I'm a Northwestern alum."

"A Wildcat. Fitting."

"I'll do you the favor of *not* introducing you to my mother."

"I don't know why not. Mothers love me. I'm adorable."

He was. She drew in a shaky breath. Released it. Finn Carstens was all manner of things, all of them admirable. Most of which she was beginning to think that she didn't want to let go of.

And that realization terrified her at least as much as the killer she was convinced was still on the loose.

———————

Dorie Hassert cooed over the doughnuts he'd brought from the Kwik-E-Station and turned to get some plates. She was a lot more amenable to being awakened in the middle of the night for a fuckfest than she was at being called at four-thirty. He'd figured the pastries would go a long way to smoothing things over.

She set a cup of coffee in front of him and he reached for it, already knowing it would be weak. When she offered him a doughnut he shook his head. "I bought those for you."

Dorie beamed. "They're just as sweet as you are."

She should just paste the damn things to her ass. From the looks of her, he was fairly certain that's where they'd end up. "I can't stay. Just wanted a few minutes with you before work."

Lifting a pastry to her lips, she took a large bite, which left her with a frosting mustache. "I heard there was something big going on in town last night."

He stilled. Gossip was the only attraction she held for him. If a mouse so much as farted in Munising, she knew about it. "How big can it be in Munising on a Sunday night?"

Her brows arched. "I have a friend who's a cook at the prison and they do the meals for the county jail. And

290 | KYLIE BRANT

she overheard that the sheriff arrested Doug O'Shea for something last night and that he spent the night in lockup. Doug O'Shea! Can you imagine?"

"Don't know him," he lied, lifting the mug to his lips again. That was fast. Damn fast. A part of him might have been a little impressed at how quickly Saxon and her special consultant had put it all together. He dismissed the feeling. Jesus, he'd practically drawn them a map. And they'd been led down the exact path he'd wanted them to go.

Adrenaline fired through his veins and he drained the cup. Set it down. Things had gelled faster than he'd expected, but that was fine. Everything was ready. All the pieces were in place.

"I'll see you later." He stood, not even hearing the woman's protests. There were people who paid big money to go on safaris or to kill a rare animal in the wild. They were suckers, all of them. They'd never know that they didn't have to go to Africa for a real hunting challenge. And they sure as hell didn't have to spend a fortune.

He had his hunt lined up right here on the UP. It would be the most thrilling kill of his life.

———

"Thanks for your help," Keira told Gary Paulus. "I'm not sure we could have found all of those spots depicted in the photos on our own without getting hopelessly lost." They'd spent hours with the man, first at her office with his computer and forestry maps and then in the Hiawatha Forest. It had been slow going, but eventually he'd helped them locate each of the areas. They'd taken daylight pictures at all of the spots.

WHAT THE DEAD KNOW | 291

Every time they'd reached a new location, she'd given a mental sigh of relief. They hadn't found Tiffany at any of the spots. It had been twelve degrees last night. She wouldn't have survived had the killer left her outside overnight.

"No problem, Sheriff." Paulus' face was unusually sober. "I figure there aren't many around here who know the forest as well as I do. I was glad to be able to help in some small way. After seeing what the guy did to the body we saw yesterday..." He swallowed and looked away. "I hope you find him." With a friendly wave, he walked toward his truck.

She and Finn headed toward the cruiser. "Now would be the time to thank me for rounding up those snowmobile pants you're wearing." Each of them was dressed similarly, although initially he had argued against the need. Some of the places they'd hiked today had had drifts up to their hips.

"Thank you," he parroted as he opened up the passenger door.

"Insincere, but I'll take it." She got in the vehicle and shivered. Despite the warm clothes, it was going to take her a while to thaw out from their excursion today. Her toes felt frozen, even with the three pair of socks and boots. Keira put the key in the ignition and started it. But before she could do anything else, her phone rang. Taking out her cell, she looked at the screen.

"It's Phil," she said in an aside before answering it. "Hey," she said to the undersheriff. "We just finished here." She listened for a couple of minutes. "Okay. Thanks for the update."

Finn reached out to turn up the heat, although she could have told him they'd be back at the office before warm air flowed through the vents. She lowered the phone. Looked at him. "Doug O'Shea just made bail."

His oath was vicious. "Unbelievable. Why doesn't that judge just give him a fat juicy kiss on the ass while he's at it?"

She winced. "An interesting visual image, and one I prefer not to contemplate. This wasn't totally unexpected. Isaacson would have been amenable to a prompt bail hearing. O'Shea's not a flight risk, as he's lived and worked in the area for decades. He also has no criminal record. Plus, we didn't find Tiffany on his property. That might have been the deciding factor."

Finn's tone was baleful. "At least tell me they put an electronic tracking bracelet on our main suspect."

"They did." And she owed the county prosecutor for that one. She couldn't afford the man hours necessary to provide around the clock surveillance on O'Shea. Keira nosed the car toward the blacktop at the entrance of the forest. "But that means he can't get to Tiffany. If we don't find her quickly, she starves." The thought struck genuine fear in her heart.

"I've been thinking about that. The killer will believe he's considered every angle. What better way to 'prove' his innocence than with an ankle bracelet or surveillance putting him at home when we find your friend?"

She mulled over the suggestion. "He'd have to have an accomplice in that case. Someone to show up in the forest with Tiffany in the middle of the night. He'd know we would check the places out as soon as possible to make sure she wasn't there." The idea was plausible. In that scenario, she had no doubt that a defense attorney could get O'Shea's charges dropped. If the killer was indeed O'Shea. "The offender doesn't seem the type to delegate the big moment to someone else."

"He would if it meant he'd be free to try again another day."

Okay, it was possible. "All this from a man who once told me he didn't deal in theoreticals."

Finn pulled his gloves off and began rubbing his hands together to warm them. "I don't know if I've ever been this cold," he muttered before switching back to the topic. "The other alternative is that the killer isn't O'Shea. He's still out there, and he's counting on leaving no witnesses when we go after Tiffany."

The second scenario seemed more probable. "Okay, either way. He knows we wouldn't arrive at any of those forest locations at three am alone. That's why he posted ten pictures, to divide up the law enforcement team we'd be sure to bring." And once he could be assured of only dealing with a few of them at a time, he'd wait in ambush.

"You've been at the center of this from the beginning," Finn said. He dragged off a stocking hat she'd borrowed for him from Brody. Her lips quirked. His hair beneath it was mussed endearingly. "It's you he wants at his final showdown. This is his big endplay. You have to be a part of it. So…how's he going to be certain you're the one who discovers the spot where he'll be with Tiffany?"

She looked at him and knew they had the same thought. "I know how I would ensure it," Keira said grimly.

"So do I." Leaning forward a little, he held his hands up by the air vents. "Head over to the county garage. Let's get under the car and see if he put a GPS device on it."

"All the spots are in the Hiawatha Forest." Keira had the photos they'd recovered in O'Shea's shed displayed on the wall of the conference room. Below each was the daylight picture she and Finn had taken of the same location earlier today. "As you can see there is ten total. No two are less than three miles apart. The furthest distance between any two is twelve miles."

"They all look alike," Phil said. "Lots of trees."

"Each area is well away from any roads or paths," Finn put in.

"And you didn't find the woman at any of these places?"

He shook his head in response to Hank's question. "Which wasn't totally unexpected. The time on the photos says three am. In the meantime, we can be fairly certain the offender is holding the victim in some sort of structure."

It was difficult to hear her friend referred to that way. *The victim.* Keira shoved away the feeling. She needed to be a cop first. That's what was going to help bring Tiffany home.

"The one thing the places have in common is there are plenty of pines in the areas," she said. And they'd been chosen with one thought in mind, she knew. Cover for the killer. There were many deciduous trees in the forest that were denuded now, and would provide little in the way of safety. She wondered if the offender had given a thought to the fact that the scattered copses of firs would furnish shelter for them as well.

"So what's his game plan?" Mary put in. "Lead us like lambs to the slaughter to these sites?"

"That's how he'll think of it, yes." The group grew even soberer at Keira's response.

"I'll coordinate with MSP and the criminal investigators from the Forest Service and the NPS. We'll want to muster as large a team as we can when we go in."

"It won't be tonight," Phil said flatly. "There's a blizzard warning advisory for the county. The wind's supposed to start blowing at eleven pm. They're predicting gusts of forty miles an hour."

Frustration slashed through her. "And we all know how accurate the weather forecasts are." Another delay. Try as she might, Keira couldn't help feel like Tiffany's time was running out.

Finn's voice was quiet. "Putting a response operation together is going to take time. We don't want to make the mistake of underestimating this offender. Earlier today we discovered that there's a tracking device on Keira's cruiser." He waited for the comments from the group to die down before going on. "We examined it for prints, but it had been wiped clean. Then we put it back in place. Keira will switch vehicles if she needs to keep her location secret, but otherwise we want the offender to think we don't suspect anything."

"That's one ballsy SOB," Hank murmured. "You've only been driving it since your SUV was in the shop. He couldn't get to it in your garage. Which means he may have accessed the cruiser here in the lot, probably when it was dark."

"He thrives on risk. Remember that." She sneaked a look at the clock. Felt tightness in her chest when she saw the hour. "Phil and Hank, you'll be calling the realtors on these lists." Keira pushed the papers across the table toward the men. "We want information on any properties in the vicinity on private lots that aren't vacant now, but are currently being rented. Ours is a small county. Chances are the real estate agents know many of the landlords. Once you get their names, split them with Mary and Brody to follow up with."

She switched her attention to the other two deputies. "We're looking for any other property Doug O'Shea may be renting." If he had somewhere else he was keeping Tiffany, it'd be close, for convenience sake. "See if you can get the landlords to give you the renters' contact information, and the addresses." They couldn't be compelled to do so, but Keira was betting many of them would. "We don't have much time. Let's get on it."

————

"Listen to that wind howl. You're going to have to give the meteorologist props for calling this one right." It was after midnight. If Keira had had her way, she'd still be in the office. Instead they were in bed. Despite the hour, Finn wondered if she would sleep. She was wound as tightly as he'd ever seen her.

"We could have been out there tonight. In a few hours, this would all have been over."

And therein lay the source of her frustration. And his. "Waiting is the worst part. But tomorrow we put the finishing touches on our tactical response." She'd contacted the agencies to be involved, and begun to devise the team. But there would be far more to be done to ready for the showdown with a madman. "The offender has been planning this for months. We have to strategize just as carefully." Finn's arms were around her, but she was stiff in his embrace, her muscles tense.

"Before I worked homicide I responded to more than my share of domestic calls." Her voice was husky. "They were volatile because of how quickly they could go sideways. I had a couple that turned into hostage situations. We had to respond with the captives' safety in mind, but I couldn't think of them as individuals. They were part of the setting, and as such defined our response. But I had to remain objective to do my job."

His arms tightened, as he understood the correlation she was making. "Your thinking has been clear throughout this case, despite your father and Tiffany's involvement."

"And sometimes that makes me feel like I'm letting them down another way." The words were a whisper drifting in the darkness. "Three days. That's how long it took to find Danny's body. And that's how long it will be if we don't get to Tiff before tomorrow night."

He knew exactly where her thoughts were heading. "It's different with her."

"Is it?"

"She isn't part of the challenge for him the way your father was. He needs her alive." He tasted the lie on his lips as soon as he uttered it. The killer merely needed them to believe the woman was alive. "We won't be too late." They couldn't be.

"The entire time we searched for my father, he was already dead. But I still felt like I failed him. I can't fail Tiffany."

"You won't. *We* won't." He brushed the hair from her face, his fingers pausing when they felt moisture on her cheeks. Finn felt his heart constrict. He knew better than most that there was a limit to the loss each person could handle. He'd do what he could to make sure that Keira didn't suffer another one.

CHAPTER 13

Keira spent hours on the phone the next morning, coordinating with the different agencies that would join them for the operation tonight, and lining up the equipment they'd need. She'd hoped to have a strategy meeting with representatives from all the entities involved. But the aftermath of the storm would make travel difficult until later in the day. She'd have to content herself with getting everyone here at nine pm to fine-tune every aspect of the plan she and Finn had hammered out. They were in the process of sharing it with her deputies.

She looked at the people gathered in the conference room. "We found ten photos of possible locations where the action may take place tonight. The killer probably selected that many to ensure that he doesn't have to deal with more than one or two of us at any one place. He knows we'll try to cover as many of them as we can."

"Are going to have twenty people?" Hank asked.

Her mouth kicked up wryly. "Doubtful. Finn and I are in the process of prioritizing the locations. Some would be slightly more beneficial for access than others. It will be a struggle to reach the areas. More so for him. He's going to be bringing an unwilling captive with him, which will slow him down. He'll have a method figured out in advance. You can count on that."

"So he set the thing up for three am. We get there a couple of hours earlier. Catch him before he gets things in place."

"Good thought," Finn said to Brody. "Unfortunately, these spots he's chosen also allow access from multiple sides. We could be watching an area, and he could show up from behind it."

"Or behind us," Phil muttered.

Keira nodded. "That might be his plan. Pen us in. We have to be ready for anything. We'll use two-man teams to cover as many of the spots as possible, focusing on those we deem high priority." She had to force the next words out of her suddenly dry throat. "There will be a civilian in the center of things. She's the bait that draws us there, and he knows she'll provide a distraction." While the offender wouldn't consider Tiffany's safety, it would be of utmost concern for law enforcement. That gave the killer an advantage.

"I'm in the process of acquiring enough Kevlar for everyone. That includes helmets." She scanned the group. She'd go over this several more times before this evening, with each person taking part in the mission. "Under no circumstances does anyone go without armor." The vests and helmets would be heavy and cumbersome. They'd also be lifesaving. "As we final' things we'll update you. Everyone will meet here th evening at ten pm. I suggest grabbing a couple of sleep after work if possible."

That got a few laughs, and Keira smiled. With anticipation running high, there wasn't a person in the room who would be able to unwind before this thing was over. And, depending on the outcome, maybe not even then. "Thanks to our talented consultant here…" she gestured toward Finn, "…we might have put this thing together faster than the killer expects. If he doesn't appear this evening, we'll try it again tomorrow. And the night after that."

"Maybe he won't come at all," Brody suggested.

"Oh, he will," she replied grimly. "This is his show. You can be sure he'll want to be in the center of it. Until then, we keep working our assignments. Where are we on landlords of rental properties?"

"We got a lot of names of renters," Hank noted. "O'Shea isn't one of them."

Keira glanced at Finn. Not for the first time she wondered if they were spinning their wheels with Doug O'Shea. Then she thought of Tiffany and her resolved hardened. If she wanted to find her friend, she'd follow every lead. "Keep me posted."

When her deputies filed out of the room minutes later, Phil Milestone remained. "Just wanted you to be aware that I'm planning on being there tonight." The jut of his jaw told her that he expected an argument. He wasn't going to get one. His arthritis might tire him faster than some of the younger deputies, but there was no one whose instincts she trusted more.

"Damn straight you are." She smiled slightly. "We need every man we can get. Wear your long johns. Finn and I nearly froze out there yesterday."

"Supposed to be another cold one tonight." He gave her a long look. "I expect we're all more than ready for this to be over."

Over. Keira stared at the man's retreating back. She'd dearly love to think about the ordeal being concluded. But only if it meant that it ended with her friend unharmed. The killer behind bars, and the rest of her team safe. Life didn't come with those kinds of guarantees.

When she looked at Finn, he was bent over his computer, engrossed in something. Keira went back to her office, but once there, she couldn't seem to concentrate. She bounced out of her chair and roamed the room, hands shoved in her pants pockets. She thought better on the move. And right now, her mind was teaming.

She was missing something. Had been all along. At least, that's the way it felt. As if something was right there, almost within her grasp before slipping away again. Going to the victimology profile she'd taped to the wall, she stared at it as if it would suddenly give her the answers she sought. The outdoors was the link that connected the victims to the killer but as Finn had pointed out more than once, they knew far too little about the offender.

Reaching up, she traced each of the victim's names with her index finger. What did the offender do with the bodies? If he were responsible for killing some of the missing persons, as they believed, his victims would number a half dozen, not counting Yembley. That man had been murdered out of rage, not because he fit a victim profile. Aside from his, only one body had been found. Her father's.

She ignored the pang the thought brought. Why had Danny's been discovered when none of the others had? Finn had once speculated that her dad had wounded the killer. They knew Danny had fired two shots. If he'd injured the other man badly, it would explain why his body had been left where it fell.

In a wilderness area. Where he'd be unlikely to be found.

Keira backed up enough to prop her hips on her desk. She was drawing closer to something now. She stared at the sheet on the wall and let her thoughts wander.

I figure there aren't many around here that know the forest as well as I do. The district forester's words came back to her. But the killer knew the region at least as well. Keira had once told Finn how many places there were on the UP where the unwary could disappear. The Hiawatha Forest housed some of those spots. The Big Island Lake Wilderness was about eighteen miles away. Her dad had died in the Rock River Canyon Wilderness area near here. People who knew the forest would be familiar with those areas.

That thought summoned another. Keira turned and sat down at her desk, bringing up the Alger Herald and typing forest in the search window. That elicited a long list of varied stories. Several, however, dealt with the same topic. *Friends of the Forest.*

The title was familiar. Keira brought up one article after another and skimmed them to re-familiarize herself with the organization. Its missions were conservation, recreation, and education about matters concerning the forest. Various agencies supported it, from what she could see, including DNR, foresters, and the National Park Service. Many of the articles had pictures. The group relied on volunteers, and its activities often revolved around kids. Offering hiking, botany lessons, reptile education… Keira stopped at one picture that showed Doug O'Shea with a broad smile on his face, a mob of children surrounding him. In his hand he was holding a flier about signing up for a tracking class.

She flipped through the articles faster, this time concentrating more on the pictures than the text. One story concerned the founding members of the Friends of the Forest. Before the article could open, Finn came into her office. His expression succeeded in distracting her for a moment. "What's wrong?"

He looked mildly disturbed. "What do you know about Roger Wilson's life before he came to Munising?"

"Nothing." Her tone was wry. "I don't know a lot about his life since he's been here, to tell the truth. He seems to live quietly."

Finn nodded. "That's what I've discovered. But he was in the military before he moved to the UP. He was a sniper for the Marines. And he received a general discharge." She must have looked blank because he continued. "That's not an honorable discharge. It means he performed less than satisfactorily, or there was some unacceptable conduct on his part."

"That's a bit hard to believe," she said doubtfully. "He seems to be a rule follower." When Finn cocked a brow, she remembered the story about the man and her mother, all those years ago. "Okay, maybe not. What sort of behavior are we talking about?"

"The military doesn't release that information."

Then it was irrelevant, as far as Keira was concerned. "Why are you looking at his record, anyway?"

Finn approached her desk, holding a few pieces of paper. "I told you I'd look further into both his and Fallon's backgrounds. I've finally gotten the results."

Annoyance filtered through her. "Hank would have had to undergo an extensive background check for this job. I'm sure it's as thorough as whatever you were able to do. Maybe more so."

She'd expected an argument. So when he said nothing, his silence alerted her. Keira wrestled with herself for a minute before giving a mental sigh. "You found something." The muscles in her belly clenched. Investigating her deputies made her feel disloyal. Especially since she never believed Hank had belonged on the list for someone with a grudge against her father.

"I think you have to know." But Finn didn't look any happier about sharing the information than she was to receive it. He set a page on her desk. "There's a rumor in town that he's having an affair."

Impatience filled her. "I don't deal in gossip and conjecture. Especially when it comes to my employees. And where would you even hear this?" If he wasn't in the lab, Finn was at her side. It wasn't as though he had time to sit in the diner with Dorie and hear all the latest scuttle about what was going on in town.

He gave her a level look. "I hired someone to come and talk to people. Just to ask a few discreet questions. The gentleman even struck up a conversation with Hank's wife at the grocery store. Talked about her son, Zeke. The flu season. The woman told him how lucky they'd been because the boy had been healthy all winter, unlike last year when he was constantly sick." He saw her expression and nodded grimly. "Yeah. I wouldn't have bothered you with this, except for that fact. If Hank's child wasn't in the hospital, why wasn't he at the forest when we responded to the call about Yembley's body?"

———

"I've got a few more names of those properties I was following up on," Hank told Keira when she summoned him to her office. "I can get them if you want."

She was at her desk. She didn't invite him to take a seat. "I wanted to talk to you about something else." Her gaze direct, she asked, "How's your son?"

He looked immediately wary. "Zeke? He's fine. I mean, he's better."

"You called Phil the morning we responded to the call about Yembley's body and said you'd been in the hospital with him and couldn't join us until later." A muscle twitched in the man's jaw. "Care to revise that story?"

He looked away. After a moment, he said, "I never lied to you."

"You lied to my undersheriff, knowing he'd pass the message on to me, so it's the same thing." Impatience filled her. "What's going on with you, Hank?"

She'd never seen him look so uncomfortable. "I've… Amy and I are having problems. There's…I'm seeing someone else." At that moment, Keira knew Finn's information had been correct. She didn't want to hear any of the details. There was only one course of action to take. "And you were with her when we got the call?"

He nodded miserably. She gave a long sigh. "Get your things and go home. You're suspended for a week without pay."

The man's attention snapped to hers. "You can't…" He swallowed what he was going to say. "I know I screwed up, Sheriff. But it's the first time, and I swear it will be the last. You need me tonight. So does the team."

"We have to have people we can depend on. Apparently that isn't you." His face darkened, but he went silent. "Get your life in order before you come back. I don't interfere in my deputies' private lives, but yours affected the job. Fix it."

After a brief hesitation he gave a jerky nod, and turned on his heel and went out the door.

Once he'd gone, Keira put her head in her hands. Damn it all to hell. The timing couldn't be worse. When her door opened again minutes later, she jerked upright. Relaxed a bit when she saw Finn.

"Now I know why they used to shoot the messenger."

He came in, dropped into a chair. "Was it bad?"

She released an impatient breath. "No, it was pathetic. He's a good deputy. Great skills, impressive instincts. How can he be so stupid?" There was nothing to be done about it now. "Lying to his superior would get him fired in most departments I know of. The fact that he's usually a damn fine investigator meant he only got a week's suspension. But he's not on the op tonight."

"He shouldn't be." Finn's expression was grim. "We don't want anyone on the team we can't trust, especially with the stakes we're facing."

"We can't afford to be down a man either," she shot back, and then shook her head. "There's nothing to be done about it now. We'll make do with the people we have."

"You were pretty engrossed in something when I came in earlier." He nodded toward her computer. "Was it important?"

With difficulty, she tried to pick up the mental threads she'd been following before he'd interrupted her. "It was something Paulus said yesterday, about knowing the forest well. And I started wondering who else might be as familiar with it. We've followed up with hunters and trappers. But there's a group called Friends of the

Forests." She turned back to her computer and selected another story and clicked on it. "Obviously, there are representatives from various government agencies. But there are volunteers in this organization who might be of interest to us." She pressed the command to print the picture and after a moment her printer began to whir.

Finn retrieved the image as it passed into the tray. Studied it. "Well, that's an eclectic bunch." When she held her hand out, he gave her the photo. Keira looked at it. Doug O'Shea was in it. Hank and Brody. Gary Paulus, Beau Chandler, Arnie Hassert, and Roger Wilson. There were a couple of other strangers wearing the uniform of park rangers. She was a little surprised to see her deputies in the photo.

She dropped the picture on her desk. An image of Tiffany's note flashed across her mind, and she snatched the sheet up again. Stared. "I think…I might have just figured out what Tiff was trying to tell me with those weird doodles in the message. She was attempting to give a clue about who the killer was. And if I'm not wrong, he's in this picture."

The sound of the door rolling open had quickly become Tiffany's least favorite noise in the world. She slid over toward the center of the pole. He flipped on a light and she winced, hiding her face in her shoulder to block the sudden glare.

She knew it was dark outside. Tiff was positioned in a way that anyone looking in either of the two windows would never see her. But paned glass let daylight in. And day had just faded, but not long ago. Maybe an hour. Time passed in a blur. There was only the constant rubbing of the chain along the pipe threads to break the

308 | KYLIE BRANT

monotony, and she was growing convinced that her plan had no chance of succeeding. The links still held strong.

"I brought you something to eat. You're going to need your strength tonight."

The words filled her with dread. "Why? What will happen then?"

The mouth showing behind the facemask curved in a chilling smile. "That's when I make you a star. Well, you have a bit part. And I doubt Saxon will earn much of a role. It's her special investigator who might make a game of it." He drew closer. Sniffed. "Jesus. You stink."

"Well forgive me all to hell." Whatever he had in his hand was hot. She could see the steam rising from it. Maybe she could throw it in his eyes. Blind him. "Your accommodations lack a few basic amenities."

"You won't have to worry about that much longer."

Terror sprinted down her spine at the answer. She'd seen his handiwork. Yembley hadn't come back once he'd left, but parts of him had. This man had shown them to her and laughed and laughed. Her time was running out. She was no closer to a plan then when she'd first been brought here.

Her mind scurried around the issue like frantic little ants. He crouched to set the bowl on the floor. Stew. There was meat of some sort floating in it, and the sight of it made her gag.

Getting up, he took a key from his pocket and approached her. He didn't unlock the cuffs, just the chain. She'd still be bound while she ate.

He unlocked the chain.

She grabbed at the links as she pretended to crumple to the ground, close enough to the bowl to send it teetering.

"Careful, you stupid bitch." When he squatted to right the dish, she gathered the length of chain in her hands and sprang. He reacted quickly, half rising at her action, but she jumped on his back and attempted to wrap the chain around his neck.

With a roar he surged to his feet, his fingers clutching at the links. Her bound hands restricted her movement, so she threw herself backward, trying to use her weight to press the chain hard against his throat. He toppled over her, pinning her beneath him, then reared forward and slammed back violently against her. Her head cracked against the pavement with enough force to have unconsciousness rushing in. He ducked out of her awkward embrace and scrambled to his feet.

There was a roaring in her ears and a gray haze across her vision. Tiffany was aware enough to see his booted foot rear back. Pain exploded again and then she knew nothing at all.

———

"Is this everyone?" Sergeant Gomez looked around the room.

"No, where's Han…" Brody's words ended on a squeak as Phil stepped smoothly on his foot.

"It looks like it," Keira answered. Two of her jailers had joined them, as well as three MSP agents. With two of the city cops, Gomez, Stevens, her deputies, and she and Finn, the group was twelve strong. In two-person teams, they could only cover six of the locations found in the pictures from O'Shea's shed.

After finding the GPS on her cruiser, she knew exactly where the killer was going to be. Wherever she and Finn were.

Adrenaline began to knock in her chest. She quickly named off the pairs that would team together, before handing out copies of the location photos and handheld GPS devices.

"What happens if the woman is at a spot we don't target?"

Brody's question was fair, and one she and Finn had debated endlessly. "There's a reason he put a location device on my cruiser." She saw members of the group who weren't in her department look up, surprised. "I think he'll arrange to appear wherever Finn and I are. He needs us engaged to fulfill this game of his. Or he may attempt to pick us all off, one member at a time."

"I'd like to see him try." The MSP agent who muttered the words looked familiar. In the next moment, Keira recalled he'd been on Danny's search team.

"If we don't show up, he might think we haven't put the clues together yet. He'll leave and come back tomorrow night." That's what she expected he would do, but one thing she'd learned working homicide was that killers were notoriously unpredictable. They were a product of their own psychoses and grandiose fantasies. No one could be entirely certain how one would react in any given circumstance. She tried to inject more certainty than she felt into her next words. "He'll need Tiffany alive to continue to engage us another time."

But once they began the contest that the offender had set in motion, Keira's friend ceased to serve a purpose. And no one was more cognizant of that fact than she was.

"Are there any other questions about this assignment?" The silence that greeted her question was not unexpected. They'd been poring over the details for hours. Her gaze went to the clock on the wall. "Then let's get our gear on. Time to roll."

————————

Each group would leave their cars along little-used skid roads and logging roads, whatever would be closest to their assignment. Keira and Finn got out of the cruiser and shouldered their department issued rifles. He carried a backpack, as well. They started walking. It would be two miles to their assigned location. Coupling the weight of their Kevlar and the deep snow they'd encounter, it would feel like twice that.

They moved silently, saving their breath for the walk. Last night's blizzard had rearranged the snow into drifts in some places, leaving other spots almost bare. The reflective strips on the back of Finn's helmet made him easy to keep track of in the shadows. Each of them was marked similarly, to lessen the chance of losing an LEO to friendly fire. She was very much aware that the strips would make them targets from the right vantage point. Which made finding cover crucial at all times.

When they reached their assigned location, Finn used his free hand to reach for hers. Squeezed hard. "Stick with the plan." He barely breathed the words, but she was close enough to hear him. They took up positions on either end of a cluster of firs they'd scouted yesterday. There was another clump one hundred yards ahead of them. If they were in the right location, Tiffany would be there, too.

The temperature hovered in the single digits. By the time an hour had crawled by Keira's feet had turned to ice. In another thirty minutes, she was doing finger exercises to keep the circulation going.

Every once in a while, she'd see the glow of a yellow pair of eyes. A doe meandered in front of them once before stopping, as if their scent had reached her even while they were hidden. She bounded away, and Keira and Finn were left alone again.

She strained her ears but heard nothing outside the occasional crack of a tree limb. Noises traveled in a forest. The sound of shots fired would reach them from all but the furthest assigned area. But getting to that spot in a reasonable time would be another matter altogether.

The branches on one of the firs straight ahead of them trembled. Keira stared hard at the place, scarcely daring to breathe. She fully expected another deer or possibly an elk to make its way out of the cluster of trees.

Instead, out stepped a woman.

Although she was dressed in dark clothes, the fall of blond hair gave her away. Keira felt her heart rate slow. She and Finn raised their rifles as if synchronized.

There was something odd about the way her friend was moving. Her arms were secured behind her back. Lifting the night binoculars to her eyes with her free hand, Keira studied her more closely. Mouth taped shut. Legs unbound. They'd have to be to walk here from wherever she and the kidnapper had come from. The snow was past her knees, but Tiffany was moving with exaggerated actions, lifting her feet high. Jostling her torso up and down.

"Got it Tiff," Keira thought silently. Only hours ago she'd figured out the hidden message her friend had tried to send her with that note. She'd known then who the killer was. But without a shred of proof, the knowledge had been useless. The woman stopped in mid-motion as if responding to a command they couldn't hear. Everyone waited as if frozen in place.

"Your move, Sheriff Saxon."

Voice changing megaphone, she realized instantly. Not loud enough for any of the other law enforcement to hear. He'd selected the different spots with privacy in mind. She knew it wasn't happenstance that she and Finn were in the right location.

Like lambs to slaughter. Mary's words flitted across her memory.

"Are you willing to trade yourself for this worthless bitch? Throw your weapon out, then come out slow, hands in the air. Or I shoot this piece of shit in the back before your eyes."

She exchanged a look with Finn. Imagined the command in his face behind the helmet guard. Going over possible scenarios wasn't the same as being confronted with the prospect of her dearest friend being gunned down. Keira inclined her head. "I'm coming out," she called. "Don't shoot."

And then she dropped to her knee, squeezing off a shot that would seem much too close to the other woman. "Get down!" she screamed. Tiffany dove to the side, rolling through the snow in a blur of motion. The cluster of firs exploded with gunfire around them.

She and Finn peppered the clump of trees with shots for a full minute after Tiff rolled out of Keira's vision. When they stopped, they heard only echoes.

"Beau Chandler!" Her voice reverberated in the space. "You are under arrest for the murder of Danny Saxon, Joseph Atwood, and Bruce Yembley. Throw down your weapon." Finn was speaking quietly into the radio, alerting the others of the shooter's location. Then he put the radio away and shrugged out of the backpack. Reached inside. Each of the teams was equipped for this exact situation. He hurled a canister of tear gas into the opposite cluster of pines. With a nod toward Keira, he took out a portable mask and, lifted the shield of his helmet to affix it. While she provided cover, he ran in a crouched arc to round the trees the man had hidden in.

A minute ticked by. Two.

"Saxon."

She froze. The voice was quiet. And much too close. A figure clad all in black rose from behind a fallen log twenty feet to the right of her. One arm was looped around Tiffany's neck. His rifle was pressed beneath her chin. "I suppose you're wearing a vest. Pussy. No matter. They end just above the base of the spine anyway."

"That's right. You like to shoot people in the back, don't you, Beau?" Keira gave one quick glance at her friend then concentrated on the man behind her. "Very sporting of you."

"Sporting will be when I cut down your armed consultant right in front of you. After I finish this bitch." Tiffany's head bent back with the force of the rifle barrel pressed against her skin. "Put down the gun."

"I don't think so." She angled around, searching for a better shot.

"Do you want her dead? Drop the fucking weapon!"

"You can't shoot us both at the same time, asshole. This forest is crawling with law enforcement. How are you planning on getting out alive? We've already radioed them your location." It wouldn't take Finn long to ascertain the man was gone. And he'd check back here first. Keira inched to the side. Chandler was a head taller than Tiffany. She just needed to keep him talking a few more minutes.

She wouldn't get them.

"You're gonna die like your old man." He shoved Tiff aside. Shifted his weapon to aim it at her. Keira moved to get clear of the woman as she squeezed the trigger. Something slammed into her chest. Knocked her off her feet. Time slowed. Sound came from a distance. Muted shots. Screams. And her name being yelled over and over.

She lay spread-eagled in the snow, struggling to breathe, staring at the night sky peeking through silvery birch branches. The pulsating pain was intense. She thought of her dad. And wondered if this was what dying felt like.

————

Keira put down her cell when Phil Milestone walked into the hospital room. "Phil." Her voice was filled with every ounce of the desperation she was feeling. "You've got to get me out of here. They took my clothes. And King, that prick, has them convinced that he's my family physician. I swear to God if the man touches me I'll shoot him."

It was one of the rare times she ever saw her undersheriff crack a smile. It was a broad grin, tinged with relief. "Figured it would be simpler to come over here than to have you call every five minutes." He came further into the room to stand beside her bed and eyed her critically. "You look like hell."

"I feel like I got kicked in the chest by a band of mules," she admitted. Kevlar had saved her life, but the impact of the bullet had left a brilliant bruise that radiated across one entire side of her torso. She still couldn't draw a breath without wincing. And she'd die before admitting that to anyone.

"Yeah, well taking a round at close range is going to pack a wallop, vest or not."

"Did Chandler make it?" Finn had been a tyrant about filtering the news that got through to her, but the last time she'd pressured Mary the woman had said he'd been airlifted to Marquette.

"He didn't survive the surgery." The man hooked his elbows over the side rail of her bed, not a flicker of regret on his face. "You hit him center mass. Damn good shot with the girl in the vicinity. Finn hit him twice more."

She'd gotten that much out of Finn before he'd closed down any discussion of the op in the forest at all. "I hate that he died without giving us answers." Regret filtered through her. Her father had deserved that much. So had Joseph Atwood.

"We're piecing together what we need to know."

The door swung open again. "Guess who gets to go home?"

The sight of her friend lightened something in Keira. "Probably the one of us wearing clothes." She took stock of Tiffany's injuries as she came in and took up position opposite Phil. Chandler had beaten her badly. Bruises covered her face and given the stiffness with which she moved, she figured the rest of her body looked about the same. "Nothing's broken," the other woman assured her, intercepting her look. "I'll be all right in a week or so. The biggest problem is my hair. He cut it so short I'd have to get a pixie to even it out."

"I still can't believe you had a chance to send me a message about the killer, and you drew Cassie Winkelman's boobs." She could joke about it now but had she been able to decipher the flourishes on the note Chandler had forced Tiffany to write sooner; they might have gotten to her much more quickly. But maybe not.

As Finn had pointed out in the office, the man had been untouchable. He'd framed Doug O'Shea with all the evidence. They would never have been able to get a search warrant.

"I couldn't draw an Adam's apple," Tiff protested. "He would have known I was describing him. I'm sure he's got a mirror." Then she sobered. "You should see that shed he kept me in. He said he liked to keep trophies. He had human ones. There were things in jars and a pair of feet."

That's where the former DNR officer had once kept the liver he'd cut out of her father, Keira thought. A souvenir for every kill. At some point hunting animals hadn't been enough for the man. That's when he'd become the worst sort of predator.

"He said some things. About Yembley being muscle and almost ruining everything by trying to kill you."

"She means muscle for Bielefeld's drug operation," Phil put in. "We found financial records kept in Chandler's Au Train house. Looks like he'd been running things for the last several months."

Tiffany's head bobbed. "That's what Chandler said. He told Yembley that Pete was small-time until he caught him with a meth lab in the forest and that it was his idea to expand."

No wonder neither Bielefeld nor Yembley had shown up on the DNR violation list, Keira thought. Chandler had caught them breaking the law but had turned it to his advantage.

"Yembley said he'd patched Beau up from a bullet wound. But Chandler was furious that he shot at you." Her friend's blue eyes were troubled. "He had other plans for you. But he underestimated what he was getting into. Fierce women." She reached for Keira's hand.

Right now Keira felt about as fierce as a church mouse, but things could have worked out far differently. She gave her friend's fingers a squeeze. The fact that they were still alive and Chandler wasn't said it all. "Damn straight."

Finn walked in, stopped short in the doorway. His narrowed gaze landed on Phil.

"Don't give me that look," the older man remarked, seemingly uncowed. "We can't get anything done in the office because she's ringing us off the hook. And if your positions were reversed, you wouldn't like being kept in the dark anymore than she does." He pushed away from the bed. "Quit coddling the girl," he advised Finn. "She's a Saxon, for chrissakes. She was a homicide cop. She can handle hearing the rest of the details of last night." He winked at Keira and brushed by Finn as he walked out the door.

"Hey, you know who stopped by my room a couple of times?" Tiffany said. "That doctor. King. I know you don't like him, but I think he's kind of cute."

Horrified, Keira tore her gaze away from Finn's. "No. Not a chance. He's a huge jerk. You don't want to get anywhere near that."

The woman settled the strap of her purse on her shoulder. "No offense but I'm done taking dating advice from you, based on your last suggestion. Because, hello, serial killer."

"Well, King isn't in Chandler's category," Keira allowed grudgingly. "But I still say you deserve better."

"After the weekend I had, I deserve Bradley freaking Cooper. But who among us get what we deserve?" She reached over to brush a kiss across Keira's forehead. "I hope you get out soon. It sucks being in here." She turned, rather gingerly Keira thought and waggled her fingers at Finn on the way out. "Take care of her, fudgie."

He watched her go out the door and then approached the bed, taking up Phil's stance at the rail. "She keeps calling me that. What's a fudgie?"

"Hmm, pretty much the same as flatlander. A tourist. The UP has tons of fudge shops, which are very popular with visitors. Hence the name."

He picked up one of her hands in his, playing idly with her fingers. "So. I guess you've been going crazy here trying to figure out what's going on."

"I've intimidated each and every one of my deputies, browbeating them for details. Turns out," she noted a little smugly, "they're more afraid of me than they are of you."

"If it hadn't been for me you'd have tried to continue running the op from your hospital bed." He looked her over critically. If he commented on her looks like Phil had, Keira thought she'd punch him. "Your color's better."

She asked the one thing that was uppermost in her mind. "Did Chandler talk before he died?"

Finn shook his head. "But Tiffany told you about the souvenirs, right? I'm pretty sure the DNA matches on some of that stuff will go a long way toward identifying his other victims."

She'd worked a few serial cases in Chicago. It wasn't unusual for such a killer to take trophies. Nor was it uncommon for a hunter to do so. Chandler had been both.

"I think you called it, a couple of days ago. You had him dead to rights. He wasn't just at home in the outdoors; he saw it as his personal hunting ground.

Some men want to pit themselves against dangerous animals." Finn shrugged. "Man is the ultimate prey."

"Any idea what he did with the bodies?"

He shook his head. "There's talk of bringing in a cadaver dog. They'll start with the Au Train property. Plenty of places to dump them on the UP, though. Maybe your father happened upon him doing just that and was killed for his efforts. We do know that Chandler had a poorly healed bullet wound in his side, another fresher injury to his arm and he was out sick for a two-week period when the search for your father was going on. I think both the Saxons wounded him. At any rate, the house in Au Train was a trove of information. His father hasn't been alive for years. Chandler had been collecting the Social Security since he died."

Shocked, her gaze flew to his. "How do you know that?"

"Because we found the man's body in the freezer in the shed, beneath packages of game. Given the massive trauma to the corpse's head, I'd guess he was one of his son's first victims."

"God," she muttered. "A regular chamber of horrors."

"It was. He was also a great record keeper. We wondered how Bielefeld had expanded his operation. The notebooks we discovered in Chandler's home have those answers and more."

"Tiffany said he'd run across Bielefeld in the course of doing his job." And had found a use for the man. She attempted to pull her pillow higher. Finn reached over and adjusted it for her. "How long has his father been dead?"

Finn shook his head. "The body would need to be thawed to make that determination. But no one has seen him around town for at least eight years, and that's when people remember Beau being there more."

"Once he took over the property, he had a base for his games." She wondered how long it had been before he'd taken advantage of that. There'd be no opportunity to understand why Beau Chandler became what he did. But Keira knew his treatment at his father's hands could have laid the foundation for it. It didn't excuse it, though. In the end, they were all responsible for their choices.

That thought summoned another. She blew out a breath. "I'm not sure how I'm going to make it up to Doug O'Shea." He'd likely been traumatized by his arrest and night in jail. She saw the small smile playing around Finn's mouth. "What?"

"He's been to your office since you've been here. Quite concerned about you, too. I suspect you might find him more forgiving than you think. He remembered being at a meeting for the Friends of the Forest and helping Beau take pictures of the kids there. Chandler probably got his print when Doug was assisting with running off a copy for each child."

Death and deceit. Chandler had been a master at both. "This case will take weeks to clear up. There has to be a mountain of evidence at the Au Train house alone." She wouldn't be sorry to give Finn a reason to stick around to see it to the end.

His next words shattered that possibility. "Since the state has a vested interest in untangling that evidence, they can run the tests on it. I have someone coming later today to pick up the mobile lab. No use you shouldering the expenses from here out."

She considered for an instant. "What about the money I already spent on that special consultant I hired?" Her smile was slow and wicked. "I'm not sure I got my money's worth from him."

His lips curved. And for the first time since he'd come in the door, his expression looked lighter. "As it happens he might be sticking around a bit longer. I have some vacation coming. And I did promise you a trip to Ohio. The place is lovely in February." And then the humor vanished from his face, and it went deadly serious. "When Chandler didn't come out of those trees after I gassed the area, I knew he was dead or gone. I went back to check on you and saw…" He swallowed hard. "You cost me a couple of lives in that moment. I got off two shots." He lifted his free hand to brush her hair back from her face. It lingered to stroke her jaw. "But you were already falling." His mouth flattened. "I realized before then that I loved you. But in that instant I wasn't sure I was going to get a chance to tell you."

Her hand came up to cover his. And the pressure in her chest at that moment had nothing to do with her injury. "I know. Sort of put things in perspective when I was lying there wondering what the heck had happened. I've learned by now that we have to reach out and hold on to things we love with both hands. And I love you, Finn. I'm not sure how we're going to see this thing through living where we do, but…"

"We'll figure it out." A smile played around his mouth. "In addition to my leadership skills, I'm also a helluva good organizer. And I plan to organize as much time together as I can until your term here is finished."

He brushed his lips over hers, and something inside her calmed. Only days ago Keira hadn't had an idea what her future would entail. Now it was taking shape around Finn Carstens, and that seemed absolutely perfect to her.

Made in the USA
Columbia, SC
21 November 2017